Fr

"Byrd's enjoyable prose transports readers into a French bakery, with all of its sights and smells. Lexi is an engaging character whose life lessons will strike a chord with anyone who's struggled to find direction in their life."

—*Romantic Times Book Reviews* about *Let Them Eat Cake*

"...readers will almost taste the French pastry as they journey with Lexi toward her future..."

—*CBA Retailers+Resources*

"Chick-lit never tasted so good! *Let Them Eat Cake* is one of those rare chick-lit novels that integrates faith elements without being preachy, and includes plenty of romance without it being the only point of the protagonist's existence. Chick-lit fans will find that this delectable mix of faith, fun, and fiction has all the right ingredients for a romantic, enjoyable read."

—FaithfulReader.com

"In this sequel to *Let Them Eat Cake*, Byrd again entertains with descriptions of delectable food and, this time, with exquisite details of France as well. Foodies will delight in this novel, and anyone who adores romance will warm to the story. It's easy to identify with Lexi's struggles in life, because they mirror so much of what everyone experiences, no matter what their age."

—*Romantic Times Book Reviews* about *Bon Appétit*

"Sandra Byrd has created a witty heroine whose search for significance and desire to follow the Lord equals her charming bonhomie. You won't regret settling down with a plate of French pastries and this delectable adventure!"

—ANGELA HUNT, author of *The Elevator*

"Byrd brings a fresh, insightful approach to women's fiction as she stretches out a welcoming hand to twenty-something readers. Bon appétit!"

—ROBIN JONES GUNN, best-selling author of *Sisterchicks Say Ooh La La!* and The Christy Miller Series

Pièce de Résistance

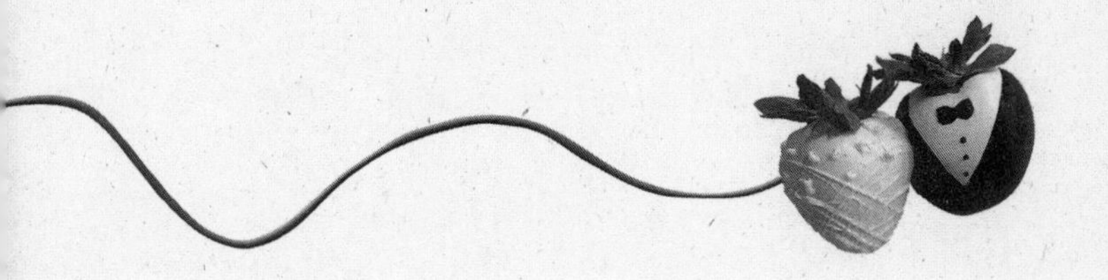

Pièce de Résistance

a novel

Sandra Byrd

WaterBrook
Press

Pièce de Résistance
Published by WaterBrook Press
12265 Oracle Boulevard, Suite 200
Colorado Springs, Colorado 80921

ISBN 978-1-4000-7329-0

ISBN 978-0-307-45830-8 (electronic)

Published in the United States by WaterBrook Multnomah, an imprint of the Crown Publishing Group, a division of Random House Inc., New York.

Library of Congress Cataloging-in-Publication Data
Byrd, Sandra.
Pièce de résistance : a novel / Sandra Byrd. — 1st ed.
p. cm. — (French twist ; 3)
ISBN 978-1-4000-7329-0 — ISBN 978-0-307-45830-8 (electronic)
1. Women cooks—Fiction. 2. Pastry industry—Fiction. 3. Seattle (Wash.) —Fiction. I. Title.
PS3552.Y678P54 2009
813'.54—dc22

2009011974

Printed in the United States of America
2009—First Edition

10 9 8 7 6 5 4 3 2 1

To Linda Rice.
Thanks for your prayers, encouragement,
and generosity which shone a light during a dark passage.
Matthew 5:16

Grace isn't a little prayer you chant before receiving a meal. It's a way to live.

—Jackie Windspear

One

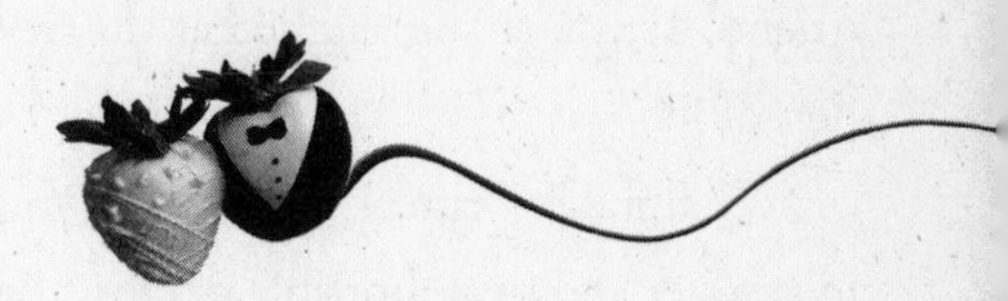

Everything you want is out there waiting for you to ask.
Everything you want also wants you.
But you have to take action to get it.
Jules Renard

If I had known exactly where and in what kind of trouble I was about to land, I'd have stayed in Paris.

"Come on, dear." A wizened woman dragged a shuffling friend past me and down the long carpeted hallway. "We don't want to get in the way of Rosa's granddaughter, even if she's sitting on *our* couch." She threw a dirty look over her shoulder.

I started to stand up and get out of her way, but she disdainfully waved me back into my seat.

"WHO?" her friend shouted as I sank back down.

"ROSA'S GRANDDAUGHTER. She's sprawling on *our* couch." I flinched at the vocal hurricane, but no one else seemed to notice. Or maybe they just couldn't hear it.

For the time being, I was crashing at the guest apartment at my nonna's retirement community. Where else could I get in on such short notice? It was twenty dollars a night, and only for a week or so…I hoped. "Well, they *do* have a lot of singles," I'd told my best friend, Tanya, as she laughed at the news. "And they do love what's left of life."

"I think it's cute," she'd said. "You can get a personalized pill container and swap horrible doctor stories."

"Ha ha," I'd answered. "Be careful, or I'll hold your bridal shower there on bingo night."

I'd stayed with my parents on Whidbey Island for the two weeks since I'd been home from France. Yesterday they'd dropped me and my gear off at the retirement community, though most of my stuff was still in storage awaiting my "real" apartment. And now I sat in the common room, not realizing I'd poached what someone considered her personal couch, waiting for the afternoon bus to take me to my new job.

I checked my watch again. To pass the time, I thumbed through the Gideon's Bible sitting on the side table, flipping by chance to the first chapter of Philippians and scanning the extra large print until my eye caught something that hooked into my heart.

> And this is my prayer: that your love may abound more and more in knowledge and depth of insight, so that you may be able to discern what is best.

Oh yeah, I thought. *Bring on the discernment.* I was starting a new job—the job I'd been hoping for all my life and at which I desperately wanted to succeed. And I found myself embroiled in a romantic crisis where I not only didn't hold all the cards, but the men involved had turned surprisingly poker-faced about their intentions.

Lost in thought, it took me a minute to realize that a kindly looking man had sat down next to me. He tried valiantly, but unsuccessfully, to clear the phlegm from his throat. I scooted over to both accommodate him and to offer us some personal space. He kept looking at me, but as soon as I looked back at him, he glanced away.

Finally he spoke. "Who are you?" he asked quietly. "And what are you doing here?"

That was indeed the question, and not only for my current living situation. I wished I had an answer.

Nonna breezed in through the lobby, snapping her mauve umbrella shut with a force that belied her age. She kissed the cheek of her companion, Stanley Jones, who tottered off to his own apartment, then came to get me.

"Lexi, love," she said. "I'm glad I got here in time to see you off. Let's wait by the door. The bus will be here soon." On the way through the foyer, she whispered, "I thought I'd mentioned, dear—don't sit on any upholstered furniture in the common areas. When you get to be my age, many of us have incontinence problems."

Shocked, I reached around and felt my backside, not caring who saw me. *Whew. Dry.*

Nonna giggled at my distress, taking everything about aging in stride, as she always did, and looped her arm through mine. "I'm glad you're home."

I grinned back at her. "Me too, Nonna."

"Why can't one of those nice young men drive you to work today?" she asked.

"I don't want to ask them. It's…awkward. I'm not sure where I'm going with either of them right now, and they both have their own jobs."

"Seems to me a man who likes a woman would offer her a ride," Nonna sniffed.

"I'm sure plenty of men hitched up their buggies and took you to work back in the day," I teased.

She grinned wickedly and leaned over to kiss my cheek. "So tell me about the Frenchman."

"His name is Philippe. He's really nice, a great baker, and has the most adorable daughter named Céline. He's taking Luc's place, the one who moved back to France."

"He's one of the owners of the bakery?" she asked, checking creds, as always.

"Yes, Nonna," I said. "He's an owner. He's Luc's cousin, and the whole family owns all the bakeries."

"What about that lawyer you were seeing before you went to Paris?"

"Dan?" I kept my voice even.

"Mm-hmm."

"He's…here still. Of course. I just talked with him a few days ago. It was his suggestion, actually, for the Delacroix Company to lease the space I'll be working in. The new bakery."

"That was nice of him. Who's the better looking of the two?"

"I'm glad to see your values haven't changed!" I said, but compared them in my mind anyway. Philippe was definitely good looking in a continental way, dark blond hair that just touched his shoulders, a bit taller than me. Dan was built bigger, taller, with broad shoulders I loved to see set off by suspenders. His strawberry blond hair perfectly matched his lightly tanned complexion.

"You're thinking about it, aren't you?" Nonna poked me out of my daydream. "Gotcha!"

She laughed, and I laughed with her as the rain slid down the outside of the window, my hometown Seattle lights blinking away in the drops. "Thanks for seeing me off today. I won't be long. Just meeting Margot and getting a quick run-through."

"Of course I'm seeing you off! Everyone is jealous that my granddaughter is here. I need to brag."

I saw the bus rounding the corner about a half mile down the road. Nonna saw it too.

"Go get 'em," she said. "And bring something home from the bakery. Anything with fruits and nuts will be right at home in this place." She grinned, but I knew she loved her home and her friends.

I walked out the door and started toward the covered bus stop. Not a moment later, though, a motorcycle pulled up and parked in front of the retirement center door a few feet away. Even with the helmet on, I recognized him immediately.

"Philippe!"

What is he doing here? Quickly followed by, *He looks good!*

"Good afternoon, mademoiselle." He hopped off the bike and walked toward me, holding out a helmet. "As your employer, it's my responsibility to get you to work on your first day at the new job, *n'est-ce pas*? And I was eager to see you again. Sophie told me where to find you and what bus you were likely to take."

"Oh, thank you," I said. I introduced him to Nonna, who'd come running out as soon as she'd seen me talking with a guy. "This is my grandmother, Rosa. Nonna, this is my...friend, Philippe."

"Enchanté." Philippe kissed her hand.

"Enchantée," Nonna responded, pulling back her shoulders and making sure the gathering crowd, their noses pressed against the retirement center's front windows, witnessed the exchange.

As I got on the back of the bike, I said, "I had no idea you had a motorcycle here. Do you also have a car?"

"Oui," he said, "I do. Luc left his car for me, and I gave him mine in France. But I thought a motorcycle would be fun too."

He sped up a little, and as he turned the corner out of the retirement center's curved driveway, I recognized the truck pulling in.

Dan!

I'd told him I'd be staying with Nonna and had planned to take the bus.

I caught his eye, and he caught mine, and I saw the bouquet of flowers carefully propped in the passenger seat. I had no time to wave before Philippe accelerated and we sped off.

I turned my head and squeezed my eyes shut to avoid seeing Dan's reaction. Nonna would explain it to him.

Nonna was liable to say anything.

A few minutes later, Philippe pulled the bike up in front of a long, black marble-fronted building in the Fremont district.

"Eh voilà!" he said, parking and then holding a hand out to me. "This is it. Do you like it?"

I took his hand, got off the back of the bike, and looked at the building. There were already two gold fleurs-de-lis over the front door, with the gold-lettered word *Bijoux*—meaning "jewels," the name of the bakery—centered over the door. Otherwise, it was a blank slate.

"It's beautiful!" I walked to the huge picture windows and looked in. The room was mostly empty, holding only a jumble of boxes and supplies, and some tarps left over from a recent paint job. But what lines, what bones. What this place could be!

"I can't believe I never noticed this building before," I said. "It's perfectly perfect."

Philippe laughed. "It's been recently restored. That's one of the reasons Luc was drawn to it...until he found out it couldn't be used for a restaurant. But, *ooh la la,* what a bakery, *n'est-ce pas*? *Après toi,* mademoiselle," he said, holding the front door open for me.

I expected to be greeted by the chic calm the exterior promised. Instead, I was blasted by a streak of blue French from the kitchen.

"Margot?" I asked in a small voice.

Philippe grimaced. *"Oui. La Margot."*

Philippe's sister Margot was the one downside to this dream job. Since she was a great baker and a member of the family, she didn't worry that her attitude might lose her a job. She didn't bother to sweeten it either.

"Bonjour," Philippe called in what I recognized as his fake singsong voice. I felt torn between my desire to see my new kitchen and my desire to flee at once. Philippe decided for me, pushing me forward.

"*C'est* Lexi," he introduced me to Margot.

"Nice to see you again," I said in English. It was the polite thing to say, even if I didn't mean it. She ignored me.

"I'm glad we'll be working together," I tried in French, an even graver lie. She didn't return the favor or grasp my hand, but she grunted. French it was, then.

"Alors." Philippe led the way toward the back of the kitchen. "This part," he indicated with his hand, "will be mostly for pastries, which Margot will do. She'll be here part time and at the other bakeries part time too." He smiled widely and indicated the largest part of the kitchen. "And this will be for the cakes and catering. That's you!"

I looked at my part of the kitchen. Marble and stainless counters, and lots of tall glass-fronted cabinets for ingredients. A pair of gleaming industrial mixers. Drawers full of equipment, but not in the easiest-to-reach places. I didn't know who placed some of the utensils and tools. Maybe the guys who'd brought equipment over from the other bakeries.

"It's everything I could want," I said. And it was. My own kitchen. Tiny though it was, it was mine.

Philippe opened an armoire. "Here's where you'll store the paperwork and computer, and the phone even fits in there. Will this be enough space for the accounting books?"

I blinked and answered, "I guess so." He'd be a better judge of that than I would.

Margot slammed a drawer, and when I turned around, I saw her grab her cigarettes and a lighter from the countertop. I wrinkled my nose. They should at least be hidden. As she headed out back, Philippe followed her. *"Un moment,"* he said, winking.

While they were gone, I turned the radio to a warm, low-key favorites station and began rearranging my work drawers. After ten minutes, I had them just so. I also rearranged my countertops and cake decorating materials so it made sense to me.

When Margot and Philippe came back in, I asked him, "How will the front be decorated? Will there be furniture arriving?"

He took my arm, and we headed to the big front room. I could already envision engaged couples choosing their cakes in a chic, refined, leather-furnished room.

"Hmm," Philippe said. "I hadn't thought too much on that topic. I am so busy at L'Esperance…" He shrugged, and I knew the burden of taking over their biggest US bakery. "Would you like to do it?"

"Would I?" I grinned. "I would!" I pictured deep blue drapes framing the windows and subtle gold cording. I'd make an appointment for a window etcher to etch the company name in gold on the glass, just like the Delacroix bakery in Versailles.

It was going to look *fantastique.*

When we got back to the kitchen, my countertops had been completely rearranged back to the previous nonsensical order. Margot's back was turned toward me, and she quietly hummed along with the radio—not the station I'd turned on. I looked through my utensil drawers. All returned to the way they'd been before I'd fixed them moments ago. I looked at Philippe. He shrugged. I determined not to escalate things and left everything where it stood—for the moment.

"Lexi?" His voice softened. "I have a few questions about some things for Céline…"

"Oh, yes, when is she coming?" I asked, delighted at the prospect of hugging that sweet little bonbon again.

"She's at her grandparents' in London but will be here in a few days," he said. "I've signed her up for the French-American school, but there are some other things..." He opened his briefcase and held out a folder. "Do you know a good doctor? a good dentist? And many other questions I need your help with."

I found it endearing to see him a little vulnerable for once; he was always so in charge. It made him even more appealing.

"Of course I can help you."

He smiled. "Perhaps we can talk about it at dinner tonight? Incredibly, I have found a quiet little bistro..."

He must have caught the look on my face, because he stopped midsentence.

"I'm sorry," I said. "I've got dinner plans tonight."

"Ah well." He shrugged, but looked a little forlorn. "Perhaps another time."

"Certainly," I said. "Anytime this week. Stop by for lunch or let me know when it's convenient."

With that, he handed me a key and took his leave, and Margot left too. I locked the doors behind them and then sat on one of the bar stools next to the counter. I looked around.

It was all mine, my kitchen. Well, and Margot's too. But I was no one's assistant anymore. I was a chef.

I checked my watch, saw I had fifteen minutes to get to the restaurant where I'd agreed to meet Dan for dinner, and went to brush my hair. On the way out of Bijoux, before turning the lights out in the kitchen, I did two things.

I put Margot's cigarettes and lighters into a drawer near her work station, and I turned the radio station back to the one I liked.

As soon as I walked into the restaurant, I saw him at a corner table. My eye caught his, and then my breath caught too. Dan was a good-looking man in any pose, but when he smiled, he was downright divine. Though he'd picked me up at the airport and taken me to my parents' house when I first got home from France, I hadn't seen him since.

"The world traveler has returned," he said, standing to pull my chair out and then scoot me back to the table.

"Do you mean from my travels in Paris or the urban oasis of Whidbey Island?" I grinned.

"Both." He held out a bottle and a glass. "Wine?"

I nodded, and as the waiter came to take our order, we shared the last few weeks' happenings, culminating in my announcement that I had been to Bijoux that day.

He nodded. "I left work early to come pick you up, but I arrived just a little too late."

I knew he would bring that up. I knew it. And yet, we weren't at the exclusive dating level yet, as far as I understood, so I didn't have to explain myself to him, right? "Philippe thought it would be good to take me to work on my first day," I said as casually as I could. "And he had the keys."

Dan nodded and showed absolutely no emotion. Lawyer's training, I supposed. A minute later, he loosened up again and asked about the kitchen and the countertops and what kind of oven it had—things nearly no non-baker would think to ask.

"Why are you interested in the ovens?" I teased.

"Because you are," he said simply and without guile. And that was even more appealing than the dreamy smile.

I asked about his job too, and he regaled me with his latest case, somehow making the law funny, something my brother was never able to do. Then his phone rang.

He looked mortified. "I'm so sorry. I thought I turned it off. It's new." He took it from his pocket and fumbled for a minute to locate the Ignore button. Before the backlight went off, I saw the caller ID.

Nancy.

I met his eye and he looked away, and then the waiter brought our salads. While he ground some pepper for Dan, I reminded myself, *You're not at the exclusive dating level yet, as far as he understands, so he doesn't have to explain himself to you, right?*

Right.

Two

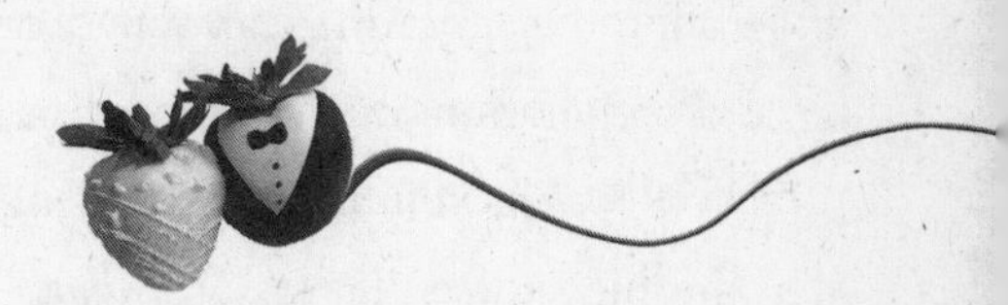

"Come to the edge," he said.
They said, "We are afraid."
"Come to the edge," he said. They came.
He pushed them, and they flew.
Guillaume Apollinaire

A week later, the last bits of January poured into February as the rain coursed down the outside of our new little jewel box of a bakery. Margot and I kept warm by sticking close to the ovens and arguing.

Bijoux was set up to cater special orders, help provide specialty pastries for the other Delacroix bakeries, and to sell high-end wedding and special occasion cakes. We'd just started whipping up our first few orders.

"What *are* you doing?" Margot shouted from the kitchen.

"I'm fixing up the front so people don't kill themselves when they come in to place their orders," I shouted back. I didn't know what her *problème* was. I'd much rather bake the birthday cakes a securities firm had ordered for pickup on Wednesday, but we were a health hazard. Rolled rugs lollygagged near the walkway, and boxes of unpacked supplies loitered next to the door. Perhaps Margot didn't understand the very American way of making money by suing people and corporations over nothing, but I did.

"Well, when you are done playing *les chaises musicales* I need help finishing these platters. *Zut alors!*" Margot muttered. "Where are the berries for these tartlets?"

Musical chairs. Humph. I left the folding chairs where they were and went to the back, then opened the doors to the walk-in. After poking about for a minute I confirmed we were out of berries and had a catering order pickup due soon.

"I'll run down to the market," I told Margot. I pulled my coat off a rack. Sophie, the assistant manager at L'Esperance and my good friend, had placed our food order with Peterson's when she'd placed her own order earlier in the week. Margot would have to get together with her to determine what we'd need from now on. Maybe Margot could chew on *that* for a while.

"Vite, escargot!" Margot hurried me along. "I'll finish the *crème patisserie* while you go. Pickup is in one hour!"

Escargot indeed. I was going as fast as possible.

We were licensed only as a commercial-order bakery, but we'd had some walk-ins stop by, hoping to buy breakfast or lunch, which of course we couldn't serve. We had no signage yet. I'd talk with Philippe about that. Didn't we need a catering brochure? When I got back, I'd make sure I wrote that on the large chalkboard we'd set up in the kitchen. The list of things he needed to do grew longer each day. I didn't want to pull overextended Philippe away from the business at hand for L'Esperance and La Couronne, but we needed his attention here too.

I returned quickly, and we nestled berries on the tartlets, rolled plump cherries onto the cream cheese pastries, and feather-dusted cocoa across the petite chocolate croissants set on silver platters I'd bought the week before. Even Margot stood back and smiled.

"They'll do," she said before heading out back to suck down half a pack of Gauloises while waiting for the delivery van to pick up the order.

As bakers, our day both started and ended early. I'd had a couple birthday cake orders the other Delacroix bakeries had sent over, and we'd done a few catering orders. After the pickup was ready, Margot flew off to La Couronne to finish her day and then to pick up Céline after school. I missed Céline. It had been almost a month since we'd said *à bientôt* in Paris.

Note to self: Arrange to pick up Céline one day next week and borrow Sophie's car to do it.

With the kitchen to myself, I busily touched up the prototypes for one of the most important cakes of my life. Just after four o'clock, I heard a knock at the front door of the bakery, which I had locked after Margot left.

I grinned as I unlocked the door. "You've arrived!"

"No, *you've* arrived!" Tanya said. "As in, this is your place." We giggled and hugged like the girls we once were together.

"It's not really my place, but it's a start. I'm just glad to work here. Of course, if they don't start shuffling some orders our way, it'll be nobody's place very soon."

Tanya hung her coat on a hook in the back next to mine. "Give me the grand tour."

I laughed because the place was so small, the grand tour could almost be done without moving a foot.

"The front, of course, is where we'll meet with clients to place catering and cake orders. I'm ready to order a couple oak coffee tables, some soft leather chairs, and a sofa—cozy and romantic, since I'm hoping lots of our business will come from wedding cakes. I'm going to put a large, lit display case here." I pointed to the far wall. "With porcelain brides and grooms, jewels, and flowers. I want it to be romantic and inviting, high end and celebratory." I swept my hand in front of the area that looked into the open bakery. "Over there, they can see us baking through the cutout, and I'm going to have a long bar in front for sampling. I've got several tables for books showcasing both cakes we can do and pastries for catering orders."

"Wow, Lex, this is fantastic," Tanya said. "And they just let you design it all?"

"Yep. It's a small room, and I guess Philippe has enough going on, being new and all, that he was glad to pass that part to me. I want to be useful; I want them to be happy they hired me. After we're set up, I'm sure Sophie and Margot will do all the food ordering, Philippe will handle the bills and marketing, and *moi*? I'll just bake."

"Great how you got that all worked out so early." Tanya leaned on a dusty folding chair.

"Well, it's not like it was hammered out, exactly," I said. "We're just flying by the seat of our pants for now. You know, new start-up and all."

Tanya crinkled her brow. “Oh. Uh-huh.” I caught a look but she moved on before I could ask about it. “So—back to cakes!”

“Yes, come back to the bakery!” I was so proud of it. The pastry decorating kit that Margot’s sister and my mentor, Patricia, had given me for Christmas sat in the place of honor in the tiny cake decorating cool room off the kitchen. So far, though, I hadn’t needed it very often.

But that would change. Philippe had probably placed ads, and soon the business would roll in. They ran two other bakeries. He knew what he was doing.

I opened the walk-in cooler and gently carried out a demo cake I’d made earlier in the day.

“Here it is!” I announced with a flourish, setting it in front of Tanya and watching for her reaction. I went back to the walk-in and took out cake number two. “And here it is!” I set it on the counter beside the first and held my breath. Would she like them?

“Oh, Lex, they’re so beautiful. This one—what’s on top? Chocolate-dipped coffee beans?” She pointed to the first cake, layers of buttery German chocolate with caramel melted between and a soft, marshmallow-based frosting foaming around the sides and top to look like coffee froth. In the froth I’d painted beige hearts, then toasted the frosting lightly with a culinary blowtorch.

“A caramel latte cake. I know Steve likes caramel lattes, so I thought maybe he’d like this as a possible wedding cake. But if he doesn’t, I will come up with whatever you guys want.”

“And this one?” She touched the tip of the next cake. “It’s so beautiful. And these pink things floating on it—what are they?”

"Candied rose petals," I said. "A dainty pink rose cake with perfectly pure white frosting for you, my perfectly pure friend."

She leaned over and hugged me before whispering, "Thanks, Lex." A few years back, Tanya had been date raped and had shied away from any thought of marriage because she felt impure, and was afraid she'd flinch away from the honeymoon and all physical intimacy thereafter. After counseling, a step of faith, and meeting a great guy, she was happily heading toward the altar.

"I know you love roses," I said. "The cake is lightly perfumed with rose essence." We took the cakes and some plastic forks to the front and sat in the folding chairs. I placed a couple boards over an upside-down flour bucket and we set the minicakes on top of them.

"So let's talk bridal showers," I said.

"My mother is already planning the basic girly thing with the women from church and her friends, so for *our* friends' shower I want…" She pulled a billiard ball out of her purse.

"Yes! Pool!" I grinned. We'd played pool together since our youth group days in junior high, and we still often met and hung out at the pool hall to talk over our lives and problems. "I can totally do that. Do you want, like, a beer cake or maybe a nacho cheese cake for the shower?" I teased.

"Ah, no, but I know you'll come up with something good. Would you do this rose cake for my mom's shower?" She polished off her piece of cake.

"Sure!" We talked about the details of her job and then her shower and wedding, but Tanya being Tanya, she already had a good sense of what she wanted. She had it all laid out on an Excel spreadsheet. I looked it over. "This looks good," I said softly. "You're so organized; I don't feel like there's much I can offer you besides the cakes."

"Lex, the most important thing you offer me is your friendship, your insight, your support, like always. *And* killer cakes. We've spent the last hour talking about me, my cakes, my shower, my wedding. You are so here for me. And now, how can I be here for you? How are things going with the guy situation?"

I put a bite of latte cake in my mouth. "I had dinner with Dan last week, and it was..."

"Great?" Tanya asked.

Putting his call from Nancy out of my head, I nodded and smiled. "Great. It feels really natural talking with him. We've been on the phone almost every night too. Philippe is charming as always, so interesting, and I feel like we're in a true partnership with this business. He came over one night, and I helped him hammer out the paperwork for Céline's school and gave him the name of the dentist I've seen since I was a kid. I was going to suggest my pediatrician, but he'd found a doctor somewhere else."

He hadn't offered how or from who, though. *Funny.*

"Sounds good!" Tanya said.

"Oh, it is! And he promised me a movie night out if I interviewed the two choices for a piano teacher, so I'm going to do that soon. I'm busy here trying to get my footing. We're having a meeting on Monday, here, so the other bakery employees can see what we are doing and what their parts will be in running it."

"And what is *your* part?" she asked, nibbling on a sugared rose petal, releasing its gentle scent into the air.

"Designing and baking cakes," I said, "and decorating and making other pastries for catering. Margot will do some too, but she's also at the other bakeries." I hopped off the chair and dug into my messenger bag. "I had an idea. I thought I might offer to do a booth at the wedding show. But it's in two weeks." I flipped through the pastel bridal guide to the glossy four-page spread for the show. "I think it might be a way to get the word out about the cakes. Not that I expect to do a lot of marketing. It's definitely not my thing."

"Yeah," Tanya said. "As I recall, you were fired from that marketing job."

I nodded. "Yeah. Lexi Stuart and business are a toxic mix, which is why I'm a baker now. But…if I do the show, will you help? Margot will scare away the customers, Sophie works on Saturdays, and I can't do it myself. It might even be too late to sign up."

Tanya bit her lip and pretended to think hard. "Do I have to wear a hair net?"

I grinned. "No hair net, I promise. We're only serving cake slices there, not baking."

"You bringing this one?" Tanya pointed at the latte cake. "It's to die for."

I nodded. "It might be a signature cake for us—you know, Seattle and all. And it's close to *café crème,* which is French."

"If you do it, I will absolutely help," Tanya said. "Plus, I can scope out stuff for my own wedding too."

"You got it. This is going to be our year."

"So both of our careers are set for now," Tanya said. "And my love life is set."

"Right." I knew where this was heading.

"So now it's time to get yours settled."

"You make it sound so easy."

"Of course it's easy. It's not my problem. Ha!"

I stood and grabbed the keys to lock up for the evening. "I just don't know how to do it so everyone is happy."

"Isn't that why you changed careers, Lex? Because you were tired of trying to make everyone else happy?"

"That's different."

She rolled her eyes at me as she stood and gathered her coat, then opened the door to the street. "Really. Who makes *you* happy, Lex?"

I followed her, silent, and locked the door behind us.

Sophie agreed to pick me up early on Monday morning so we'd get to Bijoux before anyone else. I met her at the door and hopped in her car.

"Hey, Lex," she said. She looked at the building and started laughing.

"Okay, what's so funny?" I asked.

She pointed to the sign. "Soundview Retirement Community—Where Seniors Age in Place."

I looked at the sign, still brightly lit in the early morning darkness, and cracked up with her. "I know, I know. Everyone here is very sweet, but I'm aging in place. Help me, Soph. Are there any openings in your building?"

I knew she lived somewhere affordable because she took the apartment just as she'd been made the assistant manager of L'Esperance last year.

"I'll ask, Lex. There might be a studio coming up. There's a guy I talk with at the mailbox sometimes, and I think he said he was moving back to India. You want me to check into it?"

A studio. Last year I wanted someplace with a view and a Bosch oven. Now all I wanted was someplace with a private entrance.

We arrived a few minutes before the meeting was to start, and it was with no small measure of pride that I withdrew the keys and opened the bakery. I thought back to how God had redeemed my pain of nearly a year ago when Sophie was given the keys to L'Esperance instead of me. Now I knew God had something wonderful planned for me all along. Baking!

"Voilà!" I said as we stepped in. I'd swept everything and arranged the folding chairs in a circle.

"It *is* a little jewel box," Sophie said. "I drove by last year when Luc was signing the contract, and I had no idea how he would make it work. But when he told us you'd be baking wedding and special occasion cakes and Margot would be helping you with the catering pastries, I just knew you could make it work."

I could make it work? Margot helping *me*?

"Knock, knock." I turned to see a young man in the doorway.

"Lexi, this is Andrew," Sophie said. "He took your place as Margot's assistant when you went to Paris last year."

"Hey, good to meet you." Andrew looked at me from under a

shaggy hairdo and held out his hand. He looked cute and only a year or two out of high school. "May I?" He pointed toward the kitchen and I motioned him on.

"Robbing the cradle, are you?" I teased Sophie after he left.

She grinned. "Nothing going on there." We headed back to the kitchen, the size of a tithe of the bakery at L'Esperance but fashioned especially for wedding cakes.

Shortly thereafter, everyone else poured in through the door—Margot; Carol Boyd, the assistant manager for La Couronne; a handful of bakers; and of course, Philippe.

And, unexpectedly, Céline!

"Hey, it's my California angel!" I knelt and opened my arms wide; she ran into them. We hugged each other for nearly a minute. Then I held her at arm's length. "I think you've already grown. You're going to be as tall as I am soon. We'll be, like, sharing shoes."

She grinned, her smile showing another lost tooth. "The tooth fairy found me at Tante Margot's house," she said. I'd introduced her to the tooth fairy concept last year in Paris as she'd shared with me her American dream to get to California. I bet the tooth fairy was named Papa and not Tante Margot.

We chatted together in French for a while, and she opened her backpack and showed me all of her new school gear. I exclaimed over every Hello Kitty pencil, and she hugged me again.

"I'm so glad you're here," she said.

Her dad whispered to her in French, and she nestled in a corner, nibbling the flaky horned ends of a croissant he'd packed for her to eat while we had our meeting.

We crowded into the small front space. Philippe had brought coffee for everyone as we didn't have a coffee machine—a terrible deficiency—because we had no eat-in customers. He smiled at me, then winked when he saw I wore my freshly pressed Boulangerie Delacroix chef's jacket. I smiled and winked back.

We toured the kitchen, Margot in the lead, then went back to the front and sat on the folding chairs.

"Good morning," Philippe greeted everyone. "I'm so glad you all could join us here as we celebrate the opening of our newest bakery, Bijoux. Most of you know that the bakery is a commercial kitchen only—no food service on the premises. Lexi will run the bakery with an eye toward developing a strong presence in the wedding cake market. We want to be a known name in that market—only the best for Delacroix!"

I blinked. My throat involuntarily flexed. *Lexi will run the bakery?* He must mean the kitchen—although officially, Margot was the senior baker.

"My papa, the patron of the Delacroix bakeries, has paid the lease on this space through December of this year. And, of course, we've invested in fitting out the kitchen. Lexi will decorate the front room to be a warm and inviting space. Here," he said, handing me a folder.

I looked at the tab. "Annual Budget."

"Right," he said. "It's all on this too." He gave me a disk. "I plan to streamline our ordering process in the next month or two. Carol will do the ordering for La Couronne, Sophie for L'Esperance, and Lexi for Bijoux. They will all be delivered separately, of course, but we'll have one main account with all of our suppliers. Everything will be uploaded by the individual assistant manager."

Assistant manager? As in running the place? Wait a minute, I'm a baker. I looked over at Sophie, who didn't seem to pick up my desperate *look at me* vibe. She sipped her coffee and I did likewise, if for no other reason than to appear casual—in spite of how I felt inside.

Philippe continued. "Margot does a fantastic job on the kitchen, of course, but Lexi is in charge of the front of the house." He looked pointedly at Margot, and I knew he remembered the rearranged drawers. She sniffed and looked away. "Lexi, will you please tell us what you've got planned for the front room?"

I pulled out the drawings and explained the plans I'd made. "I want Bijoux to fit in with the French feel of the other Delacroix bakeries," I explained, "to have an atmosphere of romance for ordering the wedding cakes, but also a smooth corporate feel for those who come in to order for business catering."

I licked my lips and swallowed to keep my mouth moist, trying to process the ideas on the outside while reconciling new information on the inside.

"We've got a beautiful thing going with the eat-in cafés and bread delivery," Philippe said. "We're going to shuttle all our catering business over to Bijoux, just to keep each business doing what it does best. Lexi will develop a plan to get the wedding and special-occasion cake market going. We're just in time, as wedding season approaches, eh? *Ooh la la.*"

Margot didn't bother to smile. If anything, she looked even more sour at the mention of my doing the cakes. Was she really that offended?

Everyone else, however, laughed. Each person shook my hand and said how glad they were that I was back and how fabulous the front room would look with the blue curtains and heavy oak pieces and specialty cake toppers. Philippe promised they'd be back for wedding cakes one evening when it was all set up. Most of the La Couronne crew headed on to their bakery, which was now open on Mondays.

I grabbed Sophie, dragged her back into the walk-in cooler, and closed the door.

"Did you know I was supposed to be the assistant manager?"

She looked confused. "Of course. Didn't you?"

I shook my head. "Luc said I'd be baking. I thought...well, I thought Philippe would be the manager."

"He is," Sophie said, "but he's got to manage all three. You didn't think Margot would do the ordering, did you? She's baking pastries for the other bakeries too, and, uh, vendor relations aren't exactly her specialty."

Right. It did make sense.

"Luc didn't make it clear."

Sophie understood. "Oh, Lex. But...you're still baking."

I sank down onto the stepstool. "Yes. But I have to find the markets to sell the products too? And do the books?"

Sophie nodded. "It's a smaller operation. You can do it. Remember? You wanted to be an assistant manager last year." Miss No Nonsense, that was Sophie.

"That was before I knew what I was gunning for. And that didn't involve baking too."

"I'll help. You can ask me any budgetary questions you like. And you don't have to worry about staff like Carol and I do."

But she didn't have to do marketing. I opened the folder Philippe had given me and looked at the sum I had to operate with for the next ten months. Suddenly, those blue drapes and oak tables I'd committed to in front of everyone seemed stunningly expensive.

I nodded. It was a challenge, but I could do it. Maybe. But baking too? Maybe not. My starched collar seemed too tight, and I wished I were alone so I could wring my hands, tear my clothing, put ashes on my head, and call my mother.

Instead, the walk-in door creaked opened. "Lexi?" A small voice found its way inside. Céline.

"Oui?"

"Do you want to take me to school? Papa says you can drive me." She smiled brightly.

"Let me talk with your papa." I slipped out as she nodded, leaving her and Sophie in a palpably uneasy proximity to each other.

Margot was starting some work in the kitchen; she would work at Bijoux three half days a week and split the rest of her time between the other two bakeries. The other staff had already moved on to their own restaurants. I would basically have Bijoux all to myself. Exciting...but a lot of pressure too.

"Philippe?" I said quietly.

"Come," he said to me, motioning toward two of the chairs. He leaned his head close toward mine. "I love the plans you've made for the place. I'll leave a corporate credit card for you to place orders for the bakery. Just keep a tight eye on the spending—Papa was *absolument positif* about the money he was willing to invest after Luc signed the lease on this place."

I nodded. "I, ah, I didn't know I'd be the assistant manager."

Philippe cocked his head. *"Non?"*

"Non."

"But it's a good thing, *non*?"

I didn't answer.

"I rely on you in so many ways. Helping me get settled in Seattle, as a...special companion and a business partner. Do you still want this job?"

It was clear the job was a package. And honestly, Philippe was new here. He had to work within his personal resources too. I drew in a deep breath and committed myself. *"Oui."*

He stood and kissed both of my cheeks. "You are a smart woman, a beautiful woman, and a baker *fantastique*. You won't let me down, Lexi."

I weakly nodded. "Céline said I should drive her to school?"

"Ah, yes." Philippe gently took my hand in his. "Come with me."

He led me out the back door into the small parking lot we shared with the other businesses in the strip along Feldmont Drive. Right behind the bakery loomed a large white van.

"A gift," he said.

I looked at him, and then back at the boxy, extralong, extratall, top-heavy vehicle. "For me?"

"Oui," he said. "Leased for Bijoux for delivering the cakes. Come. See." He opened the doors, and I saw the inside was set up to stabilize the large wedding cakes for delivery. The walls were lined with cooling panels. "You need to be able to fit several cakes in here at a time," he said, "right?"

"Right." Assuming I had three or four orders at once. Or two. Or one.

"You can drive it for your own personal use too, when you need to," he added magnanimously. "And take Céline today, if you like."

I nodded dumbly as he grinned, pleased with his gift. He went to get Céline and her backpack. I stood there, staring.

A marketing job. An apartment in a retirement community. An ungainly white commercial van.

That's just how I roll.

Three

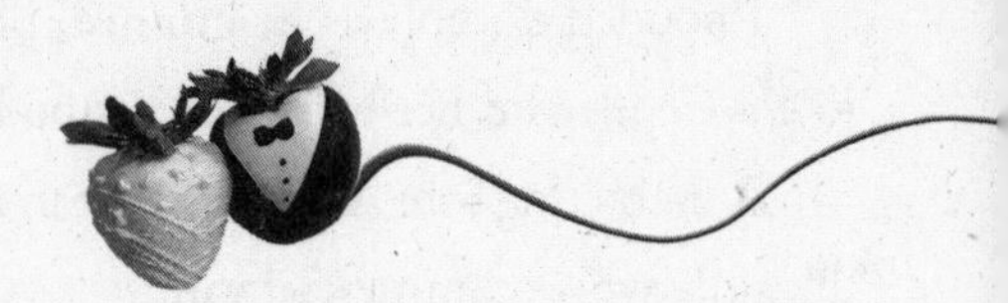

It is only with the heart that one can see rightly;
what is essential is invisible to the eye.
Antoine de Saint-Exupér

He's here!" Nonna dropped the curtains and turned back to me.

"Could you *please* go upstairs to your own apartment?" I pleaded before looking at the calendar. Sophie promised she'd know by the middle of the month if a studio was coming available at her building. Otherwise, I would have to start begging low-rent property managers.

Nonna kissed my cheek and slipped out the door, leaving it open for me to follow. I noticed that nimble Nonna feigned aches and pains so she could walk slowly toward the elevator and not miss anything. Dan entered the lobby, and the place went dead silent. I locked the guest apartment door behind me and quickly headed toward him.

Every time I caught a glimpse of him, it sent a shock wave

through my insides all over again. He smiled, and his eyes crinkled at the corners.

Oh yeah. When I'd been mentally comparing him with Philippe, I'd forgotten about the beautiful gray blue eyes.

"Hey," I said out loud. Then I whispered, "They're all very nice, but it's pretty low on the privacy quotient. We can eat here, though, if you'd like."

"Um, no, my place is better." Dan turned to see me grinning. I had no intention of having a date at *my place,* such that it was. "I'm a good eater but a poor chef," he said. "How about we stop by whatever grocery store you like, and I'll buy the ingredients and you cook?"

"Okay," I said. "But afterward I want to introduce you to Bijoux."

"Deal."

He held the truck door open for me after I got in, holding my gaze for a minute before closing the door. Cooking for him in his place was definitely a more formal step. Did he realize it? He was pretty canny.

We drove toward Whole Foods—lovingly referred to among my friends as Whole Paycheck. But it wasn't my meager paycheck this time!

"I'm eager to try out some of the traditional French dishes I learned last year," I said. "Is that okay?"

"Parisian Porterhouse?"

"No," I said, shaking my head. He sounded like my dad. I wasn't sure whether that was a good thing or not.

"How about the royalty of the beef world?" he tried again.

"What would that be?"

"Sir Loin."

"Ha. How about *coq au vin,* chicken in wine?"

He drove into the parking lot. "Sounds good." He was a good sport.

In the store, we picked out some skinny early asparagus, plump chicken breasts, mushrooms, and a knobby head of garlic. Dan's face cheered a bit when he saw me toss some bacon in the cart too. Finally we picked up a baguette—baked at L'Esperance, I proudly pointed out—and a bottle of linen-crisp rosé.

His apartment was located close to L'Esperance and really close to the church we both attended. I realized, with a start, that I hadn't been to church since I'd left my parents' house.

"How's church going?" I asked, following him into the kitchen.

"Good," he said. "I was out of town off and on for a couple of weeks, but I've committed to teaching Sunday school again for the winter term, so I've been pretty regular. I'm teaching Battles of the Bible."

I laughed. "I'm sure the boys love that. Are you going to put your armor on?"

"Oh yeah, me and my knight costume," he teased. "But only if you're the damsel in distress."

"I don't feel too distressed at the moment," I said. "But I could pretend." He laughed aloud and turned the stove top on. I waved my hand over it. Things were heating up.

"Do you have a skillet?" I asked.

"Just look around and use whatever you need," he said. It felt weird, kind of proprietary to be cooking in his kitchen. I knew attending church together would be another step toward intimacy.

Easy Coq au Vin

Ingredients

5 thick slices bacon, roughly chopped
4 chicken breasts, cut into 4 pieces each
8 ounces sliced cremini mushrooms
20 whole baby carrots, cut in half
3 cloves garlic, peeled and minced
2 large sweet onions, chopped
2 cups red or white wine
2 cups chicken broth
2 sprigs fresh thyme

Directions

Cook the bacon in a large skillet until crisp. Transfer to a large plate but leave the bacon fat in the pan. Add the chicken to the pan and cook until it's nicely browned all over, about 8 minutes total, stirring every couple of minutes. Transfer to the plate with the bacon. Sauté the mushrooms, carrots, garlic, and onions in the pan for 5 minutes. Pour the wine and broth into the pan and cook over high heat until it boils. Add thyme. Add the chicken and bacon, and simmer for 25 minutes. Remove thyme and serve. Serves 4.

During dinner we talked about work, his and mine, and our families. He told funny stories about mistakes he made as a young lawyer, and we laughed at the mistakes I'd made in France.

"You miss it, don't you?" he asked.

I thought about working for Patricia and the beautiful stone houses and fresh produce sold by old men who handled each tomato as if it were a treasure.

"I do," I said. He was silent but looked thoughtful.

After dinner we kicked back and listened to his music for a while. I'd only been in his apartment briefly before, so I looked around to see if I could get an even better idea of the man. It was simply decorated but tasteful. There were exposed brick walls in some places as the building had been restored when the Ballard area went from old town Norwegian enclave to up-and-coming young professional district. Simple brown furniture adorned the living room; I couldn't tell if it was leather or pleather. I grinned, remembering what Tanya's fiancé, Steve, had said when they bought more affordable pleather for their new apartment. "Putting the pleasure back in leather."

The sound system was good, but it was a very manly place. No female touch.

I picked up a photo on the table, the only one I could see. "Last year's softball team?" I asked. I picked out Nancy right away, standing next to Dan. At one point he'd insisted she was only a coworker, but after we decided that being exclusive was not a good idea while I lived in France, I got the vibe they'd been out at least a few times. By the way she leaned into him in the picture, I guessed she had bigger plans.

He nodded. "Yeah. We're going to start practicing again soon. Are you interested in playing this year? We can always use a good catcher." I'd already noted, appreciatively, that he'd been working out.

His phone rang, and as he took it, I headed back to the kitchen to put away a few dishes. I was trying to be a good guest, but it felt very domestic. I wondered if Nancy had cooked and cleaned up in here too.

A bit later we drove to Bijoux.

"First I want you to see this!" I said, pointing at the gold etching across the window. It read, "Bijoux, a Famille Delacroix Bakery. Distinctive Wedding and Special Occasion Cakes. Upper Crust Pastry Catering." Our hours and phone number were etched with some fleurs-de-lis.

"Very high class, Lexi," he said. "I've had corporate send a couple orders over."

"I noticed," I said, and lightly touched the back of his hand. "Thank you so much. I've got a lot to do in order to make this work."

I punched in the security code and unlocked the door, then flipped the lights on in the front room. A few pieces of furniture had already arrived, including the huge display case. There were still some boxes, unpacked as of yet. The tables had arrived but no chairs. I opened some of the folding chairs, and we dusted them off and sat down. He handed me my cup of coffee; we'd stopped at Caffé D'arte on the way.

"I found out I'm actually the assistant manager," I said. I hadn't told anyone else that yet, except Tanya.

"Great!" he said, and then he must have glimpsed the despair lurking under my smile. "Or…not."

I shook my head. "Maybe I am a damsel in distress. I'm no good at business, as has been proved time and time again on my résumé. I don't like it. I can't do it. I'm a baker."

"So you didn't know you'd be managing Bijoux? Isn't...Luc's cousin here to help you?"

"Philippe," I said, trying to keep my tone of voice even.

"Ah, yes." Dan's jaw hardened just a little. "Philippe. The day I just missed driving you to work, your grandmother told me that he'd been very...helpful...to you in France. And now here too?"

"He's helpful, sure, but he's also running the other two bakeries." I tried to steer the conversation back to business. "As Sophie reminded me, I don't have to worry about staff, but I do have to drum up some business. Here." I picked up the wedding magazine. In the middle was the contract I'd planned to submit via e-mail for the wedding show.

"I've been thinking of exhibiting at this, but the application has to be completed and paid for online...tonight. Because the show's soon. It's expensive and would take up a big share of my operating costs, but it would be a really good way to get the word out about the wedding cakes. Lots of brides go to these things, and this is the biggest show all year. And the one thing I am confident in, thanks to my training, is the taste of my cakes. If I can just get people to try them."

"Makes sense," Dan said. "Can you get it all together that fast?"

"I don't know," I admitted. "Maybe if I do nothing else. Of course, with the number of orders we have right now, I have nothing else to do anyway."

Dan leaned toward me and handed me the contract. "You can do it, Lexi. I think you're better than you believe you are. Before, at those other jobs, you didn't have anything you wanted to sell. Nothing you believed in. But now you're invested."

"Do you really think I can do it?" I realized that by leaving the contract at the bakery, I had already given in to the fear of failure.

"I *know* you can." He gently closed my hand around the contract, holding my hand there with his own, and I didn't let go of the contract when he pulled his away.

"Thank you," I said softly. And then the moment slipped away but not without leaving an echo.

"Speaking of cakes, I want to show you my kitchen." I held out my free hand to help him stand up, and as he took it, my hand felt the same kind of warmth it had while waving over the burner earlier that evening. He wound his fingers through mine. "So here's the walk-in," I said, "and the wall ovens. I'm sure you're really interested."

"I am!" he protested. "Remember? And I've never seen ovens five feet long."

I pulled him into the walk-in and presented the cakes I had chilling to frost on Monday.

"You bake them in advance?" he asked.

I nodded. "If you don't wrap and chill them for a few days, they fall apart when you cut them."

I showed him the large corkboard on the wall and an area with clipboards hanging on it. "For catering orders. I keep them all straight," I said. We laughed; we'd first met over a catering order for his company I had misplaced.

Dan saw the very few orders on the catering side. He glanced at me with concern but said nothing.

"What's that?" He pointed to the large dartboard hanging on the wall.

"Oh, that's my brother's old dartboard. I put it up for fun at first, intending to take it down, but when I saw how much it bugged Margot, I kept it up." I grinned.

He walked over and read the papers that I had stuffed into each section. I was glad I'd replaced the "man, job, apartment" choices Tanya and I had originally put up. Mine said, "bake, bake, bake, shoot pool, marketing, *zut alors*!"

"What's *zut alors*?" Dan asked.

"Margot says it all the time. It's a French saying that means something like, 'we're in trouble now,' or, 'good grief,' or, 'what in the world.'" Most of the darts were stubbornly stuck in *zut alors.*

Dan touched the large, red construction paper heart on the walk-in door that said, *"Je t'aime, Lexi,"* and, "I love you, Lexi."

"From a niece or nephew?" he asked, smiling easily.

"No. It's from Céline, a little French girl I know who moved here. They don't celebrate Valentine's Day in France, but she wanted to now that she's here."

He smiled. "That's sweet. Do you know her mother?"

"No. Her mom passed away some years ago. She's Philippe's daughter."

"Oh," Dan said. "I see."

That was all.

Four

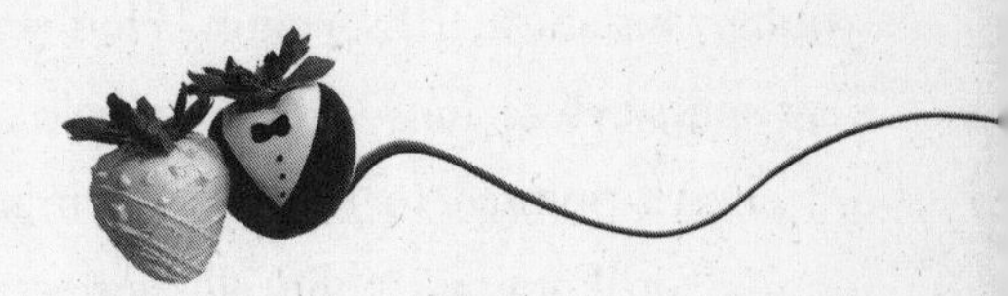

Each player must accept the cards life deals him or her: but once they are in hand, he or she alone must decide how to play the cards in order to win the game.

Voltaire

The Saturday morning of the wedding convention started early. As always. Finally, the megavan was going to get some delivery use beyond delivering me to work and back and Céline playing dollhouse on the shelves. I felt like I should crack a bottle of champagne over the rear bumper and christen it "Spinning Odometer" with great hope.

That morning, even Margot helped load the display cakes plus the nearly one thousand sample slices—all neatly packaged with an individual plastic fork and a chocolate coffee bean—into the van. She'd muttered about the stupidity of wedding cakes as she did, but I said nothing, though I thought it a crazy attitude for a baker. And I left the radio on classical music, her default choice.

I'd rushed an order for business cards and had stayed up late the past two nights taping one to the bottom of each cake sample plate. Last night, I'd slept on an armchair in the front room of the bakery after wrapping the cake slices with help from Andrew, Margot's young assistant at L'Esperance. He'd stumbled home to bed just a few hours before Tanya arrived to help out with the wedding show.

Tanya pointed to the two valentines on the bakery's walk-in door. "You know it's politically correct to call it 'Single Awareness Day' now instead of Valentine's Day."

"No way." I rolled my eyes. "I am officially aware that I'm single."

"And yet you have not one but two valentines here."

"One's from Céline," I said. "The other is from Dan. He sent it after he saw Céline's."

"Ah," Tanya laughed. "A little competition."

"You mean from Philippe or Céline?" I grinned, kidding.

"That's the question, isn't it?" she answered pointedly.

"I've been so busy trying to get everything set up for this show that I haven't had more than a quick word with either Dan or Philippe, although Philippe, Céline, and I are going to the Seattle Center next week. Children's Museum and then out to eat."

Margot came back into the kitchen. *"C'est fini,"* she said. "Everything is loaded into the van except for the decorations."

"Which are in my car," Tanya said, brushing off her black pants and white shirt.

"You're such a good friend to wear a semi-chef outfit," I told her.

"I'm just in it for the beer and nacho cheese cake at my shower."

"Thanks for taking the bakery alone today," I said to Margot.

"I think I can handle the enormous workload." She turned her back to me.

You haven't heard sarcasm until you've heard it in French.

I got into the van and started it up, and Tanya followed me down toward the convention center. I looked at my rearview mirror. My "B positive" blood donor card was tucked into the corner, where I kept it as a reminder every time I got into the van that attitude was everything. *I am trying hard to be positive, Lord. But please don't let anything go wrong today.*

My little Bible lay on the passenger seat. After I'd inadvertently flipped to Philippians in the retirement center community room, I'd decided to read through the book. At the red light I opened my Bible to the verse where I'd left off and started reading. A desperate tactic, as the light was only thirty seconds long, but I needed a boost. It was amazing—and sad, in a way—how much more reliably I read my Bible when I was worried or anxious, like I was begging God to be my supernatural Valium or on-call Mr. Fix-It instead of following His leading as Lord.

I found my place and read, "Whatever happens, conduct yourselves in a manner worthy of the gospel of Christ."

I hate it when a verse seems to promise trouble. I felt my confidence scatter like billiard balls all over the table. What was going to happen that I'd have to watch my behavior?

Lord, please let things go well today. Please let everything work out right, let a lot of people sign up for cake consultations, let a lot of orders come out of this show. I need it to work. I don't know what else to do. You've told me to rely on You, and I'm doing that.

I never doubted God's ability to pull anything off. Only His will to do it the way that I wanted—needed—it to happen.

After I prayed, an amazing, palpable peace relaxed me in a way that would have seemed unbelievable just a few minutes before.

We pulled into the underground offloading area for the wedding show. The show ran from eleven o'clock that morning through seven o'clock that night. We took everything to our booth—a little out of the way, due to my late registration, but still well placed. We had two front tables smoothly covered with starched white tablecloths and then skirted with light beige. "Perfect!" I said. "This will look fantastic with our dark brown, royal blue, and gold trim."

"And with the latte cake," Tanya said, "which Steve is dying to taste."

"Is he stopping by?" I spread the brochures out over the front of the table and set up the display cakes on the oak table I'd brought from Bijoux.

"No, he can't come. He's working," Tanya said. "Aren't those cakes going to melt?"

I shook my head. "They're made of Styrofoam and a kind of cement. It's just to show you what the cakes look like. I also brought a photo album of some of my other cakes, but I'm hoping what will really sell them is the taste."

"The taste is going to do it," Tanya agreed.

We set about two hundred and fifty of the sample slices on the rack I'd rented from the convention center. The rest would remain in the van with the cooling panel inserts until we needed to restock. Then I ran down the street and bought some balloons—in dark brown, royal blue, and gold—and tied them to the corners of the booth.

Lastly, I lint rolled my black pants and neatly starched Boulangerie Delacroix chef's jacket.

"Ready?" I asked Tanya.

"Ready!"

Brides, grooms, maids of honor, and moms trickled in right after eleven o'clock, and a low hum of excited voices thrummed through the hall. I'd walked the room before the official start. There were about a dozen other bakeries displaying. Not too many; I felt hopeful. I stopped by most of them, wiped my clammy hands down the sides of my pressed pants, and introduced myself as the new kid on the block. I left a brochure, which I knew they'd scope out later, and took theirs to do the same. Most of the bakers were really kind, but one or two were a little chilly. One woman was downright cold and threw my brochure into her minitrash before I'd even left. I was new competition—if only they knew how little they had to fear at this point!

There were also DJs, bands, dresses, and lots of caterers. I stopped by a few of those, amazed at the size of their booths. Then I raced back to my own before the show started.

"You go scope the stuff," I told Tanya, "before it gets busy. They're sampling food at some of the catering booths and there are lots of DJs. It'll give you a good chance to figure out what you want for your wedding. Get brochures! We'll shop!"

Tanya grinned and took off.

"Would you like a piece of caramel latte cake?" I asked a young couple who came toward the booth.

"Caramel latte, yum!" The groom held out his hand and took one for him and one for his bride. He gently put the first bite into her mouth. I melted just looking at them, practicing feeding each other wedding cake.

"This flavor is so unusual, with toasted frosting. The best one we've tried and we've already been to one other wedding show." The bride took a brochure. "Do you have a sign-up list for consultations?"

"I do!" I handed over my clipboard, and they left their name and number. "I'll call next week to follow up." I flushed with joy. Within the next few minutes, several other couples stopped by and exclaimed over the cake.

Then the cold woman from the competitive booth showed up.

Was I supposed to offer her a piece of cake? And why was she snooping around the back of my booth?

I decided to take the high road. "Would you like a piece?"

"No thanks, sugar." She flicked a disdainful look at my topper arrangement and left the booth.

What was wrong with my cake topper display? I'd ordered a variety, from fine porcelain brides and grooms to whimsical modern art representations. I toyed with a few of them, placing and replacing them.

Tanya snuck up behind me. "Well, I see you've got the bride in the right place. Were you testing out whether she looked better with the strawberry blond American or the darker Frenchman?"

"Just making sure everything looks okay."

"I brought you some samples. Looks like you've had a good start!" Tanya eyed the sign-up sheet, and I grinned.

"Yep, and the day is young."

A minute later, a pair of suited men walked up to the booth. Were they a wedding party? I'd heard there were alternative couples here too.

"Hello. We'd like to speak with the booth owner," one of them said in my general direction.

"That would be me," I answered. "How can I help you?"

"We're with the health department," the man said. "We're here to inspect your hand-washing station."

"My hand-washing station? We didn't prepare any food on site. It was all done at my licensed bakery," I reassured them.

The second man took out a contract. "If you'll note on the bottom of the fourth page of the contract—I assume one was e-mailed to you—you must have a hand-washing station installed at your booth in order to serve cake."

Tanya melted into the background, serving two new couples that had come up while I handled the crisis. Or mishandled it.

A contract *had* been e-mailed to me. I must have overlooked the fine print. I'd been so bleary eyed with details I'd skipped over some of the legalese. "I don't have a hand-washing station. Can I get one now?"

He shook his head. "No, I'm sorry. It has to be set up before the show actually starts. Otherwise it disrupts the other vendors and the visitors."

I panicked. "So what do I do?"

"You can still hand out brochures and take names," he said, "but you can't serve food."

"Nothing?"

"Nothing." With that, they shook my hand and backed away from the booth.

I left Tanya to fend for herself and slunk toward the back of the booth, squeezing my eyes shut. I had about nine hundred and fifty slices of cake that couldn't be served. I could stand in a booth all day and hand out brochures, but it would look odd with everyone else proudly serving cake.

I felt a hand on my back. "You okay?"

I nodded but didn't trust myself to speak yet. When I could, I told her, "We have to take the slices back out to the van."

"I heard. Do you want me to stay here and man the booth while you do it?"

I nodded. I needed a minute. I needed a week. I needed back the several thousand dollars I'd invested in this wedding show.

I took the slices tray by tray to the van and slipped them onto the shelves before returning to the booth and putting on a smile.

It didn't take long before Catwoman returned. "I decided I'd like a slice of your cake after all, sugar," she said sweetly.

I knew who had pointed the inspectors my direction. "I'm sorry, I can't hand slices out right now. Stop by my shop," I told her, handing over a brochure. "I'll give you an entire cake." Visions of dumping that cake square on her head crossed my mind.

She took the brochure and left.

Tanya and I stuck it out, but with no samples to share, we signed up very few people interested in a consultation. At the show's end, we packed everything into the van.

"I'm sorry, Lex," Tanya said as she took off for a date with Steve. "You sure you don't want me to cancel? It's no problem at all."

"No, go on," I said. "I've got to figure out what to do with the cake slices."

I sat in the cab of the van for a while after she left, exhausted. A fair chunk of my annual operating budget gone. I looked down at the Bible, bitter. *Why* had He given me such peace when this was worse than anything I could *ever* have imagined?

"I mean this in the most respectful way," I told God, "but I don't get the point of this at all."

I tried to figure out what to do before going home to the retirement center. Nonna was at St. Rita's soup kitchen, serving as she did every Saturday night. Maybe I could take the cake there.

I dialed her cell phone. "Nonna, can you guys use about nine hundred and fifty slices of cake?"

"What? Why?" she asked.

"I'll explain later."

"No, no, that's too much for us," she said. "Hold on a minute." I heard her muffled voice as she talked with Pete.

I sighed.

"Pete says try Community Table. They're bigger. Maybe the biggest. I don't have their number. You'll have to look it up yourself."

"Okay. And, Nonna, don't tell Sophie I called, okay, when she comes to bring the bread?"

"Oh, Sophie didn't come tonight. I think she has a date. She sent someone else instead. So don't worry, lovey."

I drew a long breath before dialing directory assistance and getting the number for Community Table. A nice man answered, and when I explained my situation, he said he'd be thrilled to take the cake. They served about five hundred people each Saturday and

Sunday night. Guest chefs came in and donated the food and time to prepare and serve main courses and salads, but rarely dessert too.

The location was not far from Bijoux, actually. I pasted on a smile.

"So glad to meet you," the manager greeted me at the loading door. "This will be a special treat for our guests. Most of them are homeless, and a fair share of our workers are, or were, too. I'll be glad to write you a receipt for tax purposes."

He motioned over a group of young workers to help me unload the van, and they did so, willingly and cheerfully. Most of them were men, but I noticed two young women working together too. They looked barely out of high school. And already homeless.

I pushed past my self-pity. I was glad they would enjoy my latte cake that night.

As soon as they'd brought in all the cake slices and went back to help that night's guest chef, I turned off my phone. I didn't want anyone calling or texting to ask how the big day went. I drove back to the retirement home and soaked in my tub with installed stability rails.

Then I finally cried.

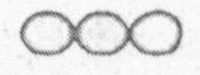

The next week was better, more hopeful, as I followed up on some of the leads the conference had generated. Margot and I still seemed unable to move toward a civil working relationship.

"I told you, wedding cakes are not going to do it," she said. "Better to concentrate on what French bakeries do best."

Not only would she not let me arrange the utensil drawers according to my work needs, she refused to let me check in the UPS orders each day.

"I can get the order," I told her as I heard the brown truck pull up. "You're busy."

"Non," she said. "I always check in the order."

This time, I stood my ground. "Even at L'Esperance? Even at La Couronne?"

"No, certainly not," she said. "Sophie and Carol do it there."

In other words, I was the only incompetent.

The driver got out of the truck, and I stationed myself at the door. I opened the door to meet him, and he set down four or five boxes. As I read over and then signed the manifest, Margot opened each one and ensured the contents were whole.

"Thank you," she said. In English! Then she dismissed him, and me, with a wave.

At that moment I became aware that I had inherited my father's blood pressure issues. But I'd at least taken an inch of ground. I resolved to work in silence or to classical music, but I would not get into a catfight.

Philippe picked me up one day after work—a very good day, actually. I was happy he came early, because he saw the Delacroix delivery truck taking out some catering orders. I delivered the cakes, because they had to be set up and decorated by me. The delivery truck took all the others.

"Ah ha!" He strode into the bakery and then kissed me on both cheeks while holding on to my shoulders. "An order going out!"

"Two," I said proudly. "Big ones. And I have two wedding cakes next week too."

"Ah," he said. "The wedding cakes. *Très bon.* You're going to do another wedding show?"

I began switching off my appliances. "Maybe. It's smaller than the event I, ah, went to last weekend, though," I added softly.

We drove to the French-American school Céline attended. She was in an after-school piano program, and I could hear amateur plunking bouncing through the empty hall.

"Papa! Lexi!" She ran to the music studio door and greeted us. "Come here. I want you to hear something."

She sat at the piano and picked out the first few uneven lines of "Chopsticks."

"Une génie!" Philippe said. *"Une génie musicale."*

Céline the Musical Genius beamed, though Madame the Teacher peered over her halfrims to discourage inordinate praise. In that, Philippe was already more American than French.

We got her little backpack off the hook, and she slipped into it before grabbing our hands. We three walked out together, swinging arms.

"Au revoir, bonne famille," Madame called out after us.

"Au revoir," Céline called back, squeezing my hand. Philippe didn't look at me, nor I him, after being referred to as a good family.

"To the Children's Museum?" I asked.

"A museum?" Céline cried in despair.

"This is a different kind of museum," I promised. "Wait and see."

We parked at the Seattle Center and hiked up the long concrete walk. We strolled into the museum, and Céline's face brightened the early evening.

"This is not a museum!" she declared.

Philippe paid for us, and we followed Céline's happy skipping into the first exhibit—forestry.

"Ah yes, I must put my boots on," Philippe said. We pulled on pretend boots and clomped after Céline through the Pacific Northwest tree exhibit.

"Attendez!" she called, motioning for us to duck. "Watch out for the bats. And the lava!"

I pretended to be afraid of the falling lava, which delighted her even more. I laughed too.

Next we went into the exhibit where she could try on costumes. She found some other girls to dress up with as Japanese princesses, and then she and a boy climbed into a pretend Metro bus.

"Watch out!" she called. "Crazy bus driver. *C'est moi!*"

Philippe and I sat on one of the benches with the other parents—um, adults—and chatted.

"She's really adjusting well," I noted.

"*Oui,* she is. Margot drops her off in the morning, and with her after-school programs, I can pick her up each night. Every day I find her with more children, some French, some not. She's the half-British, half-French girl who now calls herself *l'Americaine,* an American girl. It's funny," he said, looking at me, "how you were an American girl who dreamed of being French, and she's a French girl who dreams of being American."

I nodded and agreed outwardly, but something inside bugged me. I loved France, but I was an American.

"How are you adjusting?" I asked. "I feel like we hardly ever talk!"

"*Bon,* I am fine," he said. "So much to do, but I like it, I like it. The business is going well. La Couronne is smooth, and L'Esperance is, how do you Americans say it, humming along?"

I laughed to hear that phrase in a French accent, "homing along."

"Sophie is an excellent manager," he said. "Almost like a Frenchwoman, like Maman or Patricia. The customers are happy, the money balances perfectly, she is so careful, and we are in better shape than we were when Luc ran the bakery. He made a good decision, making her an assistant manager."

I blinked a few times, thinking of my quick perusal of the books at Bijoux a few hours earlier. They were leaking dollar signs. Philippe caught the blinks but misunderstood.

"Don't worry, Lexi, I will come look at the Bijoux books soon. In a few weeks, everything will be humming along there too. How go the wedding cakes? I can tell, they are special to you. Weddings are special to you, *non*?" He looked me straight in the eye and held my gaze. It was intimate and questioning, but I wasn't sure what the question was. The intimacy caught me off guard.

"They are special to me," I said, and switched tactics. "But not to Margot. She doesn't seem to like wedding cakes very much. Or me," I finished, rather pointedly.

Philippe nodded. "Margot was stranded at the church, you know?"

Stranded at the church? I shook my head. "What do you mean?"

"Her fiancé, he left her just before their wedding. Married her friend instead."

Ah. Maybe it was weddings she didn't like, not wedding cakes. But I noticed Philippe did not refute that she didn't like me. Instead, he switched topics too.

"Did I tell you? My papa is coming from France to visit. He really misses Céline but says he is coming to check out the bakeries. Ha! I know better." Céline called to her father, and he stood to check out her latest adventure.

We followed Céline to the next exhibit, the Imagination Studio. She imagined herself riding horses in the country like a cowgirl. I imagined what I would say to her *papi* when he arrived at the end of March.

"Come on," I said after another half hour. "I'm starving. Let's go have dinner."

"Okay," Céline said. "Where should we go?"

"I thought Dick's Drive-In would be fun," I said. "It's a real Seattle restaurant with great cheeseburgers."

"Yeah!" Céline said.

Philippe was quiet.

"Is that okay?" I asked him.

"I don't really like the McDonald's," he said, shrugging.

"It's not McDonalds," I explained. "It's different and very American."

Philippe smiled wanly and shrugged again. "All right. But I don't really like the cheeseburger."

"Oh, okay. Well, how about Le Pichet?" I suggested.

His face warmed. "*Oui,* that would be excellent." He put a gentle arm around each of us to shepherd us back toward the car.

I looked at Céline behind her dad's back. She looked back at me and coolly shrugged in a perfect imitation of her father, as if to say, *What can we do?*

Céline loved America, but she was very French. And so was Philippe.

Five

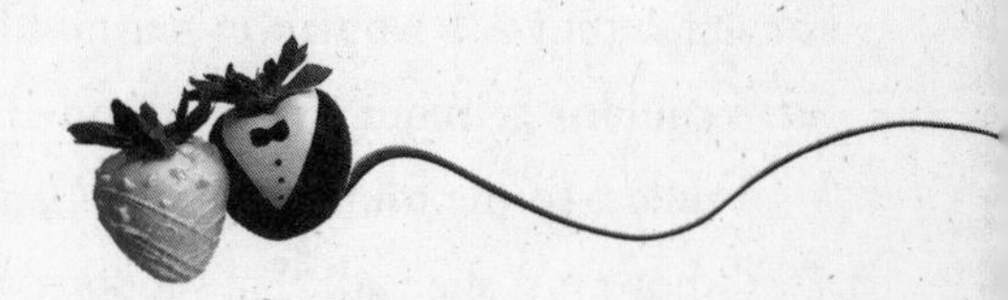

Man cannot discover new oceans unless he has the courage to lose sight of the shore.

Andre Gidé

Sunday morning I was at the bakery early. *I'm responsible and know what I'm doing.*

I knew what I was *really* doing. Avoiding church.

First, I was still angry with God about the way the wedding show had turned out. Next, I felt totally out of place at church. In France, I expected to feel like the odd woman out because I was a foreigner, but because of that, people had gone out of their way to make me feel welcome. Since coming home, I hadn't really connected at church. Of course, I hadn't tried much either.

"Just jump in!" my mom had told me over the phone. But Mom was a joiner; I wasn't. Did I have to pretend to be someone I wasn't in order to find my place in a Christian community?

Whine, whine, whine. I'll go next week, I thought, *when I'm caught up. Oh, but next weekend I'll be busy moving into my new apartment—out of the retirement complex and into my own place! Maybe church the week after that. Or the week after.*

A few minutes after I'd turned back to the food order I needed to finish, I heard a knock on the front window. I peeked through the kitchen cutout—a woman in her midthirties waved and smiled at me. I couldn't help but smile and wave back.

I unlocked the front door. "Hi. Can I help you?"

"I hope so," she said. "I'm supposed to bring refreshments to my singles group this morning and totally forgot. I remembered there was a new bakery here and hoped I could pop in and buy something. I've got to be there in fifteen minutes." She checked her watch.

"We're a commercial bakery," I said and watched her face fall as flat as the first *brioche* I'd ever baked. Then I remembered I had a plate in the back from a catering order that had been paid for but never picked up. "I do have some pastries I might be able to give you," I said. I opened the door and let her in. "Wait here and I'll check."

I stepped into the walk-in and found the leftover platter. It'd be a risk sending it with a stranger, as I didn't know if she'd return the silver tray. My gut said to go for it.

I walked back to the front of the bakery. She sat in one of the leather chairs. I unwrapped the tray and presented it with a flourish. "I have these."

"Oh, so pretty!" She admired the emerald kiwi tarts, the tiny lemon puffs, squiggled mini *éclairs,* and *macarons.*

"Will this work?"

"Will that *work*? Absolutely! I'll be the hit of the class. How much do I owe you?"

I shook my head. "Nothing. Someone already paid for them and then didn't pick them up. Just bring the platter back."

"No, not *nothing,*" she said. "I won't feel good about that." She turned on her heel and looked again at the front room, which was now completely set up. It had a warm, lodgey kind of feel, north-western and yet still elegant. I'd teased with Tanya that it would be easy to auction off the furniture when I ran out of capital.

"The entire neighborhood was so pleased when you guys took over this building," she said. "It's been empty and run down for some time, and now look at it. Gorgeous."

"Thank you," I said. Then I blurted, "Business is a little slow building up."

I regretted it as soon as I said it. Was I turning into Terri Too Much Information? Maybe because I had so few people to talk to about it. I couldn't tell anyone else at the bakery without making them nervous. I didn't want to bother Tanya too much in her pre-marital bliss. Didn't want to freak out my parents. Didn't want to let Dan down.

"Really? With these great pastries? And your front sign says you do wedding cakes too. Does your Web page bring in much business?"

I shook my head. "I don't have a Web page." Why hadn't I thought of that?

She reached into her pocket and pulled out a card. "Maybe I can help. Let's talk when I return your platter."

I looked at her card. Natasha Vogler, Web designer for Blue Nile, a jewelry e-tailer located downtown. "Okay." I couldn't afford her, but at least I'd get my platter back.

She looked so happy to be meeting with friends that morning. I locked the door behind her and realized that maybe I missed Christian community more than I'd realized. I grabbed my keys, headed out to the van, and took off.

As I pulled into the parking lot, it looked like church was just about to begin. I scoped out the sanctuary from the back and saw a couple scattered open seats...and then I saw Dan.

I made the decision quickly and slipped in next to him.

"Hey. Do you seek here often?" he teased, tagging a pickup line for church.

"Who says I'm seeking anything?" I teased back. I already felt better being there. He pointedly put his Bible on the other side of him so that we sat side by side. The space between us crackled with the lack of distance.

We'd never been in the same service together. He was either teaching Sunday school or I wasn't there or we'd gone to different services. There was something powerful and intimate about worshiping together. For the first time I realized just what my mom missed going to church every week without my dad. She'd told me a hundred times as a kid not to marry someone who didn't share my faith.

Yeah, yeah, yeah, I'd thought then.

Yeah, I thought now. *Yeah.*

Dan felt something too. As we stood, our arms touched from shoulder to elbow. Neither of us drew away.

During the singing and Scripture reading, I closed my eyes and, as the Spirit led me, lifted my hands in worship, connecting to God on a higher plane, adoring Him as His name was praised. Afterward, I opened my eyes and we sat down. I noticed Dan didn't look disturbed that I raised my hands, though to the best of my knowledge he had not raised his own.

He passed that round. I had the feeling I had too. The pastor spoke briefly and powerfully from the Bible, and it seeped into the worried cracks in my soul, softening me, reassuring me. I closed my eyes and asked God's forgiveness for my self-pity and lack of faith and asked Him to help my unbelief. I thanked Him for sending a Web-designing angel to push me forward this morning.

After the service, Dan spoke up. "I'm going to teach my Sunday school class. Want to stop by?"

"As in…help?"

He shook his head. "Nah. If a woman stuck around to help, they'd all clam up and try to be on their best behavior. Or show off. Maybe I just want to show off for you." He grinned.

His honesty disarmed me. "Sure. I'll come until your class starts." I risked some honesty of my own as we walked down the hallway. "Then I'm going back to work. Things still aren't going so well." I'd told him about the wedding show fiasco, of course.

"I'll talk to the office manager about sending you more catering orders," he said.

"Thanks," I told him, touched but a little embarrassed in case he thought I was hustling him for business.

We entered his classroom, and the few boys who had arrived looked at us and fiddled with their camo- or steel-covered Bibles. One leaned over and whispered to the other, "I think that's his girlfriend."

I kept my eyes straight ahead, and Dan did too, but I saw him struggle not to smile.

I spent a moment watching Dan with admiration, the easy way he talked with the boys and the way they opened up, wanting to please him. I waved and began to slip out the back door, sorry to disconnect from him for the day.

"Wait." He caught my wrist. "I have a business dinner to attend this weekend. Would you be available to come with me on Saturday night? I know it's kind of last minute."

"I think so," I said. "I'm moving into a studio in Sophie's apartment building next weekend—she just found out yesterday that the tenant will definitely be gone in a week. I'm taking over the rest of his lease. But I should be set by Saturday night." I grinned. "I don't have much to move, after all."

"Great," he said. "I'm really, really glad you can come. I'll call you soon to talk about the specifics."

I wondered if Nancy would be there. "Will your whole office be coming?"

He nodded. "Yes. Is that all right?"

"Sure."

He reluctantly let my wrist slip away, and I backed out of the room. I stood around the corner where he couldn't see me and listened to him teach for a while. Last November, in Paris, he'd told me he was interested in moving on to the next phase of his life, and he'd made it pretty clear that meant marriage and a family, though he hadn't said he wanted it to be with me. Listening to him, now, I could see he was a natural fit with kids.

I, on the other hand, was not a natural fit with kids. With the exception of Céline, I had little idea of what to do with young children. And like pack animals, they usually sensed my vulnerability and closed in for the kill.

I walked down the hallway toward the sanctuary. I nodded to a few people, and they nodded back, politely, but then turned back to chat with people they already knew. This didn't feel like a home to me in any way. I felt like I should keep parking in the visitor spaces every week.

"Just jump in!" I heard my mother echo in my head.

At the end of the hallway, I saw a sign-up sheet on a bulletin board.

HELP WANTED!

Sign up below to volunteer in the following areas: sound system, janitorial services, Tuesday morning coffee service, van driver for feeding homeless, or Sunday school substitute teacher.

Name	**Phone Number**	**Area in Which You Wish to Serve**

Got an idea of your own on how we can serve others? Let us know!

Couldn't do Tuesday mornings; I worked. Didn't know anything about sound booths. I was driving a van way more than I wanted to at this point, saving up for a car. I looked again at the list of service options, my eyes stopping on substitute Sunday school teacher.

You know, maybe it's just that I never had a chance. I was always overshadowed by babysitter extraordinaire Tanya. I could be a completely fantastic, newly emergent Sunday school teacher.

I jotted down my name and number, hoping they'd never call.

Six

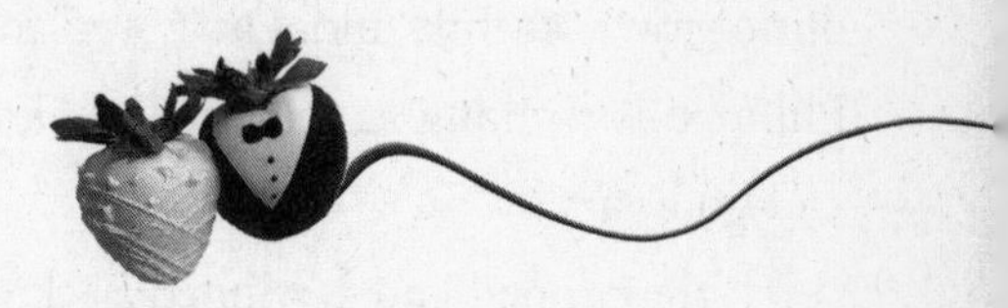

The desire of the man is for the woman,

but the desire of the woman is for the desire of the man.

Madame de Staël

"I think I twisted my ankle," my brother Nate moaned as he stumbled into my new studio apartment with the second-to-last box. "Leah, will you check it out?"

I looked at Leah, his wife, and rolled my eyes. She winked back. The difference between a wife and a sister, I guessed.

She bent down as he pulled his shoe off and said, "I think it's good. And we're nearly done."

He nodded. "Thanks, honey." He kissed her cheek. They were still newlyweds, but married life didn't seem to have cured him of his lifelong hypochondria. In fact, being—and marrying—a lawyer made him more aware of every tiny detail. I was rafting through life on a sea of attorneys.

"Say, how come that lawyer friend of yours or the French guy isn't here helping you move?" Nate asked. "Seems like you could pull some favors with either or both of them."

I punched his arm to give him something legitimate to complain about to Nurse Leah later. "Dan is working today—they have out-of-town clients, and I'm going to their dinner later tonight. Philippe is working at the bakery. Not everyone has cushy come-and-go hours."

Nate grinned and I grinned back at him. I knew he worked a really heavy load.

"We'd better head back and clean up the guest apartment for Nonna," Nate said.

I grabbed my purse. "Should we take two cars?"

Leah shook her head. "Nate and I will do it for you. You've got a lot to do here. What's family for?"

"Thanks," I said. Nate waved good-bye and headed out the door, but I held a finger up to indicate that Leah should hang behind for a minute. "Come in here," I said, motioning toward the bathroom. I showed her the dress hanging from the shower rod. "Ta da! What do you think?"

It was a wine red sheath dress, close fitting but not form fitting, with a light spray of gold undertone catching the light in little shimmers.

"Do you think this will work for the formal dinner tonight?" I'd laid off the baguettes all week so it would fit just right.

Leah sang in her best karaoke voice, "She's a brick...house."

"So I take it you approve?" I grinned.

"Approve? Oh yes," she said. "He won't want to let you out of his sight!"

"That's the idea," I said, laughing with her. "Thanks so much for everything today. Let's have lunch really soon—text me next week."

Not five minutes after she left, I heard a knock on my new front door. No security buzzer, though, so I knew it had to be someone who lived in the building.

I opened the door and found Sophie. "Hey!" I'd seen her on the go since I'd been back, but hadn't noticed until now how much she'd changed. She still had medium length hair, but wore it tousled now and looked more feminine. She'd removed all but two earrings from each lobe. She still had her nose pierced, but it was a tiny diamond that winked in a gentle way. She just looked…softer. "Come on in," I said. "It's my guardian angel."

"Nah," she said, but she looked pleased.

"Yeah," I contradicted. "I am no longer 'aging in place' thanks to you."

"I brought you coffee as a housewarming," she said. "And my elbow grease! I took the afternoon off in case you wanted help moving in. The books and payroll are all set at L'Esperance anyway, and I've got everyone 'homing' along, as Philippe says. Including him!"

"You are so competent," I said with only a tint of envy. "But thank you so much for coming to help. You're a great friend." I reached into the box I'd set on the dinette. "I found my expensive little Dale Chihuly bud vase." I handed it to her. "Would it be okay if we kept this in your apartment until I have everything unpacked? I'm afraid of breaking it."

"No worries," she said. "I remember your telling me about this." She held the vase in her hands.

"It's a vase I bought when I had very little money, intending to put it up in my place when I got the perfect apartment, the perfect job, and the perfect man," I said.

Sophie looked around. "And this is the perfect apartment?" She tactfully left unspoken the questions about the job and the man, though I bet she wondered.

"Uh, no." I smiled. "Grateful as I am. But I decided it needed to be out anyway, wherever I was. I'll bring it with me to the 'perfect' place too, if that ever arrives!"

"You bet," she said, and ran the vase upstairs. I started unpacking my books, thinking back on the last time I'd done this with Tanya when I thought I was hopelessly parked in my parents' house forever. I pulled out my childhood Bible, doodled-on cover and all, and opened it to Philippians. In the past month or more I'd only made it to chapter two. Okay, so I was savoring the read.

> Do nothing out of selfish ambition or vain conceit, but in humility consider others better than yourselves. Each of you should look not only to your own interests, but also to the interests of others.

I felt that tug at the threads in my heart. What *now*? I was going to have to stop reading the Bible if it kept asking me do things I didn't want to do.

Sophie came back in. "Can I put the books away for you while you do the kitchen? I know you'll want to put your cooking and baking stuff away yourself."

I nodded. "I don't have very much, but thanks a lot. I noticed the place is pretty clean."

"They had the crew in here right away after Chandar left," she said. "I asked them to make an especially good pass on the upholstery." She had a teasing gleam in her eye as she disappeared into the living room.

Even though the place came furnished, I had a few dishes and pans of my own. I unpacked my special baking rack, my sauté pan, and my knife set. I put a few serving pieces in an open cupboard with the chipped Prairie Girl Corelle I'd picked up at Goodwill. I wasn't going to spend a lot of my limited capital on dishes I wouldn't use forever.

I was kind of hoping to do a wedding registry of my own someday. No Corelle.

It didn't take me long to kit out the kitchen, so I joined Sophie in the living room. The place was decorated seventies style—gold, burnt sienna, and avocado. Sophie's place was a lot nicer because it wasn't furnished and the leases were longer, but I was glad to get into any place at all.

"How's work going?" Sophie asked.

I sighed and sat on the floor next to the boxes of clothes. "It's…okay. Don't get me wrong. The baking is fantastic. Margot is a pain in my neck, but I knew that was going to be the case, and we both have the same goals, so we deal with it."

"And the business end of things?"

"The numbers aren't good yet," I admitted. "I spent half of yesterday cold calling caterers to see if I could bring by a small cake and let them see and taste my work. I called up one of the nicest bakers I met at the show—I'd taken her card. She told me most of her wedding cake business comes from two places. First, wedding shows. Especially the big Valentine's Day one."

"Oh," Sophie said.

"Yeah. Oh. And then she said she got a lot of business, maybe most of her business, through caterers. She'd built up relationships with them over the years, and when people hired them to do their food for the receptions, they'd send them her way for the cakes."

"That sounds promising," Sophie said. "It sounds like you're learning a lot."

"Yeah," I said. "But nobody has asked me to send over a cake. I don't know if I have enough time to turn things around. Especially before Philippe's dad comes in a few weeks."

Sophie didn't answer nor catch my eye, but after a long silence she said, "You've met Philippe's father, right? What's he like?"

I realized I was the only nonfamily member in the bakery who'd met him. "He's nice, he's formal, and he's French. I'm pretty sure he and Philippe have wrestled a bit over who does what and who runs what. But that's only natural, right? I mean, two strong men with ideas of their own. Especially since Philippe's mom isn't there to intervene anymore."

Sophie kept her back to me. "The mom died when Céline's mom died, right?"

"Yes," I said. I pulled out my sweaters, and a puff of cedar filled the air. I put them on the top shelf of the armoire that stood next to the foldaway bed. "A couple of years ago. I think Céline has done really well since then."

"Do you want me to start breaking down the boxes?" Sophie asked. We were nearly done.

"Yes, thanks!"

She tore the tape off with one motion, and it ripped into the apartment's silence. "You seem to get along really well with Céline. I—I have to admit I was an only child, and I don't know how to relate too well to kids. Even though I love them!"

"What, are you kidding? You're always handing out cookies to the kids who come into the bakery," I teased.

"But that's not one on one," she said. "It's from behind a counter."

I turned my back and folded my jeans. The only sound in the room was the muffled *pop* of the cardboard as she wrestled it into place. I, on the other hand, wrestled with myself. Sophie was so good at everything. *Nearly a Frenchwoman,* Philippe had said as he'd praised her managerial abilities.

"Consider others...," the verse I'd read whispered to me. Suddenly I had the answer, and I knew it wasn't for me but for her.

I cleared my throat and said softly, "Maybe that's the problem, Soph. You stay behind the counter, you know, figuratively speaking. I'm just guessing, but maybe it's because I always come close and get down on my knees. That way she's not looking up at me but across to me."

She turned and looked at me, and a smile spread across her tired face. I realized she'd probably opened the bakery very early this morning and was still here helping me. "You're right, Lexi! I think that's it. Thank you."

We'd barely finished getting everything in order when I heard the security buzzer go off. For my apartment!

I ran over and buzzed back. "Yes?"

"*C'est moi,* Lexi!" a little singsong voice warbled. Céline!

I buzzed them in and turned to Sophie. "Did you know they were coming?"

Sophie grinned. "Philippe said he'd stop by with lunch."

They walked into the room, and Céline ran to me and gave me a hug. I saw Sophie drop to her knees out of the corner of my eye, and I gave Céline the tiniest nudge in her direction and winked at Sophie.

Céline went to Sophie and gave her a hug too—not quite as warm as mine but not as standoffish as I'd seen them at other times. Maybe I did have a way with kids after all!

"Hungry?" Philippe handed me a small box.

"Famished!" I stood and took the box before kissing him on each cheek. "Thank you so much."

"It's for heating the house," he said.

I looked at him quizzically. "Oh, housewarming!" I laughed.

He laughed back. "*Bien sûr,* housewarming." I loved the way he dropped five years and his serious mask when he laughed. I could see Céline so clearly in him, then.

We sat at the table and chatted. It was clear from the conversation that Philippe was still very busy getting the bakeries in top shape before his father came, as well as just handling the steep learning curve of taking over everything from Luc, who had run things for years.

"Which means I am very bored," Céline said crossly. "School, bakery, homework, Tante Margot. That's all I do."

I felt bad. I was one of their only friends here. I should have done more to help them adjust. It's not like I had been a slacker, but I had more resources than they did.

"How about if we three go out somewhere soon?" I offered.

"Yeah!" Céline said. "Maybe to a movie?"

Philippe looked a bit uncomfortable. "Maybe...soon. Things are so busy and Papi will be here soon."

"Did you know my papi was coming?" Céline asked me and Sophie at once. I had the feeling Philippe had just suavely diverted the conversation, but I went along with the flow.

"Can I play your electric piano again, Sophie?" Céline continued without waiting for an answer to her first question. "I like the sounds better than the one at school."

"No, we have to get back to L'Esperance, *ma petite,*" Philippe said firmly. He stood, and we tidied up the lunch mess. I looked at my watch. I wanted to rest a bit before getting ready for my night out.

"Thank you again for everything," I said to them at the door. "For lunch, for helping me unpack."

"Of course," Sophie said.

"De rien." Philippe kissed both of my cheeks with gusto, then did likewise for Sophie. "We will see you very soon. I am hearing very good things about Bijoux. I will be in on Tuesday, *n'est-ce pas*?"

"See you then." I closed the door behind them.

As soon as I did, I had two surprising thoughts. *Sophie has a piano. And Céline has played it.*

OOO

I was ready early. My hair was perfect. I had mood lighting on—such that it was in the Partridge Family–era living room I currently resided in. I sat on the sofa and then got up again and looked in the sunburst mirror on the faux wood-paneled wall, checking my lipstick and my hair once more.

This wasn't a first date. Why was I so nervous?

In a way, though, I acknowledged, it was a first date of another kind. It was the first time Dan would introduce me to his colleagues, as a significant person, as an escort on an official date. We'd kept everything pretty low-key since I'd been back, but my lips had a memory of their own, and they could feel the kiss he'd left on them in Paris.

The security buzzer startled me out of my reverie. I pushed the Call button. "Yes?"

"It's me," Dan said. I buzzed him up.

I opened the door, and he greeted me with a hug and a kiss on both cheeks, French style. As he came close I inhaled the subtle, manly spice and polish of his cologne and for a moment it disoriented me. Or maybe it was just the closeness that did that.

"Your time in Europe is rubbing off on you," I teased, trying to regain my equilibrium, and he smiled.

"You're teaching me," he said. He stood in the door while I got my purse.

"It's kind of 'Age of Aquarius,'" I said, apologizing for the apartment. I didn't want him to think this was my preferred decorating style. "But I could get right in, and it's not forever."

"It's okay," he said. "Besides, who's looking at the apartment? *You* look fantastic."

I shrugged and said, "I clean up good," but I was happy he'd noticed. I did have a little more sparkle and poise since I'd come back from France. The bakers at the other Delacroix bakeries gave me less lip, and a few more heads turned on the street when I walked by.

"Ready to go?" Dan asked as he opened the door.

I nodded, flipped out the lights, and followed him downstairs. As we were on our way down, Sophie was on her way up.

"Hey, Lex," she said, glancing at Dan. "I was just bringing up your vase. I didn't want to be responsible for the cat knocking it over or anything."

"Oh, thanks. Soph, you remember Dan, right?"

She nodded. "Nice to see you again," she said, and then she turned and grinned at me. She seemed extraordinarily happy to see us dressed up for a date. Giddy, almost, which is not a setting I thought Sophie dialed to.

I took the vase back to the apartment and met them in the hall. As we parted ways, she gave me an enthusiastic thumbs-up when Dan turned his back.

We drove to the Union Square Grill where Davis, Wilson, and Marks, the law firm Dan worked for, had rented a huge room. The char of prime beef and the clink of real crystal filled the air with a sense of power. I looked at the people in the room and realized, French chic or no, I was in a whole other world. Auntie Em and the bakery were far behind.

Dan took my hand as we made our way through the crowds. Politically astute, he walked over to his boss first. He stood with several others, two men and a woman.

"Dan," the man said, holding out his hand. I looked at him—fifty-something with the chiseled look that said he was used to getting what he wanted. A gold watch. He looked at me appraisingly, and I got the feeling that I "passed."

"I'd like you to meet Lexi," Dan said. "Lexi Stuart, Rod Thompson."

I held out my hand. "Nice to meet you."

"Where have you been hiding her?" Mr. Thompson asked Dan teasingly, although we both knew he had to answer the question.

"Lexi's been living and working in Paris for the past six months," Dan answered.

"Ah, I see. Well, I'm sure Dan is glad you're back," Mr. Thompson said before introducing Dan to the others in the small group. They were investors and partners with the firm that had just contracted with Davis, Wilson, and Marks to represent their legal interests. The dinner this evening was a celebration of the contract signing.

As soon as he could break away, Dan led me to another group several tables away. I could feel him relax as we approached them. "Now *these* are my friends," he said.

"Hey, champ," one of the guys called out. Dan reached up to clap him on the back and as he did, I saw he wore his trademark suspenders under his suit jacket, which I loved.

"We saved you a seat." He motioned to the chair next to him. "Uh, two seats, I mean," he said as he glanced at me.

"Thanks." Dan took care to introduce me to all of them, protectively keeping his hand on the small of my back. They were mostly lawyers with a couple of spouses, and they were all pleasant and kind to me, especially Chip, Dan's closest work friend. I got the feeling he and Dan had discussed me, but it wasn't a bad feeling. He grinned at me in a friendly way.

The Davis, Wilson, and Marks people spent a lot of time chatting about the deal that had just been closed. One of the lawyer's husbands, an aspiring writer, cornered Chip's date as soon as he found out she was a literary agent, and never let her up for air. I stood around looking nice and smiling and making small talk with the people nearby but didn't feel like I had a lot to contribute.

The salads were finally served, and each of us sat at the table. Wine and water were poured, and the conversation turned away from legal topics. A few people were still circulating, and one woman came up and put her hand on Dan's shoulder.

I recognized her right away, of course. Nancy.

She leaned down toward him on the opposite side of me. "Talk later?" she asked. "Coach." Somehow she made the term sound personal and intimate.

He nodded. "Yeah, after dinner. And congratulations on your work today. Nicely done."

She grinned. The dark side of me wished she were unattractive or unfeminine or repellent in some way, but she wasn't. She was a mix of lawyer smarts softened by the girlish spray of light freckles across her fair skin. The other men at the table looked admiringly at her too.

Dinner was served, and afterward Mr. Thompson and some others sent out a few rounds of hearty congratulations and welcome to their new partners, Axel and Silversmith, then invited us to mingle and talk.

"I hear you're a literary agent," I said, neatly steering Jen, Chip's date, into a semiprivate conversation away from the aspiring author.

"Yes, and you bake?" she said. Under her breath she added, "Thank you for rescuing me. I owe you one!"

We sat down together and started talking about work, what kind of books she represented. I told her about Bijoux's opening. She promised to stop by the next time she had a big book signing and get a plate of pastries catered. Dan looked pleased I was talking with Jen, and I was glad to have made the connection for his sake too. Out of the corner of my eye, I saw Nancy come up and begin a conversation with Dan. I couldn't hear exactly what they said, but I did overhear her say she had to get home early tonight to prepare for the Sunday school class she was teaching the next day.

Of course. How perfect. She taught Sunday school.

Dan appeared pleasant but not overly interested in her.

Jen must have caught my flicker of interest toward Nancy. "Don't worry," she whispered. "She can't cook."

The fact that she felt she needed to reassure me told me there had been some interest between—and talk about—Dan and Nancy. Nancy went to talk with some others as Jen slipped away and left me with Dan.

The lights were raising and the evening winding down. Dan took my elbow, in a gentle but proprietary way, as if to guide me from the room, when Mr. Thompson approached us with another man.

"Dan, if I may borrow Lexi for a minute?"

Points to Mr. Thompson for remembering my name in that crowd of people. I supposed he hadn't scuffled his way to the top without an impressive set of interpersonal skills.

"Sure," Dan said. It wasn't like he had a choice.

Mr. Thompson pointed to the man by his side. "Monsieur DuPont is one of the partners with Axel and Silversmith. He's from Paris."

Mr. DuPont, for a partner, was relatively young and oozed the charm and flirtatiousness that was the birthright of every Frenchman. "*Enchanté,* mademoiselle," he said. "It IS 'mademoiselle,' *non*?"

I knew Dan couldn't speak French, but he seemed to get the gist that Monsieur DuPont was asking if I was married or not.

"Enchantée aussi, monsieur. Oui, je suis une mademoiselle," I answered. "I'm a miss and not a Mrs."

"I'll leave you to talk for a few minutes. Hervé misses speaking his native language, and I knew I had a solution." With that mandate, Mr. Thompson slipped away.

Monsieur DuPont chatted to me about Parisian politics and their new president and my baking recipes and was generally very pleasant. I was happy to talk with him—mainly because I felt I could be an asset to Dan in this way. I sure couldn't talk legalese with him, but this I could do.

The conversation went on for more than a few minutes, and I looked at Dan, standing silently and awkwardly behind Monsieur DuPont. I wasn't sure what to do, since I'd clearly been assigned to talk with Monsieur DuPont. I knew he understood, but I also knew he was ill at ease.

A minute or two later, Dan spoke up softly. "I'll leave you two to French while I go finish up some softball business."

"Bien!" Hervé said before turning his back to Dan and continuing his conversation with me.

I tried to keep my mind on a French track and appear gracious and interested. But my heart and mind strayed as I watched Dan approach a small group that included Chip, Jen, and Nancy, and then saw him relax.

Seven

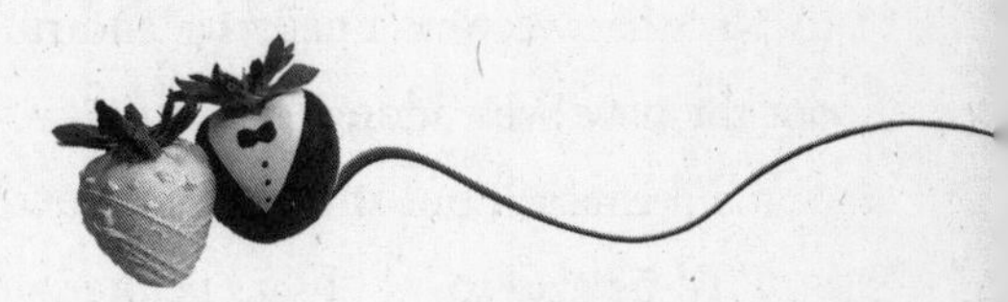

Act, and God will act.

Joan of Arc

I loved my mornings at work, mixing up cakes and trouble, but the afternoons were something different. Tuesday afternoon was just like Monday before it and Friday before that. I hoped I could keep the names straight as the calls all seemed to begin—and end—the same.

"Hello, may I speak with Jennifer Leischke?" I asked for the owner of the catering company.

"This is she. Who's calling?"

"My name is Alexandra Stuart, I'm the assistant manager of Bijoux, a new French bakery. We specialize in wedding cakes, and I wondered…" I didn't get a chance to finish before she cut me off.

"I'm sorry, Miss Stuart, but we've been working with Seattle's Best Pastry for a while, and I'm quite happy with their work."

"Can I send you a brochure?" I pressed, hating that I had learned to do so. I heard the sigh on the other end.

"Do you have a Web site?" she asked.

This was where this day was different from the others. Thanks to Natasha, we were finally up and running. "Yes," I said, spelling out the new Web address.

"I'll check it out and let you know."

"I'd be glad to…," I said before she hung up. It was my turn to sigh. I dog-eared the yellow pages three-quarters of the way through the caterers and hung up the phone. Margot, only feet away, kept her eyes fixed on the mini lemon tarts she was finishing for an afternoon tea catering gig.

For the ninetieth time, I wished we had a private office so I didn't have to make my calls from the front or the kitchen. But then the rent would be even higher.

I went back to the dartboard and threw some darts. I hit "call caterers" a few times and kept playing until I hit "develop new recipe." I promptly moved to obey.

"You don't want the other sheets of paper?" Margot asked, not looking at me.

"What other sheets of paper?"

"In the drawer, for the dartboard. I had to look in there to find my cigarettes."

I turned my back and blushed. The papers in there read, "Dan" and "Philippe." I guessed she'd paid me back for keeping the dartboard in her pristine kitchen.

Zut alors.

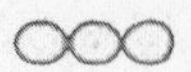

Wednesday afternoon I skipped the calling altogether and met Leah for lunch at the park near her office. The daffodils determinedly pushed their bonnets out of the ground, and there was just enough sunshine to deceive us into believing that spring might pull the curtains back early this year.

Leah settled on a bench below a Japanese plum tree still guardedly squeezing its blossom buds tightly shut.

"How's work going?" I asked as I unpacked our lunch.

"It's good. I'm grasping my way up the twenty-foot company ladder one rung at a time. They tossed me a low-level account this week, so at least I don't feel like the water girl anymore."

"It's hard to think of you as the water girl," I teased. "You're always so professional, so with it."

She unwrapped the sandwich I handed her. "Yum, Lex, thanks for bringing lunch. I pay next time we go." She tore a bit off the baguette and held it in her hand. "I've got everything under control at work, but I've, ah, spent a little too much at home."

I nodded. "You mean on that fabulous apartment?" When I moved to France, I gave the lease to the incredible apartment with a view I'd scored to Nate and Leah.

"Yes, on the apartment. And work clothes. And technology. Nate and I sat down a couple of nights ago and decided on plastic surgery."

I nearly choked on my Coke. "For who? He's not still worried about that tiny mole on the back of his neck, is he?"

Leah laughed and stretched out on the bench, turning her face like a sunflower to catch the best rays. "Yes, he's still worried about the mole. We actually have a digital photo history of his moles so we can track changes."

"No," I said. "I don't know how you put up with it. I mean, I love him, he's my brother and all, but…"

"I find it kind of endearing," Leah answered. "Things that would annoy me in someone else don't with Nate."

"Like my and Tanya's ear-shaving test," I said. Tanya and I had agreed that when you found a man whose ear hair you were willing to trim when he was an older man, you'd probably found a man worth marrying.

"Exactly," Leah agreed before taking another bite. "But by plastic surgery I meant cutting up the credit cards. I always thought I wouldn't fall into the trap of overspending. But I guess, well, I guess I did."

"How did Nate take it?" I asked, knowing his compulsive financial tendencies.

"He took it well," she said. "He was really encouraging and said we'd work together to make it right."

"Wow. I'm impressed. Love in action."

"Yeah," Leah said. "So, speaking of love in action, how is life going for you?"

I picked and poked at my sandwich but didn't take a bite. "It's…progressing. I've got the new Web site humming along. Natasha—remember that marketing woman from Blue Nile I told you about? She just finished it up. I wish I could show you."

I unwrapped two cupcakes I'd made with the recipe I was perfecting for Tanya's shower as well as for Easter. I handed one to Leah.

"Let's look at the site," she said, pulling out her micro laptop.

"Wow—expensive laptop. I need to be a lawyer."

Leah raised her eyebrows at me and we both grinned. "No."

As she called up the site, my cell phone rang. It was Céline's number. In the middle of the day.

"It's Céline," I said. "Do you mind if I take it?"

She shook her head. "No, go ahead. I'll navigate your site."

"Oui?" I answered.

"C'est moi, Céline," she whispered into the phone. "I am having a small *problème,* Lexi. There is a girl here who is being very mean to me."

"Where are you calling from?" I heard a distinct echo in the background.

"The bathroom," she said. "We're not allowed to use the telephone in the school day." She flushed once for good measure, and I held the phone away from my ear until the din died down.

For the next rushed minute she blurted out the bully tale, and I cooed some condolences before reminding her how mean Odette had been to me when I'd been new at the bakery in France.

"But I got through it, remember? I made a nice friend named Anne, and suddenly it didn't matter so much anymore."

"*Oui,* I will try to sit with a new friend," she said, sniffing. "Thank you for letting me call. Don't tell my papa."

"Just between us girls," I promised and then hung up. When I did, Leah looked hard at me even though she couldn't understand the French we'd spoken.

"You're pretty tight, you two."

I nodded. "She doesn't have a mother. And only Philippe and Margot here."

"She needs a mom," Leah said.

I nodded a silent agreement but set my face, warning her not to say anything else. "How do you like the site?"

Leah grinned. "It's perfect! Calling the wedding cake part of Bijoux '*the pièce de résistance*' was perfect."

"I sure didn't think of it," I said. "I am so not a technorati. I used to think ROFL meant 'running out for lunch,' not 'rolling on the floor, laughing.' Natasha thought of it. She's the marketing genius. She did the site."

"Was it…expensive?" Leah asked. "I don't mean to pry. I probably just have money on my mind."

"We bartered," I said. "She did my Web site, and I'm hosting a girls' baking night out for her and her friends at Bijoux this weekend. I can't afford to pay anyone anything. I have to be extremely, extremely conservative with money. We're not even making enough to meet the monthly expenses yet."

"I don't know why not, with food like this." Leah licked her fingertips as she stood. "I'd better get back to work. Got any more of these yummy cupcakes?"

I left Leah and headed back toward the bakery. Dan texted me, "C U in an hour for dinner…hungry for your company." I smiled and kept walking. A couple of blocks from Bijoux, I passed the Community Table building. I'd forgotten about it—and that it was so close. I hadn't really given it another thought since the night of the Great Wedding Show Disaster.

I passed it, then turned around and walked back. Some brochures hung in a plastic box next to the front door, and now that I'd cooled off, I wanted to know more about what they did. I pulled one out and stood there, reading it.

After a couple of minutes, a young woman came to the front door, neat brown ponytail swinging, broom in hand. "Oh, hi," she said.

"Let me step out of your way." I figured she meant to sweep off the front walk.

"Take your time," she said. She looked at my Boulangerie Delacroix chef's jacket. "Hey, I remember you. You're the chef that brought by that coffee-flavored cake with caramel filling. Right?"

I smiled. It still thrilled me when people referred to me as a chef. And she remembered the cake! "Yeah, I did."

"That was the best cake I've ever tasted." The young woman said it like she meant it. She wiped her hand on her apron and held it out for me to shake. "My name is Jessica."

"Nice to meet you, Jessica," I said.

"Are you interested in our guest chef program?" she asked. "We have chefs donate meals for our weekend guests."

I liked that she called the homeless *guests.* I liked her open face and enthusiasm and memory. If only I had the budget to guest chef. She didn't know I'd only donated out of desperation last time. "I don't think so right now."

"We have other programs." She pointed to the brochure I'd been reading.

Welcome to

Community Table

We're a Christian ministry that serves meals to Seattle's homeless and disadvantaged, as well as providing job training and guidance for culinary careers. If you'd like to help by...

___ being a guest chef for the homeless
___ donating financially
___ training our staff in the culinary arts
___ providing a job for one of our graduates

...fill out the information below and return to Community Table, and we'll contact you about serving opportunities.

"I'll take the brochure and look it over," I promised.

She nodded. "I'd really love to visit your bakery sometime." Wistfulness vined through her voice. "I'm about ready to graduate from the program. Would you mind if I stopped by?"

I knew what she was really asking. I recognized the hungry look that had been on my own face only a year before, though I hadn't been homeless or disadvantaged.

Was there any chance she could apply for a job?

When I got back to Bijoux I was surprised to find Philippe there. "Hi, what are you doing here?" I asked, coming in through the back door.

"I told you I'd be by this week to help, and at least once a week from now on," he said, hugging me and kissing both cheeks. "I wanted to see for myself how everything was going. Am I not welcome?" he teased.

"*Bien sûr,* you're always welcome," I said. "If I had known you were coming, I would have taken a shorter lunch." I pinned the brochure from Community Table on to the bulletin board.

"I am glad you took a long lunch. Margot says you almost never take lunch. That is not very French, you know," he admonished.

I knew she'd meant it as an insult. "I will change that immediately, sir!"

He handed me a coffee, and we went to the front to sit in the comfortable chairs, side by side. "How are things going?" he asked.

I grimaced. "Okay. Not perfect, but okay. I've been developing more recipes."

"Why?" Philippe looked truly puzzled.

"Natasha, the marketing woman who did our Web site, told me we needed an edge. And when she said that, I knew what it was going to be. I do a good job decorating cakes, but so do most of the people in the business. We can't slash our prices and probably don't want to anyway. What we can do is offer flavors that are both delicious and unusual. Right now, half of the wedding cakes served look great but taste like whipped Crisco. I want them to remember the taste as well as the look."

"*Oui, c'est si bon.* But new flavors? In France, we have the same flavors we've always had. Tradition."

I leaned back and sipped my coffee, feeling more confident than I had in a while. "But in America, people want their weddings to be memorable and maybe a little different from what everyone else does. Offering a wedding cake that isn't just vanilla bean or pink champagne flavor is a way to set Bijoux apart."

Philippe smiled. "Yes, it's good to have an American partner. I see that now." His praise warmed me, and we smiled at each other for a minute before he drizzled on the mood. "Do you want to look over the books next?"

"I don't want to, but I suppose we should."

Together we walked to the armoire in the kitchen where I kept all the business information. I took out the expense accounts and went over them with him. His jaw hardened a little, but I knew it wasn't personal.

"How many orders are coming in?" he asked.

I showed him the catering clipboards for the following few weeks with the bottom line highlighted. "Better," he said. "But not enough."

"I know," I said. "I figure if we can do four large weddings every weekend and four to five catering events during the week, we'll break even. Anything beyond that would be pure profit. Anything less than that..." I shrugged like a Frenchwoman. "I'm trying."

He put his hand over mine. "I know you are, Lexi. I am impressed with the work you're doing here. It's just that maybe this place wasn't a good idea. Maybe we should have just done the work out of one of the other bakery kitchens."

"The kitchens are too busy as it is," I disagreed. I could tell he wasn't conceding that point yet.

"Any luck on the caterers?"

I nodded. "One new, one from the Web site. I am taking a cake tomorrow. They do two to three weddings per month. A new accounting firm—we're catering their shareholders' meetings. Davis, Wilson, and Marks, the law firm, has stepped up their orders."

"It's a start," he said, but he didn't look too hopeful.

I heard the front door open and peeked through the kitchen cutout to see who'd arrived. Dan!

"A customer?" Philippe asked.

"No," I said, not bothering to explain the relationship. I went to the front to meet him.

"My boss, Philippe, is here," I said to Dan. "Uh, come on back." We walked through the homey oak front room to the cool stainless kitchen.

"Philippe, this is Dan. Dan, this is my boss, Philippe."

"Your boss, eh? True, but a little formal." Philippe stuck out his hand. "Nice to meet you."

"Pleased to meet you too," Dan said. He didn't look pleased. "I've heard a lot about you."

Yeah, from Nonna.

"Yes, yes." Philippe looked into space and then snapped his fingers. "I know you. You're the lawyer, right, who signed this lease for my cousin, Luc?"

"I helped him, yes," Dan said. My mind went back to Philippe's doubt about the wisdom in said lease just moments before.

"Ah, *oui,*" Philippe acknowledged but said nothing more. "Lexi, you're doing a fine job with what you've been handed." He glanced at Dan.

I closed the books. "I've been here since four," I said. "I'm going to head out soon. Okay?"

"Moi aussi," Philippe said. "But I'll be back. To keep Margot in line."

"Zut alors!" I said and he laughed before kissing both of my cheeks. He shook Dan's hand and Dan shook his back, professionally but not warmly. And then Philippe left.

"Ready to go?" Dan asked. "Our destination is a surprise."

"Cool!" I went to use the restroom, but when I got back his face was crestfallen.

"What's the matter?"

"Apparently, I made reservations for the wrong night. And they're booked."

"What would be booked in the middle of the week?"

"The Space Needle restaurant," he said. "I thought it might remind you of our date at the Eiffel Tower."

I took his hand, overcome by the desire to comfort him, maybe for the first time. "That is so sweet. It was a fantastic idea. We can still do it another time, right?"

He nodded but looked disappointed, like a little kid. It was both endearing and really attractive.

"And that means I won't have to go home to change. Lucky me! How about we go on a picnic? Maybe Green Lake? I have some sandwich stuff in the walk-in because I made lunch for Leah today. They're really good. Caprese."

"Caprese?"

"Baguettes with fresh mozzarella, basil leaves, and tomatoes. And balsamic dressing."

"Oh. Good," he said, but I think a sandwich to him meant something more meaty.

I grabbed the food, and we headed out to his truck. On the way to Green Lake we passed the Space Needle. I waved to it as we drove by, and he blushed.

"I'm just teasing," I said. "A picnic will be really fun."

The ground at Green Lake was wet.

"Let's tailgate," I suggested. "I haven't done that since I was in college."

We put the gate down on the back of his truck, and he threw a blanket from his cab over the bed. I laid out the sandwiches, cupcakes, and bottles of water. I had only picked at my lunch with Leah, so I was really hungry. We talked about his work and about church and about his family.

"You never answered me about softball," he said. "Are you interested in playing on our summer league?"

I'd been a catcher for many years, and we'd teased, when we'd first started dating, that I'd only play again if I could find the right team.

"On your team?"

He smiled. "Yes. Practices start soon if you're interested." He gave no hint of having picked up my double entendre and I didn't push it.

"I'm interested," I said. "Let me know the dates when you get them nailed down." I handed him a cupcake. He held it between finger and thumb with his pinkie raised.

"Been a long time since you ate a cupcake?"

"Yeah," he said. "It's not really a guy thing." He popped half in his mouth at once. "But this tastes really good. Even if it looks girly." He winked and finished off the other half in one more bite, then crumpled up the wax wrapper. "It looked like you'd been going over the books with Philippe when I arrived at the bakery."

I nodded. "It's growing, but slowly. I keep waiting for more orders to come in."

He nodded. "I know you're trying. Maybe you can't wait any longer. Maybe you need to act."

"I don't know what to do anymore," I answered. I heard the spring's first frogs clear their throats in the distant thickets of up-and-coming cattails. I'd read once that their croaking was a mating inquiry. I shivered a little in the falling dusk, and Dan drew closer to me. It felt nice to be nestled beneath his arm during a difficult time.

"Zut alors." He mangled the French badly, but it endeared him to me that he even tried.

"Zut alors," I said, laughing back.

We packed up the evidence of dinner and got back into the truck. On the way out of the parking lot, we passed a billboard, and it clicked.

Success doesn't come to you. You go out and get it.

Eight

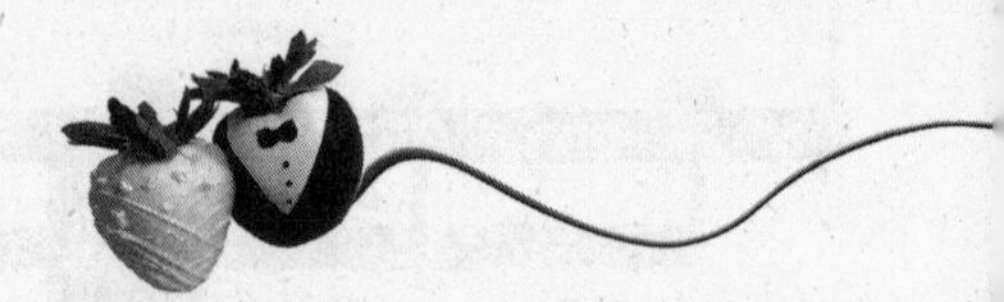

Life is thickly sown with thorns, and I know no other remedy than to pass quickly through them. The longer we dwell on our misfortunes, the greater is their power to harm us.

Voltaire

I placed eight deep, round cake pans on the marble counters, eight bowls, tubs of flour and sugar, and three sets of simple directions—homemade cloud cake, death-by-chocolate torte, and fruit tarts. I cranked the music in the kitchen and tied an apron on. I checked the clock a couple of times and then made sure all of my prep work was done. Along the back wall in the kitchen I'd already set out cheese and bread on silver trays, tiny petits fours, and some wine. No coffee. I continued to rue that we had no machine here.

Right at five o'clock Natasha knocked on the front door. I opened it and greeted her.

"Come on in!" Two other women trailed behind her.

"Hey!" She gave me a hug. I hugged her back and basked in the glow of admiration the others gave as they looked at my front room.

She introduced me to each of them, and in short order her other five friends arrived. One ran her fingers down the long bar on the other side of the kitchen cutout.

"I recognize this!" she said. "I work for a winery. We use these for wine tastings. Do you use it for tastings too?"

"No," I said.

"Maybe that's an idea," another friend pointed out as she tied her red-checked apron around her waist. "Cake tastings!"

The group laughed, but I didn't. I set the thought aside for a few minutes. Actually, if I could pull it off somehow, it was a very, very good suggestion.

We walked into the kitchen, and I lined everyone up along a stainless steel countertop. "First things first," I said and handed each woman a hair net. They laughed, and Natasha snapped some photos as they pulled them on.

"Ladies, start your mixers," I said and pulled out the first recipe. We'd start with the angel food cakes—so much better than the metallic-tasting boxed mixes and easy to make. An hour later, we pulled eight tall pans out of my oven and hung them upside down on Coke bottles. They looked like puffy silver hair dryers from the sixties, lined up along the countertop.

While they baked, I taught and washed up after them. I was used to both baking and cleaning up, but it seemed different this time.

Cloud Cake

A fine reworking of a traditional angel food cake—the taste makes it well worth the effort to do it homemade.

Ingredients

2 cups measured egg whites (don't substitute Egg Beaters or Liquid Egg Whites)
2 teaspoons cream of tartar
¼ teaspoon salt
1½ cups confectioners' sugar
1¼ cup cake flour
½ cup powered sugar
1 teaspoon vanilla extract

Directions

Preheat oven to 350 degrees. Sift cake flour and confectioners' sugar together and set aside. In a large bowl, whip egg whites with a pinch of salt until foamy. Add cream of tartar and continue beating until soft peaks form. Gradually add sugar while beating, and continue to beat until very stiff. Add vanilla. Quickly fold in flour mixture.

Pour into a 10-inch tube pan. The mixture will fill the pan to the top. Bake for 45 minutes, until top browns and cracks. Flip pan upside down over bottle and let sit until nearly cool. Remove bottom of pan and then cake. Serve with macerated berries and whipping cream.

Natasha came up behind me and tugged on my netted ponytail. "Can I help you wash up?"

"No way," I said. "This is your party; you're the guest of honor. I'll just do what needs to be done now so we can finish our recipes and then stack the rest in the sink for later."

"We're having a great time," she said, licking chocolate batter from between her fingers before running them under the sink. "How is the Web site doing?"

"Good." I ran my soapy sponge around the inside of a steel bowl we'd use to make crème patisserie for the tarts. "I've had several orders come in through it—and a lot more inquiries from individual brides. It's a great point of contact, but I've got to figure out how to drive more business to it."

"Can't help you there," she said, tightening the bow on the back of her apron. "But I do agree."

I helped each woman decorate her death-by-chocolate torte and then showed them how to stabilize their whipped cream so they could use the real thing and not sully their wonderful cakes with Cool Whip.

As the evening wound to a close a couple of hours later, I transferred each of their cakes to a silver- or gold-foiled cardboard rounder and then lined them, along with the tarts, under the lights on the "cake bar." Eight chefs stood behind them, arms around one another, and I snapped a final photo.

Natasha promised to send me the pictures. "Maybe you could hold baking nights?" she said as she pulled on her coat. "You're a really good teacher, and that might be a way to make more revenue. These little cakes look perfect and taste even better. Who can resist them?"

As each of them precariously balanced their cardboard boxes on the way out the door, one of them teased, "Do you deliver?" We laughed, and I waved to them as they made their way back to their cars.

I closed the door behind them and went back to the kitchen to go over the evening. It had been fun to teach, and they were eager and excited students, but I'd lost money. Of course, I'd done it as a barter for the Web site. Even if I'd charged, it wouldn't have made enough to cover what wedding cakes brought at six dollars or more per slice for several hundred people four or five times a week. I had to figure out how to get customers in the door.

As I sighed over the train wreck in the sink and on the counters, I heard a knock at the front door. Had someone forgotten her purse? I peeked through the kitchen cut out and saw a fresh, smiling face just outside. I recognized her but couldn't remember where we'd met.

As I unlocked the door, her name came rushing back to me. "Jessica, from Community Table, right?"

She beamed. "Yes! I'm surprised you're here. I've come by a couple of times on my way home, but you're usually closed."

"We keep early hours," I said, smiling. "But I'm cleaning up tonight." She stood there and I stood there. She said nothing, and I realized she was waiting for me to take the lead. "Would you like to come in?"

"Yes, please," she said.

I showed off the front room and the kitchen areas and then told her I needed to wash some dishes.

"I can help," she said.

Tired and not in the mood for conversation, I was about to tell her no thank you, when I saw the anxiety lurking behind her eyes and changed my mind.

"Sure," I said. I was glad for the help, really.

"I'll wash if you want to put your stuff away, since I don't know where it goes," she said.

"Don't you have a date or something to get to tonight?" I teased.

"No." She turned on the faucet in the industrial sink. "I've got other things on my mind. My six months at Community Table is coming to an end soon, and I've got to find a job," she blurted.

Which is why you're here, I thought.

"Tell me about your program," I said, snapping the lids back on the cake flour tubs and nibbling on a bite of leftover Brie from the cheese platter.

"Well, Community Table serves weekend meals to the homeless, as you probably remember," she said. "And those of us who work there are in, um, difficult times too. Some of us are homeless or were. I timed out of foster care six months ago, which is how I landed there."

I offered her some cheese, which she refused. She kept her eyes on her work while she talked about herself, never meeting my eye.

"Timed out of foster care? What does that mean?"

"You have to leave when you're eighteen or finish high school, unless your foster parents want you to stay," she said. "Mine didn't. I don't have money for college, so..." She shrugged.

"And now you're 'timing out' of Community Table?"

She met my eye. "Oh, it's not the same thing. They did a lot for me, but they've got other people to train. Trina and me have been looking for a new job..."

"Trina is your friend?"

She nodded. "Yes..." Her voice trailed off. Something else was behind it, but I didn't press her.

My cell rang and I pulled it out of my pocket. When I saw a number I didn't recognize, I let it go to voice mail.

"I'm going to clean up a few things in the front," I said. She nodded and went back to the dishes.

As I picked up a few crumpled napkins from the cake bar—I was already thinking of it that way—and gathered the aprons for laundering, I thought about the energy of the night. It was fun to have other people at Bijoux. Margot and I worked together in the morning, but our relationship was more of a truce—we had yet to win each other over. She worked at the other bakeries in the afternoons. Some days I was by myself.

But how could I hire Jessica? How would I pay her, and what would she do?

I wiped down the cake bar. I'd be doing tastings, definitely. But that, again, was trying to get people in here, expecting them to come to me, just like the Web site. How could I go to them?

Through the cutout I could hear Jessica humming along to the radio while she scoured the pans.

I looked to the left, at the yellow pages dog-eared at catering companies.

I could take cakes to them. With a business card. I'd lose money on the ingredients, and I'd have to work extra hours to do that *and* keep up with my current baking. Who would deliver them?

I peeked through the cutout again. "Jessica? Do you have a driver's license?"

She nodded. "Sure, of course. Just no car. I'm staying with a cousin of my foster family for now. I take the bus."

"Okay." I walked out back to take the trash to the Dumpster and think. If I hired her at minimum wage for a month, or at most two, I could give it a go. She could deliver the cakes, I could bake them, and she could help. We'd stay out of Margot's way. We'd take a small cake to every caterer I thought I had a chance with, starting in concentric circles around Bijoux. I'd also put a small ad in some local papers offering cake tastings. I'd do one more wedding show. I'd try my best to build up the business within the confines I'd been given.

Hiring her would cost money, using up my operating fund in maybe nine months instead of twelve. But then, would three more months really matter?

I stood there for a minute, thinking, and caught a glimpse of a bumper sticker plastered across a painful-looking dent on the back of a car parked across the alley.

That was true. When you drive, you know where you're going. Would I get where I was going by my design or God's, or both? Or by accident?

If I could make it work, we'd have a business and Jessica and I would both have jobs. If not, neither of us would.

I walked back into the kitchen as she was finishing drying the dishes and putting a sparkle on the sink. She was cleaning the *sink.*

"Come in the front room when you're finished," I said. A few minutes later I saw her dry her hands on one of the aprons, and then she came and sat across from me in one of the comfy chairs. "Thanks for helping out," I said.

"No problem," she said.

"I've been thinking of hiring someone," I started. I didn't need to tell her I'd only been thinking about it for the last fifteen minutes.

Her face lit up, and I held up my hand to dim the wattage before she fully understood where I was going with this.

"We're a start-up, and I'm not sure how long we'll be around. I'll be honest with you—I have a limited amount of time to make the bakery profitable, and if we can't make the numbers work, then we'll close it down."

"That's okay," she said. "It's somewhere to start. And I can help. So could Trina...if you wanted her to."

I shook my head. "I don't have enough work or salary for two people right now. You'd be on your own with me and Margot, the senior baker."

She looked troubled but then nodded. "Okay. What would I do?"

"You'd be doing a lot of clean-up and prep work, and driving sample cakes to catering companies as I try to get their business over the next month. When we do catering, you'd come along and help set up and serve."

She looked nervous, and I recalled my first days in front of an oven and behind the counter at L'Esperance. Everyone seemed so competent and I so inept.

"Don't worry," I reassured her. "I'll show you everything to do. I think you're a really good, hard worker." I specifically did not tell her that I knew she wouldn't let me down. I was dealing with the fear of disappointing others myself, right now, and didn't want to pass that burden along.

"The pay would be minimum at first," I told her, "but you could start right away."

"I understand." She looked like she was going to lean over and hug me but caught herself and fixed a more professional look on her face. "Thank you, Chef," she said.

"You're welcome," I told her. "I'll call your boss at Community Table on Monday, and if your references check out, you can start next week."

She nodded and promised she'd do exactly what I needed her to do, and I took her at her word. We finished a few details before I showed her out the door.

I could hardly imagine what Margot and Philippe would say. I was sure they would think I was crazy—first, upscale decorating, now hiring someone I barely knew when we had very little money. But I had to do something to make this work. I hadn't been getting anywhere by accident, so now I was going to follow a map, a map I hoped I was reading right as I made my way through Philippians and discerned a plan for my life.

My cell beeped to remind me I had a message. I pressed 1 and held it down to access my voice mail.

"Hello, Lexi? This is Jamie with the church's children's department. You signed up to be a substitute Sunday school teacher, and we need help tomorrow morning with the four-year-olds. They meet in the Noah's Ark room. The senior teacher will be there, so you'll just be a helper. Thanks again, looking forward to seeing you!"

Oh no.

The next morning I dressed carefully. I wanted to wear something casual and comfortable so I could play with the kids, but also church worthy. I finally settled on a pair of khakis and a light sweater.

I got into the van and headed to church, getting there early. I entered the nearly empty sanctuary; the praise team strummed and hummed quietly in the background. I saw the table set up for communion and was glad. The Lord's Supper. The holy meal, the French said. I looked at the elements and thought about how we would all kneel before them and eat a meal together, a meal provided by the sacrifice of Someone else for the care and keeping of His flock.

Community Table, I realized, was much like the Communion table. I felt drawn to both.

"Hey, anyone sitting here?" Dan tapped my shoulder.

"Just you," I said, trying to project more confidence than I felt at that moment. "I'm helping in Sunday school this morning."

"Great!" he said.

I didn't disabuse him of the notion. I knew he was good with kids, wanted kids, and in general, being good with kids was a point in a woman's favor.

We sat through the service together, and he put his arm around my chair at one point. I wanted to, but didn't, lean into it. It was comforting and supportive and intimate.

But then there was Philippe. And more importantly, I admitted to myself for the first time, there was what Tanya had been hinting at. There was Céline.

After the service we parted ways—he to his class, me to board Noah's Ark. I had a feeling the great disaster was just about to begin raining down.

"I'll look for you afterward," Dan said as he headed down the elementary hall. I, for my part, looked for the rainbow that promised a staying hand from disaster.

"Hi, I'm Lexi Stuart," I said to the woman at the door of the Noah's Ark room. I was relieved to see she was about my age and not a matronly woman with years of child rearing under her belt.

"I'm Tabitha." She held out her hand. "I'm so glad you can help today!" She had me fill out some paperwork and then unlocked the gate to let me into the room.

I wasn't sure if the locked gate was to keep the kids or the adults from escaping.

A few kids sat coloring at a desk, neatly dressed girls with bows in their hair and patent black shoes. Two boys shouted in a corner, one exuberantly building towers while the other just as determinedly kicked them down. Finally the builder started to cry. Tabitha stayed at the gate, checking in new kids, so I went to separate the two boys.

"Don't kick his tower down," I said as gently as I could. "Let's build another tower together, shall we?"

"No!" Demolition Kid said, aiming another kick. As I moved to protect the first boy's tower, I took the kick in the shin.

"Ow!" I yelled. Both boys dissolved into giggles. I refrained from glaring. Why was the first kid laughing? Didn't he know I was trying to help him out?

"What's your name?" I asked El Destructo.

"Bob," he said.

"And yours?" I asked the builder.

He looked at his friend. "Larry."

"Bob and Larry, let's build a tower together." Both boys began giggling again, and I looked behind them at the video monitor. VeggieTales was on.

Oh. Bob and Larry.

I left them to their own devices and went to hold the hand of a crying girl who had just been dropped off. That freed Tabitha to finish checking the other kids in.

"Would you like to play ball?" I asked the girl, picking up a large, tie-dyed ball. She nodded.

I threw it and she ran to catch it. We did that a few times while I kept my eye on Tabitha. Distracted, I threw it one more time and said, "Fetch the ball, girl. Good job!"

The little girl dropped her hands to her side and looked at me for a minute. Her eyebrows waggled and her mouth puckered, lemon style. "Fetch the ball? I'm not a dog!" Then she burst into tears again.

I put my arm around her. "Oh no, I didn't mean you were a dog." She didn't look as if she believed me but quieted down.

I was never so happy as when Tabitha gathered them around her and told the story of the disciples fishing and catching no fish until Jesus told them where to throw the net.

"Did Jesus make the fishes be there, or did He just know where the fishes live?" "Bob" asked. A smart question. I was surprised to hear him ask it, although my time with Céline had taught me that kids were a lot deeper and more thoughtful than I had realized.

"I don't know for sure," Tabitha answered. "But I do know that when they were tired and ready to give up, Jesus brought them to the fish."

After the story, we passed out paper cups of goldfish crackers while the kids watched a movie. I rested, glad for the respite, and thought about the Lord telling His skeptical disciples to fish in previously dead waters. Tabitha and I chatted quietly for a few seconds. She was only a year older than I was, newly married, and worked in real estate.

When the movie was over, I handed out refills of goldfish crackers while Tabitha took one of the little girls to the restroom. Bob took that to mean it was time for a free-for-all and started throwing crackers at Larry. Larry threw some back, and soon the rest of the kids joined the fray. By the time Tabitha returned, there were more flying fish in the ark room than at Pike Place Market. She calmed them down just as the first parents returned to pick up their kids.

I helped keep the kids occupied while Tabitha checked them out, but did overhear the little girl I'd played ball with magically start crying as soon as she saw her mother come to the gate.

"That lady called me a dog!" She pointed accusingly in my direction. I ducked my head and tried to look loving and attentive to a little girl who was coloring, but not before I caught the look of outrage on the mother's face.

Afterward, I helped Tabitha clean up, and she assured me I'd done fine. "They're a lot of work but very sweet once you get to know them," she said. "I hope you'll come back and help again."

I wasn't sure if she was being nice or genuine, but I wasn't going to commit to anything right now. It hadn't felt like my thing. I think she knew it too.

After grabbing my Bible and purse, I headed down the hall. I zipped past Dan's room, and I could hear him wrapping up. I wanted to get out of the church before he was done so I didn't have to admit what a disaster my time in the classroom had been. By the sound of things in his room, I wasn't going to make it to the van in time.

Instead, I slipped into a small, empty side room that overlooked the sanctuary. "Cry Room" was written on a piece of paper taped to the back of one of the chairs. It was supposed to be for mothers of babies, I supposed, but it was apropos for me too.

I admitted to myself the thought I'd had for months, and it grew stronger as time went on. *Maybe Céline is the only child I will ever feel right with, connect with.*

A minute later I heard a tap on the window. It was Dan.

He walked into the room. "Hiding?"

I nodded. *Might as well admit it.*

"Didn't go too well?"

I shook my head. "Nope. A free-for-all of crying, kicking children that Tabitha was able to calm but Lexi was not. The lesson was good, though, about Jesus providing fish for His disciples."

Dan sat beside me. "I guessed."

"You guessed I wouldn't do well?"

He shook his head. "No. I guessed at the lesson topic." He pulled a goldfish cracker from the back of my hair and handed it to me. "Badge of honor?"

That made me smile. "More like spoils of war."

He laughed as I popped it into my mouth.

A couple of days later, a large FedEx box was delivered to Bijoux.

"What's in there?" Margot asked as she signed for it and handed it over to me. I hadn't ordered anything to be shipped FedEx for the bakery.

"I don't know," I said. The return address was Davis, Wilson, and Marks, Dan's law firm. I peeled the tape back and opened the box. Inside were bags of every kind of goldfish cracker available.

Nine

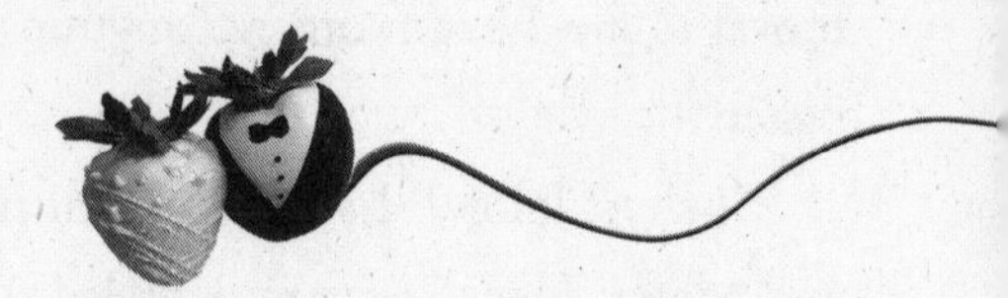

Suave molecules of mocha stir up your blood, without causing excess heat; the organ of thought receives from it a feeling of sympathy; work becomes easier and you will sit down without distress to your principal repast, which will restore your body and afford you a calm, delicious night.

Tallyrand

The morning slipped into consciousness with sweet bird song gliding through my window screens, preparing the way for April. I gathered my thoughts as I woke. I'd starched my hat, and I'd had my Boulangerie Delacroix coat professionally dry-cleaned. The night before, I'd stayed late at Bijoux making sure the books were absolutely accurate and that the kitchen shone. Monsieur Delacroix was coming to visit.

In spite of it all, I made time to read my Bible that morning, just a few verses, and then I meditated on them while I was in the shower. While I dressed, I prayed and asked the Lord to bless my day and to help me bless others, and then I locked the door and went to greet the day.

As I turned the corner from my apartment building to head toward the parking lot, I saw Philippe's motorcycle disappear into the dawn. Had he come to take me to work and I hadn't heard the buzzer? I puzzled over it for a minute and then put it behind me.

I arrived at Bijoux and was the only one there for about an hour until Jessica arrived. Her paperwork had checked out, and I had a final sign-off with her former boss at Community Table later that morning. Her uniform was crisp and clean but her demeanor a little shaky. I'd impressed upon her the importance of showing Monsieur Delacroix the professionalism that we strove for at Bijoux. Bijoux had become my hill to conquer or die on.

"What are you doing?" I asked her as I mixed up some cake batter for a wedding that weekend.

"Rearranging the catering orders alphabetically," she said.

I grinned. "He's not that detail oriented. Just be yourself and it will all be fine."

Margot arrived a few hours later, after having dropped Céline off at school, and got to work on several large pastry orders. She was even more crisp and clear in her tone than usual, though I noticed she'd been speaking a lot more English since Jessica arrived, which pleased and surprised me.

"Zat over zhere," she said, pointing to the dartboard. "Does it remain?"

I nodded. The rest of the bakery was picture perfect, Delacroix-cloned. I needed something that said, "Lexi works here." Technically,

Margot could have taken it down if she wanted, but she hadn't mentioned it in the past few weeks. The first thaw.

At ten o'clock I untied my apron. "I'm heading down to Community Table," I said to Jessica.

"Oh, today?"

"Yeah," I said, "but there's nothing to be upset about. He's already given you excellent references, and Margot and I are happy with your work. Don't worry."

She nodded but didn't look reassured. I took two more small catering orders off the Web and tossed them onto the bulletin board. Jessica immediately put them in alphabetical order. I smiled and let her do her thing.

On the way to Community Table, I made a couple of calls to ensure everything was in order for Tanya's shower at the Belltown Ballroom in a few days. I made a note to buy a few boxes of macaroni and cheese, cannibalize them for the cheese powder packets, and make a fake nacho cake.

It was just the kind of prank we'd always played on each other. We'd talked less and less over the past few weeks, and I supposed it was natural. She was busy getting married, and we were both busy working. I missed her.

I approached the door to Community Table and knocked—it was locked because it was so early. They didn't begin serving the public until dinnertime. A few people were sweeping and cleaning inside. Max, the manager, came to open the door.

He looked in his midthirties, and he and his wife had managed Community Table for a few years. "Lexi, come on in," he said.

We sat down together and went over Jessica's paperwork.

"Did she tell you her story?" he asked.

"A little," I answered. "That she'd timed out of foster care."

He nodded. "Her mother abandoned her and her younger sister when they were barely teenagers. Her father wanted nothing to do with her from an early age. Someone adopted her sister but felt Jessica was too old for them to make a commitment. Her foster parents were adequate but not loving. She's a hard worker, and you won't be sorry you hired her."

He couldn't have known I'd had second thoughts only that morning—not because Jessica was a poor worker but because I was offering her such a short-term position—and possibly working myself out of a job too. Maybe the few months extra her salary, pittance that it was, would cost me would be the few months I'd have needed to turn Bijoux around.

The verse I'd meditated on came back to me then, Philippians 2:4. *Each of you should look not only to your own interests, but also to the interests of others.* Lately Scripture had been convicting me. This time, instead, I felt His words as a reassuring touch on the shoulder. I hoped I was interpreting them right.

"And you plan to hire Trina too?" Max's voice brought me back to the present.

"I'm sorry?" I said, certain I'd misheard him.

"You're going to hire Jessica's friend Trina too?" Max restated.

I shook my head. "No, not at all. I don't need two people, just one. Did Jessica say I was hiring Trina?"

Max looked confused. "No, Trina told me that. I'm certain of it." He shook his head. "Maybe I got it wrong. A lot of the young people follow Jessica—she's a leader in many ways. But Trina, particularly, clings to her. I think it makes Jessica uncomfortable, but since Jessica lost her sister, I think she feels kind of responsible for Trina." He folded the manila file with Jessica's paperwork in it and stood. "No matter, I have it wrong, I'm sure."

He held out his hand and I shook it, aware that Monsieur Delacroix would be at Bijoux shortly and I needed to return.

I arrived not a moment too soon. As soon as I'd hung up my coat and gotten the paperwork in order, I heard Monsieur Delacroix and Philippe come through the door. I straightened my collar and went to greet them in the front.

"Bonjour, Monsieur Delacroix," I greeted him. He kissed me on each cheek, and I saw him look approvingly over his shoulder at the gold etching and fleur-de-lis on the window. *"Comme Versailles,"* I said.

"Oui," he agreed in French. "Just like the bakery in Versailles."

I showed him around the front room and explained that we'd be doing our first cake tasting next month, along the lines of wine tastings, which he, of course, thoroughly understood.

"But no spitting the cake out," he teased, and I grinned. Winetasters routinely spit out the samples so they could taste the wine without drinking too much alcohol. He had a sense of humor! Who knew?

I showed him into the kitchen. Monsieur Delacroix greeted Margot professionally, but not as warmly as I'd expect a father to greet his daughter. Jessica was just leaving to deliver two dozen sample cakes to local caterers.

"Who is that?" he asked.

Philippe cleared his throat. He hadn't been too happy when I'd hired Jessica, but he hadn't asked me to let her go either.

"She's an employee," I said.

Monsieur Delacroix stared at me, his nearly black eyes unwavering. "An employee? You are so busy already? *Merveilleux!* If we are hiring employees, we must be making a big profit already. Correct?"

"Not exactly," I said. "We are not making a profit yet." I confidently explained to him how I was developing new flavors, fresh and tasty but not too far out. He nodded appreciatively. "I have many ideas and just a short time to make this work, so I need more hands to make it happen."

He snorted. "*Bon.* But if it doesn't work within the year, then..." He shrugged, and I saw where Philippe got it from. "Business is business, *non*?"

"Oui," I said. "And thank you for asking me to be the assistant manager. I appreciate your confidence and the chance to make it work."

His caterpillar-like brows waggled a little, and then he broke out in a smile. "But of course, mademoiselle." I felt like I had scored a point with him and that he'd liked the show of strength. "And now, may I have a cup of coffee?"

I'd forgotten how much he liked coffee. In fact, for my pastry school presentation, I'd made a special "cup" cake out of a coffee mug for him as a thank-you for sponsoring my education.

"I'm sorry," I said with genuine remorse that I'd overlooked one important detail. "Because we don't have customers here, I've saved money by not having an espresso machine."

He looked disappointed but said nothing else. We went over the books and the plan with Philippe, and I showed them where the money had gone and how many orders were booked.

"I saw the catering board," he said, pointing to it. "Organized and alphabetized. I like that."

I grinned and made a mental note to tell Jessica about her *coup* later on.

"But according to your figures, you must have more orders." He snapped the book shut. "Philippe and Patricia are certain you can make this work. I, on the other hand, am not sure at all." Then he excused himself to use the men's room. I noticed he hadn't even mentioned Margot, the third sibling.

Philippe leaned toward me. "Don't take it personally, Lexi. He liked everything about the place. It's just that the bottom line is the bottom line to him, as you Americans would say. He would say the same to me too."

"I know," I said, but I knew what the books looked like at L'Esperance, and I was sure Sophie wouldn't be sweating the accounting details. "Thanks for the encouragement."

They left shortly thereafter, and I redoubled my efforts to get cakes to caterers and drew up an ad for the first round of cake tastings.

The next morning I arrived at Bijoux and was greeted by two surprises.

The first was a *café express* machine, with a card that said, *Bon Courage. Monsieur Delacroix.* It touched my heart, but when Margot saw it, she scowled and grew even colder toward me.

The second was a telephone message from the groom of someone we'd privately dubbed the runaway bride, canceling the order for a four-hundred-piece wedding cake.

Ten

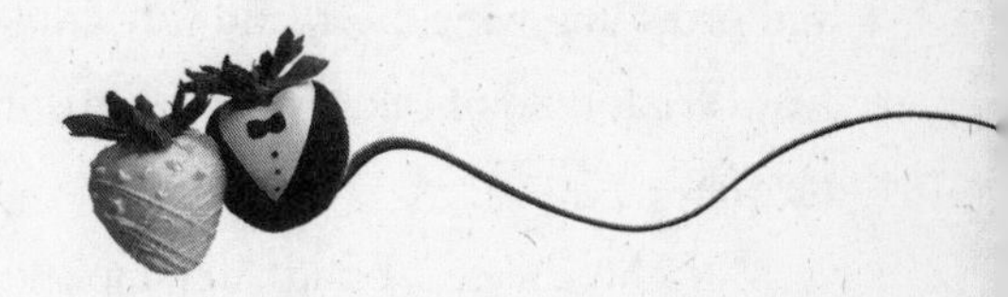

How slow life is, and how violent hope is.

Guillaume Apollinaire

I left work early on Friday night and headed to the Belltown Ballroom. I was meeting one of Tanya's work friends there, and we were going to set up the back room for the bridal shower.

Good thing I had the van! I packed it with the nacho cheese cake, the real cake, and some decorations. Then I stopped and bought a few dozen balloons.

The Friday-night crowd was starting to trickle in when I arrived, and Tanya's friend Christine was already there, waiting.

"Can I help?" she asked.

I pointed her toward the balloons, and we struggled to get them into the party room. Once in, we closed the door.

"I was thinking of making the balloons into billiard balls," I said, handing her a permanent marker.

"Great idea!" We sat in one of the booths and colored numbers on several of the balloons. "I think I'm getting a little high on marker fumes," she teased after a few minutes. I had to agree, the smell was overpowering.

We took a break and set the cakes out on the long buffet table in the back of the room. The ballroom was catering typical pub fare and providing wine, beer, and soft drinks too.

"What kind of cake is this?" Christine asked, pointing to the little one.

"Nacho cheese," I said. "It's a joke."

She laughed. "This is the most unique bridal shower I've ever been to. At a pool hall!"

"She's a unique woman," I said, and suddenly I felt the pain of the moment. For the first time, it dawned on me that in a very real way, it wasn't just the parents who gave the bride away. Her friends did too.

"Knock, knock." Tanya peeked her head in. "Am I welcome yet?"

"Of course!" I waved her in. "You're the guest of honor!"

She laughed at the loopy billiard ball balloons and took some pictures of the set up. Within half an hour, the other guests had trickled in and we were racking up the balls.

"Hi, Lexi."

I turned at the familiar voice. It was Jill, one of the leaders of the singles' group at the church I'd gone to as a girl.

"Hi, Jill," I said. I looked at her finger. No ring yet. She saw my glance, and I felt kind of ashamed. It was just that she'd seemed so close to marrying Bill last year when I'd left for France.

She drove right to the point, as she always did, but this time, I admired her for it rather than becoming annoyed. "Bill and I broke up," she said. "I thought it was a sure thing right up until the month before our wedding. Then he moved on to another church and another woman at the same time."

"I'm so sorry, Jill," I said. "I didn't mean to pry."

She nodded. "It's for the best, I think. I…I can be a little uptight, and he can too. Maybe we both need to relax." She didn't look as convinced as she tried to sound.

I leaned over and gave her a hug, and instead of the stiff, social hug she'd always offered in return, she gave me a genuine embrace. Seeing her here, more honest and vulnerable than she'd been in a long time, reminded me of the girl she once was, the girl with perfectly combed hair whose mother didn't let her wear eye makeup and always dropped Jill off early and picked her up late so she could run half the programs at church herself.

Grace, Lexi, err on the side of grace.

"I want you on my team," I said, handing her a pool cue. "I have a feeling you're a shark in the making." We were already on the same team, no matter that we worshiped at different churches—she at the church of our childhood, me at the church where I was starting to feel at home. She grinned and awkwardly chalked her cue. I looked behind me and saw Tanya working the crowd as hostess extraordinaire, becoming more and more comfortable in her own skin.

We turned on some good chick music and divided ourselves up among the pool tables, music keeping time to the beautiful sounds of pool balls clanking and women having fun. The tang of garlic fries and buzz of happy voices filled the room.

The games were different from your typical bridal shower games, but we still had prizes, all wedding themed.

"The winners of the first round each get a small bouquet of flowers from Blooms on the Way, the florist for Tanya's wedding," I announced.

Squeals of delight erupted as I handed out the gift certificates for the flowers. Second-round winners got a bottle of champagne each, or sparkling cider if they didn't drink alcohol.

"I'm going to announce the winners for this game," Tanya said, commandeering the center of attention after the third and last round. "Each person on the winning team gets an eight-inch cake baked at Bijoux, in the flavor of her choice, by Chef Lexi. If you haven't tried her cakes, you should. They're terrific—not quite as good as Safeway's, but a close second."

A groan of laughter sounded because everyone knew what a food snob I could be. I was the girl who insisted on using Belgian chocolate chips in the cookie-baking fund-raiser, and even though I wasn't the most popular girl in the crowd, my box lunches always got a big bid at the high school social.

"Safeway indeed," I grumbled to Tanya as she came over to me. "You deserve the cake I made you tonight."

"Oh yeah?" she said, her interest piqued.

"After dinner. You'll see."

We sat down, and Tanya made the rounds among all of her guests while we ate some burgers and pizzas and played a wide variety of women-empowering music over the sound system.

Afterward, I brought Tanya up to cut her cakes. "First, Tanya has to take a large slice of this one," I said, indicating a cake frosted with guacamole and decorated with pinto beans.

"What *is* this?" she asked as I sliced a piece for her and handed it over on a billiard-ball plate. She took a bite. "No way, nacho cheese."

I nodded. The guests had a good laugh and then went back to their own conversations. I cut the cake and handed a piece to Tanya first as Christine helped pass pieces out to everyone else.

"Mmm, this is good, Lex. New flavor?"

"Yep," I said. "I told you I'd think up a new one just for your shower."

"What is it?" She started on a second piece.

"Passion fruit." I grinned.

She laughed out loud, and there was no tonic in the world better than that. I was the one who held her, literally and figuratively, after her rape. I'd been to the counselor with her; I'd listened to her fears and watched her back away from intimacy anytime a guy drew close. And now here she was, laughing and looking forward to her honeymoon and beyond.

"My gift goes along with the cake," I said.

We opened the gifts last, and she got a wide variety of things from her and Steve's registry. Then she opened my gift.

There were plenty of catcalls and whistles from these wonderful church women, professionals, young mothers, and friends all. Tanya, for her part, played the blushing but happy bride.

"You have to come with me," she told me. "After all, you now work with French lingerie."

I laughed. Her family had thought—with horror—that I was going to specialize in French lingerie, not work at a French *boulangerie* when I'd first started with the Delacroix bakeries.

At the end of the night, we all smeared a little blue pool chalk under our eyes, like football players, and had one of the Ballroom staff take our picture before guests started drifting out the door, hugging Tanya one last time before leaving.

"So, once again, we're left on the cleanup crew," I teased Tanya, looking at the detritus of the evening's party and of our mutual singlehood.

"Yeah, that seems to be our place," she said. Normally she and I were so busy talking when sign-up sheets went around at an event that we ended up doing the leftover jobs.

I wrapped up the few pieces of leftover cake and tossed the napkins into the trash. We popped the balloons, which caused some of the staff to look in. At the end of a long week, a long night, that dissolved us into laughter. We sat down and finished off a last cup of coffee.

"It's getting closer," I told her. "Only a couple more months. I feel like we have so little planned together in that short time."

She nodded. "There's so much to do. Finish up the school year. Get all the paperwork done. Plan the honeymoon and the wedding, get the furniture..."

I squeezed her hand for a minute. "It's kind of bittersweet for me. On one hand, I'm so glad you have Steve. I really, really like him. On the other hand, we've always been best friends, and now he needs to be your best friend."

She nodded. "I know. I hope that's okay…" She looked divided.

"Of course that's okay," I said. "It's supposed to be that way. You need to go to him first with your thoughts and worries and all that now."

She finished off the last dregs of coffee. "In some ways, I think God made it easier by sending you to Paris last year. With some distance between you and me, there was space for me to grow closer to Steve. And now that you're back, everything is in the right place."

"I totally agree," I said.

"Someday soon we'll be having a bridal shower for you too," she reassured.

I smiled back at her, not wanting anything to dampen the evening. But an uncomfortable thought crossed my mind, one I kept to myself.

That's what Jill had thought too.

The next morning I arrived at Bijoux early. I had two wedding cakes to put the finishing touches on and then deliver to the wedding sites. I had invited Jessica to come along if she wanted. I could use the help, and I was hoping to train her to do setups too, so if we got busy, she could do more than just deliver cakes.

I pulled out a traditional pink champagne cake and the pillars that would support its many layers. "Can you get the cake topper?" I called to Jessica, who was in the front room.

"What does it look like?"

"It's that free-form African sculpture of the man and woman flowing into each other," I said. I made a few finishing touches with a piping bag and then carried the layers out to the van.

The UPS truck arrived, and I saw Margot head toward the door. Suddenly, all the color left her face and her hand reached up toward her neck.

"Are you okay?" I called, worried she was having some kind of stroke. It was so unlike her. She looked afraid.

She nodded and headed toward the walk-in. I met the UPS man—a fill-in guy, not our usual—and signed for our boxes.

"Does Margot work here?" he asked, peeking into the kitchen.

"Yes...," I answered, wondering how he knew. He must have picked up on my hesitancy.

"I deliver to La Couronne too, since it's just a few blocks away. Or, I should say, I did. I was injured six months ago and had to take some disability. I'm back on my route now, though. Have a good day, ma'am." And with a tip to his hat and a honk of his horn he was off.

I went to the walk-in to find Margot, who insisted she was fine but still looked flustered. Jessica still wasn't in the back. I looked through the cutout and saw her talking with another girl I recognized from my cake drop-off at Community Table. Trina, I bet.

After a few minutes, Jessica ran into the kitchen with the sculpture. "I'm sorry it took so long," she said.

"It's okay. Was that Trina?" I asked.

She nodded. "Yeah, but she's gone now." She looked at me and bit her lip. "We haven't seen too much of each other since I left Community Table. She's still looking for a job."

I nodded. "You ready to get the second cake in the van?"

"Yeah. I'll get it out of the walk-in and set it up for you on the counter so you can make sure all of the pieces are here."

I'd taught her that assembling wedding cake layers and pieces was like putting a puzzle together. Some of them flowed into one another, some of them were connected by marzipan, some cakes stood alone. Before we left the bakery, we assembled everything on the counter to ensure we had everything we needed. Then we broke them down again and put them in the van. Philippe had recently upgraded the van with a GPS unit so we'd never get lost. He'd bought it for me when he bought one for the L'Esperance delivery truck, so it hadn't come out of my budget.

Very sweet.

My phone rang. I was expecting a call from the florist for the first wedding. We normally tried to arrive at the same time, as the brides often wanted flowers around the cake, but if I had more than one to deliver, I couldn't guarantee I'd be able to hang around.

I answered the phone without looking at the number. "Bijoux, Lexi here."

"Hi, Bijoux Lexi here." It was Dan.

"Oh, hi, Dan," I said, softening my voice. "I can't talk long—I'm delivering some wedding cakes."

"I know," he said. "Big day. I wondered what time you'd be done? We're having an informal meeting for softball."

"I thought you were going to play on Tuesday nights. If you guys meet on Friday and Saturdays, I probably can't do it. So many weekend weddings during the summer," I said, disappointed.

"I know. We do have some Saturday games, but not many. Don't worry. Today we're just having a quick meeting since I'm going out of town next week for about ten days. I want to get things settled before I go."

"Oh...I didn't know you were leaving. And for that long."

Jessica motioned that we were missing a strip of green marzipan for the floral cake. I pointed her toward the walk-in, and she went to look.

"I just got it finalized yesterday," he said. "Boss doesn't want to go—fiftieth birthday party—so he's sending me. Can you come today? It's going to be beautiful out. Sunny and wonderful and the cherry blossom trees are blooming."

"I don't think so," I said, wishing it were different, especially at the mention of cherry blossoms, a reminder of one of our first dates. "After the cakes, I have to go somewhere with some people from work."

"Oh," he said. "I'm sorry. Where are you going?"

I hesitated before answering. "Mini golf. I promised Céline I'd take her out. She's been here so long, and I hardly ever see her."

"People from work, eh? I'm not a labor attorney, but I think there are laws against having children work at bakeries," he said teasingly.

"Her dad is coming too," I admitted.

"Of course. I understand," he said.

Did he?

"Dan?" I said quickly before he could hang up.

"Yes?"

"Would you be able to come to the cake tasting at Bijoux tomorrow? It's my first one. I'd really love to have you there." I motioned to Jessica to get the marzipan from a plastic storage tub, then turned my back to her while I waited for his answer.

"Yeah, Lexi, I'll be there. I'd love to come."

I sighed with relief and gave him the details before hanging up. Then Jessica and I piled into Spinning Odometer and headed off to our first setup.

We pulled up in front of a clubhouse on a local lake. There were already vans there—the food caterers were setting up.

"I'm going to drop you off here with the pieces for the big cake. You can set up the tables, and I'll be back in an hour to help assemble," I said. "I'm going to drop off the small, garden-themed cake, and then I'll be back."

Jessica nodded and I backed the van up to the door.

"Do you want my phone number," I asked, "in case you need to call me for anything?"

"Sure." She turned her phone on and typed my name and number into her contacts. A minute later, a beeping noise alerted her to a text message. I saw her push a button to ignore it.

We carried the pieces in and I gave her the linens, then I left to drop off the smaller cake for a church reception just a few miles away. I set the cake up on the table, arranged a few flowers around it, and checked with the wedding planner. Then I returned to help Jessica.

After setting up, we stepped back. The ivory cake looked stunning; five large squares secured one against the other with tiny sprays of pink icing flowers cascading down the sides. I had coordinated with the florist to have a few extra pink and white flowers that matched the bride's bouquet to scatter on the table for a finishing touch.

"Looks nice," a voice said behind me.

"Thank you," I answered, turning to see a fiftyish woman wearing a chef's outfit. "I'm Lexi Stuart, pastry chef for Bijoux." I held out my hand.

She shook it. "Cathy Paquay, chef for Delectably Yours. The cake looks very nice, simple yet tasteful."

"Taste is the name of the game, isn't it?" I said.

She smiled at the pun. "It certainly is."

"Do you get to taste the cakes at weddings?" I asked. My job was to deliver the cake and do the setup. I didn't get to see what happened afterward.

"Not usually," she said. "If there's extra, sometimes the wedding party offers it to us. But mainly they send it home with their guests."

"In that case, may I send you a cake next week so you can give it a try?"

"Certainly," she said, surprised. She handed me her card, and we chatted politely for another minute until she had to attend to the finishing touches on her luncheon.

Jessica and I got back in the car. "You did that really well," she said. "Smooth."

"Thank you. I guess now I can unlock my knees and start breathing again."

We laughed our way back to Bijoux. When we had unpacked

the van, I got ready to meet Céline and Philippe for early evening mini golf.

"Thanks for everything," I told Jessica. "You can clock out now."

"I don't mind staying to clean up," she said eagerly. I could see the young girl who never had her efforts recognized still working hard to seem valuable.

"Jessica, you did a great job today, as always. And you're very helpful. But being overly responsible for things that are not your responsibility is not a good thing, either. The rest is up to me."

"Okay." She untied her apron, looking confused but relieved. I had the strange feeling that I, who had always been the little sister, was now a big sister. And Jessica, who had always had to be the big sister, got to sit back and be the little sister for once.

After she left, I finished putting away the baking materials and then made a few calls for next week's deliveries. Half an hour later, Philippe and Céline showed up.

"Bonjour!" came her singsong voice through the kitchen. *"C'est moi."*

"Non!" I said. "I thought it was a movie star. You had me totally fooled!"

She ran into my arms. "Someday I will be a movie star and live in California, and if you're very, very *gentille* to me, I will let you stay at my mansion and swim in my pool."

I laughed and kissed her cheek. "Is that so? I will work hard to be *gentille* then."

Philippe grinned. "Let's get going to the mini golf. *Allons-y!*"

We took his car and talked about Luc and Marianne's baby, which was due any day.

"I want a baby too," Céline pronounced. "I won't even complain if it's a boy. And he will let me dress him up and tell him what to do."

Philippe laughed. "And just where are you going to find this baby?"

"You're going to get married and give one to me, Papa," she said.

The silence in the car was palpable.

"Let me show you how to get there," I interrupted the quiet. "By the way, thank you for the GPS for the van. We made the deliveries with no problems at all today."

"Bon!" Philippe said, cheered as always to hear about a business success. "And how are things going?"

"Good," I said. "Picking up. If we could just get a few more serious accounts online, we'll be set."

He nodded but didn't say anything else. I'd been saying the same thing about getting a few more serious accounts for a month, but he didn't seem to understand that these things took time. I turned slightly away from him, putting my shoulder in the space between us.

We pulled into the mini golf course, and Céline clapped her hands. Even Philippe loosened up and smiled. It was hard not to smile with the sun on our heads and Astroturf beneath our feet.

"You want to keep score?" I asked Céline. "I'll show you how."

Philippe paid and we headed to the first hole.

"So what's new with you?" I asked him. "Are you enjoying Seattle?"

"Oui," he answered. "A little. I've been at the bakeries quite a bit, but Céline and I have been...doing a few other things. Piano

lessons. We've gone to a movie, and one of her school friends asked us over for dinner."

"Oh, that's nice!" I enthused. We walked to the next hole, where I putted. Céline tried to get her ball into the hole with about fifteen swings. We laughed, but there didn't seem to be a lot to say. I tried again.

"Have you found a new place to live? Or will you stay with Margot?"

"It's fine with Margot, for now. We'll have to move at some point, naturally, but I'm not worried about that right now." He was polite but either disinterested or distracted.

Céline jumped up and down as she knocked her ball into the hole, and we clapped for her. Philippe stood aside and took a call, which irritated me.

"Your turn, Lexi," Céline called. I putted one in with four strokes, then took the card from her while she took a turn and bumped her father until he was done with his call.

FAMILY MINI GOLF

HOLE	1	2
PAR	3	3
NAME: CELINE	2	
PAPA	1	
LEXI	4	

Eleven

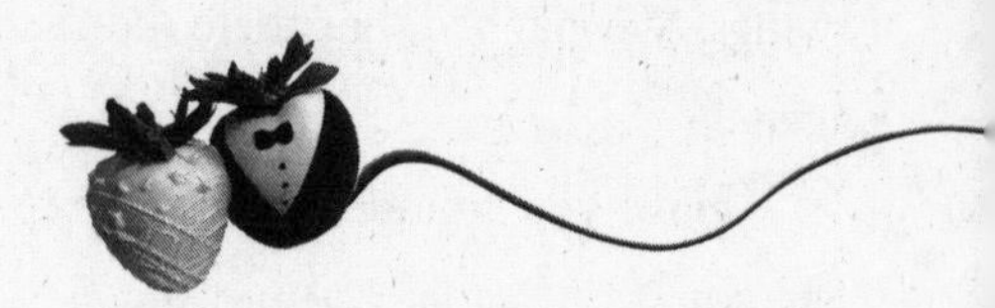

Hope is a risk that must be run.

Georges Bernanos

Dan wasn't in church on Sunday morning, but he'd agreed to come to Bijoux for the cake tasting and hadn't called or texted to tell me otherwise.

I'd run to the bakery right after church and gotten the place set up. I put some mood music on the rotation and arranged oval silver trays of bite-sized pieces of cake on the cake bar. I calligraphied the names of the cakes on ivory cards and set one in front of each tray to indicate the flavor of the sample pieces. Then I made "score cards" for my most popular, fresh, and tasty flavors. The guests could check off which cakes they preferred and leave a name, phone, and e-mail for me to contact them later.

I set some pretty pens nearby and made sure the walkways were clear. Then I went back to the kitchen. A few minutes later, Margot appeared.

Cake	Comments
Café Latte: Caramel Filling, Chocolate Icing	______
Rose of Sharon: Rose-Scented Butter Cream	______
Passion Fruit: Tropical Filling, Banana Icing	______
Vanilla Bean: Vanilla Butter Cream	______
Deep Chocolate: Dark Chocolate, Choco Ganache	______
Almond: Cherry Filling, Cherry Blossom Icing	______
Carrot: Lemon Filling, Cream Cheese Icing	______

Name:

Phone/E-mail:

10% discount if you reserve your wedding date at the cake tasting!

"What are you doing here?" I asked, surprised. "You never work on Sunday."

"*You* may not be aware of it, but I *do* work on Sundays," she said. "I am certain you'll need help keeping the kitchen running while you are up front, *non*?"

I nodded. "Thank you. Jessica is coming to help out. I didn't want to bother you."

"Pfft. That one can use some help. She's a little green, *non*?"

I smiled my thanks and agreement, but Margot waved them away with a dismissive hand. I'd seen her noticeably soften since Jessica had joined us, which surprised me. When I brought it up one day, she denied being tender with anyone at all. Later, though, over a cup of café crème, she'd casually mentioned that she'd left home at fifteen to apprentice in French kitchens for a few years after a fiery disagreement with her father, and that as he'd never loved her, she'd never had a father, really. It was much the same with Jessica. That explained both the coolness toward her father and the warmth toward Jessica.

A few minutes later Jessica came in, flustered. "I'm sorry I'm late."

After glancing at the clock I said, "You're okay. We won't open for a few minutes."

"Do you need any more help? I mean, anyone to come and work, even for free?" she asked.

I shook my head. "No, we're set. Who did you have in mind?"

"Trina asked if we needed any help. I told her I didn't think so but that I'd ask."

"No," I said. I would have to address the Trina situation at some point, I feared. My gut told me something was wrong there. Then I felt bad. Maybe the kid just needed a hand up. "If we cater a big event sometime, maybe."

Jessica nodded and tied on her apron. I told her what I needed her to do, and Margot prepped a few more cake trays, just in case.

I went to the front room and waited. What if no one showed up? There were three employees here, and I'd be so embarrassed if no one came. What if Dan came and he was the only person here? How embarrassing would that be?

I laced my hands together and flexed my fingers back and forth. I watched a young couple walk down the street, approaching Bijoux, and then keep walking right on by. I swallowed my disappointment. They'd looked so nuptial.

I ran to pretend to check on next week's cake fillings in the walk-in, something I'd already checked three times. I snuck a look at the ad I'd placed in the local papers to make sure I'd got the date and time right. I had.

"Lexi, *vite,*" Margot hissed into the cooler. "People are here."

She gripped my hand on the way out, and I knew she really wanted this to succeed for all our sakes, no matter how cool a customer she might seem day to day. I straightened my collar and headed toward the front room.

Not one but two couples waited there!

"Hello, and welcome," I said. I handed each couple a scorecard and a pen, and explained the cakes. "Please have a seat. Can I get you an espresso?"

"Yes, thank you," one man said and his fiancée agreed, as did the other two, who had already moved toward my topper display.

I asked Jessica to make four coffees and blessed Monsieur Delacroix for his gift, grateful I'd purchased some inexpensive but nice-looking demitasse cups at World Market.

Fifteen minutes later another couple strolled in, and just as the first couple left, promising to check back with me via the Web site, a fourth couple came in. The second couple left without placing a deposit, but the third couple loved the latte cake and signed up for their wedding date on the spot. Before I could ask for help, Margot was at my elbow with the datebook. I didn't let them see me write in it—viewing all those open dates might deflate their confidence. They ordered two hundred and fifty pieces, a very respectable amount.

They left and a single bride trailed in. As I chatted with her about the rose cake, I saw Dan arrive.

The mood changed for me the minute he walked in the door. I looked at him and smiled, and he held his hand up as if to tell me he knew I was busy and would greet him as soon as I could.

There was a short lull after I'd taken one more order, and I went to talk with him.

"I'm so glad you could come," I told him. "I was worried when I saw you weren't at church that you might not make it."

"I had a meeting this morning with the team that's going to South America for this deal, but I knew I'd be done in time." He looked over the cakes. "New flavors?"

"Yes, a couple," I said, feeling less confident and more shy for some reason. I think we both sensed this might foreshadow something.

He grinned. "Do I get to taste some?"

"Of course!"

One couple sat at the tasting bar, marking thoughts down on their scorecard and feeding each other cake.

"Hey, you're not supposed to do that until the wedding," I teased them. They laughed.

"I want to make sure he gets it right before the big day," the woman answered, and her fiancé lightly elbowed her as he gently lifted a piece of the almond cake into her mouth. They held each other's gaze while she ate it, and I could feel the burn of intimate heat and anticipation from several seats away.

I looked away and turned back to Dan, who had been looking

steadily at them too. "What kind would you like to try?" I asked softly.

"I haven't decided," he said.

I gathered my thoughts and put a few bite-sized pieces on one of the porcelain plates I'd set out.

"Which is your favorite?" he asked.

"That's not a good question to ask the baker," I joked. "Maybe you should tell me which one is your favorite." I held on to the plate for a second before handing it to him, just steps away from the couple feeding each other.

"My favorite is the baker," he said, taking the plate but holding my gaze.

After the cake tasting—a clear success—we cleaned the place up.

I high-fived Jessica in the kitchen. "You did a great job staying on top of the dishes."

Margot backed away from me, letting me know she was not up for a high-five. Still, she'd stayed to do prep work for the next week and she hadn't needed to. I think she really wanted to be supportive and knew I had the smaller wedding show soon. She'd worked on a few cakes for me too.

She and Jessica left, and Dan and I sat together in the front room.

"Two big orders." I waved the papers happily. "It's a start, anyway. People will hopefully spread the news, and I'll do this one weekend a month until we're fully geared up." I pushed away the memory of all the blank dates in the wedding cake order book.

"Maybe you should have named your Web business Word of Mouth instead of Pièce de Résistance," Dan said.

"Hey, that's catchy," I said, flushed with happiness. "You'd be a good marketer."

"What does 'Pièce de Résistance' mean, anyway?"

"It's the most important dish of the meal," I answered. "Usually served last with great flourish. Like the wedding cake!"

He looked considerably lighter than when he'd arrived. "Do you want to go for pizza?" he asked. "It might be the last time we'll get to go out for a couple of weeks. I'm not sure how long it will take to wrap things up in South America. There are four or five of us going."

I would not ask if Nancy was going. It wasn't my business at this point and it would seem petty. But I still wondered.

"I would love pizza," I said. "Let me just lock things up."

I looked over my orders and the work for the next morning, made sure the walk-in was tightly closed, and then set the alarm.

He led me toward his truck. "Alki?" he asked, talking about a local beach area that also had a couple of great pizza joints.

"Sure," I said.

We stopped at Pagliacci Pizza and split a pie, talking about movies and books we both liked, and he mentioned a few titles he hoped to read on the flight if he could get out to buy them ahead of time. Then he told me a bit more about his trip.

"I don't have to travel as much as I used to, so that's good, but this was a trip I couldn't avoid. New clients, and they're my account."

"I'll miss you while you're gone," I said, and he softened.

"I'll miss you too. But I'm sure you'll keep busy with work and other things."

"The bridal show is next week," I said, "and since I couldn't spend Easter with my parents, my mom is coming to stay with me for the weekend to help out."

"Got your hand-washing station?" he teased.

"Yes, yes," I said. "You and everyone else has asked me that."

"Just checking."

He dished out another piece of pizza for me and asked the waiter to refill my Coke. We talked comfortably about his work and who was taking over his Sunday school class.

"I would have asked you, but I didn't think substituting was your thing." I shook my head. It was still a sore subject. I think he noticed and moved on to another topic. "How is your new employee working out?"

"Good," I said, wiping the corners of my mouth with my napkin. "She's a very hard worker, and I've been thinking about how I might do more with Community Table. There's something strange between her and her friend, though. She wants a job, and I just can't give her one. I never really wanted to do marketing, I never wanted to manage employees, and here I am doing both."

"But it's for something you care about, and you're doing well," Dan said as he called the waiter over for the check.

"I know. Jessica's a hard worker, but sometimes she feels answerable for things outside of her responsibility. That takes energy away from the places she really could fly. I'm afraid Trina might be one of those situations for her. She needs to figure out what part of it is her problem and what part is not."

We changed subjects then and talked about his work, the day's news, and the local elections. We had a lively political discussion. He was more conservative than I was, but we had a happy give-and-take, and then we talked about our faith lives, where we were more in tune.

"I've really just started reading through whole books of the Bible in the past year," I said. "A couple of the gospels. Right now I'm reading Philippians. Just this morning I felt encouraged by the passage I'm on. 'Forgetting what is behind and straining toward what is ahead, I press on toward the goal to win the prize for which God has called me heavenward in Christ Jesus.' In spite of the finances, I'm going to press on."

I only had three months left of operating budget. May, June, July.

Dan nodded. "Philippians, eh?" The way he said it came out *Philippe*-ians.

"Oh! I just stumbled across the book early in the year and decided to start there," I explained. Secretly, I was glad he was a little jealous.

After paying, we walked outside and I noticed the softball gear in the back of his truck. "I'm sorry I couldn't come yesterday." I think he noted the real tint of regret in my voice.

"We missed you," he simply said. I spied a catcher's mitt in with his own gear. Had he been planning ahead for me?

"An extra mitt for your spare catcher?" I kidded.

He caught my eye and teasingly threw the gauntlet right back. "Having a backup is smart. Smarter maybe than someone who wants to play for two teams at once."

I wasn't a catcher for nothing. I caught the challenge and kept it. "Want to throw the ball on the beach for a while?"

He looked delighted at the spontaneity of the idea. "Yeah, I do!"

We took the mitts and the ball onto the nearly deserted beach and played catch, kicking up sand and laughing as the ferries slid by on the Sound in the distance. After the sun had nearly set, he brought out a blanket and we sat together on the beach.

"You're pretty good," he said admiringly. "Have you played lately?"

"No," I admitted. "Not for a while. Frenchwomen in general don't play sports. There wouldn't have been a lot of places for me to play while in Paris last year.

"When I was a girl," I continued, fingering the worn leather of the catcher's mitt, "I always wanted one of those bright pink mitts Wilson makes. Really girly and bold."

"Why didn't you buy one?" he asked.

"My dad thought it was a waste of money. It was like twice as much," I said. "But that's okay. I used a Magic Marker to glam mine up. Tanya thought it looked crazy, but I liked it."

We sat in silence for a minute, and he leaned over and took my hand, lightly tracing his finger over each one of mine before enfolding it in his own hand.

"How was golf yesterday?" he asked quietly.

I'd told him I wasn't going to play on two teams. It was time to speak up.

"I had a good time," I said. "With Céline."

He nodded once and looked out over the water, which lapped a bit closer to us. A few scattered shells and starfish lay at our feet. "Maybe like Jessica, you're trying to be answerable for responsibilities that might not be yours."

I didn't answer out loud, but as I squeezed his hand, a seemingly contradictory verse floated through my mind. *Each of you should look not only to your own interests, but also to the interests of others.*

Twelve

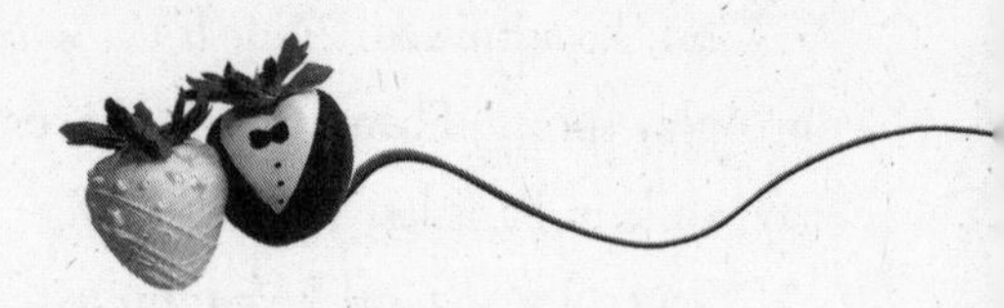

I like reality. It tastes like bread.

Jean Anouilh

I can't tell you how fun it is to have you here," I told my mom as we walked around Bijoux before anyone else arrived. "Can I get you a coffee? Margot left some breakfast pastries for us yesterday."

Mom sat in one of the big chairs. "I'd love some coffee. And I've been dying to see your place, of course. Oh, Lexi, just to call it 'your place' is such a thrill for me." She ran her hand down the side of the leather chair.

I pulled her a café crème and then pulled one for myself before putting a few breakfast pastries on a small silver catering tray. Then I sat down across the table from her.

"I don't know how you keep so trim working here all day," she said, biting into a cheese danish topped with sweet cherries. "I certainly don't need more than one of these, but I'm going to eat more than one."

I pushed the tray closer to her to encourage her to eat whatever she wanted. "I stay trim by running around twelve hours a day hustling business," I teased. "And moms are supposed to have jiggly arms."

"So are grandmothers," she said pointedly.

"Is Leah pregnant?" I feigned innocence. "She hasn't told me."

Mom sighed. "No, not yet."

"And you're not saying anything to them, right?" I scolded her. "They've been married less than a year."

"No, I'm not saying anything," she said. "Anyway, Nate's going to be an anxious handful the entire time, I'm sure, so just as well they wait a short while." She emphasized the word *short.* "Speaking of hustling business," she continued, "how's it going?"

I knew this question would come, and I'd decided last night that I would be honest. I didn't want to worry her, but if we were ever going to have a true, intimate relationship, we had to be able to talk honestly. Otherwise, we'd always stay superficial.

"Even though we've got the lease through the end of the year, I've only got about three months' worth of operating capital left," I admitted, tearing off a small piece of an almond croissant.

"And then what?"

"And then I close the doors. Margot goes back to working solely at L'Esperance and La Couronne, Jessica finds another job, and so do I."

"Would you go back to L'Esperance?" she asked, draining her coffee and nearly smacking her lips. Monsieur Delacroix knew how to buy a machine.

"There's no job for me there," I said softly. I tapped the furniture. "But I could probably outfit my apartment pretty well for fire-sale prices."

I heard the back door open and Margot walked in. I introduced her to my mother.

"Margot, this is my mother, Margaret. Same name!" I said.

"Enchantée." Margot kissed my mother on each cheek. My mother cooperated with her but was only slightly less surprised than I was. Since when was Margot so warm?

"Gee, I'd have told you my name was Margaret if I'd known I could have this kind of treatment," I told her.

"Mais oui," she said, wagging a finger at me. She went on in English. "A mother is a treasure, is that not so?" I remembered then that her mother had died in the car crash with Philippe's wife. Perhaps there hadn't been the same kind of antagonism with her mother as with Monsieur Delacroix.

Margot was a good hour later than she usually arrived, but she'd been staying a bit later every afternoon too. At least until Fred, our new UPS guy had left. She'd also been curling her hair and wearing liquid eyeliner. I knew the signs when I saw them, so I let her have complete control over the UPS orders. In return, she left the radio on soft favorites. No UPS delivery on Saturday, so Margot's hair was straight, but she still had a lilt in her walk and she'd stopped snorting at the wedding cakes.

The three of us loaded the van, and my mother disappeared into the restroom to change. I stepped into the walk-in to cool off and straighten my chef's jacket, then checked that everything was in order. When I emerged, I was shocked by my mom's appearance.

"Wow, you look fantastic!" I said. She had on a midlength dress of summer sky blue and a pair of low pumps to match. She'd even touched up her eye makeup a little. "Hey, I recognize that dress. It's the one you wore to Nate and Leah's wedding!"

Mom blushed. "I thought if I dressed as a mother of the groom—or bride—it might make the moms coming to the show with their daughters feel more at home."

I hugged her. "Thank you, Mom. That was very thoughtful."

Jessica arrived, and I introduced her to my mom too.

"Got the hand-washing station?" Margot asked. I rolled my eyes and nodded. The twinkle in her eye told me she'd already known I had it.

I took the last cake to the van and noticed the car parked in the parking lot with its "You don't get anywhere by accident" bumper sticker. Then Jessica, Mom, and I took off.

By the time we pulled up at the convention center, I felt like an old hand. Even though I'd only done this once before, I at least knew what I was doing this time. We unloaded and brought the cakes up on a trolley, using the elevator. The part of the convention center marked off for this event was much smaller than for the last show.

"I think there's only half as many vendors here this time," I told them as we set up the booth. "It's a smaller show because so many June brides have already made their decisions by the end of April. We're really shooting for last-minute planners, quick weddings, and people getting married in the autumn."

Jessica set up the silk plants I'd brought from Bijoux. I thought they were classier than balloons. "So that's not too good for us, right? Because we won't get as much business?"

I nodded, wanting to be honest about her odds for the future of her job as well as my own. "But we're going to try our best."

I set up the hand-washing station in the back and put my extra papers and pens back there, as well as some spare brochures. I noticed my Bible on the shelf too. As I picked it up, my mom came up behind me.

"I hope it's not cheesy," she said. "It was under the rest of the papers on the passenger's seat when I got in the car. I just scooped it all up and brought it in. Maybe it will make a difference."

"It's not cheesy," I said, glad to have a mother who had faith. I opened the Bible to the sticky-noted page where I'd left off.

> Rejoice in the Lord always. I will say it again: Rejoice! Let your gentleness be evident to all. The Lord is near. Do not be anxious about anything, but in everything, by prayer and petition, with thanksgiving, present your requests to God. And the peace of God, which transcends all understanding, will guard your hearts and your minds in Christ Jesus.

The same peace I'd had last time I was here settled on me, and *that* made me wonder what might lie ahead.

Lord, thank You for getting me here. Please bring in some clients somehow.

"First, I'm going to make the rounds to the caterers," I said. "Mom, you hand out cake slices to anyone who comes up. Jessica, you explain the flavors just like we went over, get names and numbers, and hand out brochures. I should be back before it gets too busy."

Mom looked nervous, but Jessica looked eager. I noticed she stuck pretty close to my mom's side.

I loaded a silver catering tray with a few pieces of cake and some brochures. There were other cake bakeries there too, but they didn't seem to be delivering cake to the catering booths. One caterer had already sent me a few weddings, and I stopped and chatted with her for a while, thanking her for her business. Several others were people I'd already contacted with mini-cake deliveries or ones who had been here last time.

One caterer, though, dominated the room. I hadn't noticed them last time, but maybe I'd just overlooked them after my spectacular fall from grace. I looked at my tray—I had a couple of pieces left. I held my breath and moved forward.

Someone already stood at the booth, chatting with what looked to be the head chef. Oh great. The woman who'd turned me in to the health inspectors last time.

"Well, sugar, you're back," she said. "Got a hand-washing station this time?"

Surely she wouldn't be tacky enough to announce my mistake to this man I had never met.

She turned to the chef. "This young woman is fairly new, and for the last show she forgot to set up a hand-washing station. Of course, they had to shut her down." She turned to me. "It takes a long time to learn the business. You'll figure it out eventually, I'm sure. We're all new and green at some point."

"Thanks for your encouragement," I said, and she drifted away to talk with one of the other workers at the booth. I introduced myself to the head catering chef.

"Hello, my name is Lexi Stuart." I held out my hand.

"Ted Jacques," he said. A French surname!

I tried to work some damage control. "It's true that our wedding cake bakery is new, but we're part of the Delacroix bakeries, and we've been baking in Paris and Seattle for decades."

He nodded. "But you're new, yourself?"

"Fairly," I admitted. "I returned from pastry school in Paris just a few months ago." I could see him getting anxious to talk with the increasing crowds gathering at his booth. He had a big dinner operation. He probably charged twenty-five to forty-five dollars a plate and catered ten or more events in a weekend. At least he wouldn't be scared of my upscale slice fees.

"Would you like to try a piece of one of our signature cakes?" I said. "Caramel Café Latte."

He looked at me. "I'll take a piece Miss...Stuart, but I have to be up-front with you. I'm a pretty established player, and I don't usually use new bakeries. Too much at risk for me with my particular clientele."

My heart sank but I kept my smile genuine. I handed him both pieces of cake and a brochure before slipping back to my booth.

"How did it go?" Jessica asked eagerly.

Right now we all needed our spirits boosted. "Made some new contacts," I said. "We'll see!"

"I got three people to sign up for a cake tasting," she said happily. I hugged her, not wanting her to know that that was about ten percent of what we needed. We needed not only tasters, but people willing to make a deposit.

Mom handed out more cake, and it was true, many mothers of the bride looked very comfortable with her.

"Your mom is really nice," Jessica said wistfully.

"She is," I agreed.

"I always wanted a mother," she said. "After my mother left us, I kept hoping she'd come back, or at least that my foster mother would be like a real mom to me, but she never was."

"I'm sorry," I said. She shrugged, and I watched the gates slam shut over her eyes again.

"I'll help with the sign-ups," she said.

A few hours later, feet aching, I watched as Ted Jacques walked by with one of his associates. I smiled and waved, and he slowed down.

"That cake was pretty good, young lady," he said. In spite of the French name, he had a Texas accent. "I'm impressed."

He'd taken off his chef's toque and looked more like a "civilian." Jessica approached him with a sign-up sheet. "Is your son or daughter getting married?" she asked sweetly. She looked him in the eye and he looked back at her, and they didn't look away from each other.

"Do I know you?" he asked. "You look very familiar."

I could see that she suddenly recognized him. "I used to work at Community Table. I helped you out both times you were a guest chef."

He snapped his fingers. "Yes!" He looked at me, then looked at Jessica, then back at me before taking a brochure. "Well, I'll be a thick-skinned bull at a shoe-leather shop. I guess you're better at giving newcomers a fair shot than I am, aren't you?"

There was no diplomatic way to answer that, so I simply offered him another piece of cake. He ate it and then took a second brochure. I assumed he'd tossed the other one shortly after I'd left his booth.

"I'll look into your services," he said, "and call you if I need anything."

Thank You, Jesus.

In response I heard, *You don't get anywhere by accident.*

It wasn't a promise, but it was hope. And hope was keeping us alive.

Easy Caramel Latte Cake

Ingredients

Cake:

1 18.25 ounce package yellow or golden butter cake mix
1 small package French vanilla instant pudding mix
1 cup full-fat sour cream
½ cup brewed espresso
½ stick butter, softened
4 large eggs

Layer:

1 jar of high-quality caramel

Topping:

2 cups whipping cream
1 cup powdered sugar
1 tablespoon vanilla

Directions

Cake:

Preheat oven to 350 degrees. Have all ingredients at room temperature. Grease and flour a 9 x 13 pan, or spray with flour-added nonstick cooking spray. Combine all cake ingredients in a large mixing bowl. Slowly beat for 30 seconds to incorporate, then beat on high for 2 minutes. Pour into pan and bake for about 35 minutes, or until just set in the middle. Cool cake in pan for 25 minutes. Cake is heavy, and will pull away from the sides of the pan. Spread ⅔ cup of caramel over cake top.

Topping:

Place all ingredients in cool bowl and mix on high until cream holds soft peaks. When cake is completely cool, spread topping over caramel, or serve slices of cake with topping mounded on top.

Hours later we slipped our shoes off our aching feet, put on some comfy clogs, and loaded the van back up. We dropped Jessica off at her cousin's apartment and then brought the materials back to Bijoux before Mom and I headed out to a late dinner.

After ordering, I thanked my mom again. "You looked lovely as a mother of the bride today."

She broke and buttered a piece of bread. "I'd love to be mother of the bride. I wouldn't even care who the groom was."

"'As long as he's a Christian and he loves you and treats you well.'" I echoed the mantra I'd heard all my life.

"Exactly. How are things going, anyway?"

"Dan is out of town," I said. "For business. We went out last Sunday night before he left, and I sent him a couple audio books he'd mentioned as a gift before he left. He's e-mailed once, but I know he's pretty busy."

"Before you went to Paris, you thought Dan might be a little... typical. Didn't you tell Leah there are men who are bread and men who are cake?"

I forked up another piece of my caesar salad and chewed it slowly. "I think I grew up a lot in the past year. Man cannot live by bread alone, but a constant diet of cake might get sickening. And I should know!" We laughed as the busboy cleared our salad plates.

"One woman's bread is another woman's cake," Mom said thoughtfully. I thought of my dad, a sure and steady provider. But I'd also caught him dancing with my mother in the moonlight on their new patio.

"Besides," I answered, "maybe Dan is like...brioche." I saw Mom's look of confusion. "Brioche is a very, uh, cakey kind of bread.

Bread, but with something special, something more. It took awhile for me to master it in France. In fact, it was Philippe who helped me understand how to best handle it."

"And how about Philippe?" she asked after the waitress delivered our entrées.

I sighed with the fatigue of the day and the unanswered questions in my own mind. "I like Philippe a lot. He's been really supportive of me at Bijoux, he's funny and nice. But the more time we spend with each other here, the less connected I feel. I don't know. We really didn't know each other that well in Paris before we came here."

"There is that sexy French accent." Mom kept a straight face.

"Mother!" I laughed. "Yeah, but I rarely hear it. We almost always speak French, so I'm the one with the accent. I like Philippe a lot, but maybe some of his appeal was that it was adventurous to date a Frenchman. Paris was exciting and different, and his appeal was a little exotic, you know what I mean? But when we got down to spending time together, the conversations got harder, not easier, and it just feels more like I'm always 'on' with him as opposed to being myself."

Mom took another bite of her steak Diane. "Isn't that what dating's for, getting to know someone enough to decide if you want to go further or not?"

I nodded. "Yeah. I guess I've done so little of it that I still feel bad if it doesn't work out."

"And then there's that little girl…"

"Céline." I filled in her name with affection I knew was reflected in my voice.

"Dad thought you were pretty attached to her. *I* think you're pretty attached to her."

"I am," I said. "I—I feel kind of maternal toward her in a way. I know she's needy for a mom, and I think she feels like I'm a sort of mother to her. She's bonded to me."

We sat for a while, and then Mom changed the discussion back to Dan, inviting him to Whidbey to visit their new house when he came back from his trip. We declined dessert—we'd had enough cake that day—and she picked up the tab.

"You don't have to pay," I protested. "I should be paying. You helped me out so much today. You drove all the way from Whidbey. You dressed up as the mother of the bride!"

After flagging down the waitress and paying anyway, she replied, "That's what mothers do, honey. They choose to do the very best for their children, no matter the cost to themselves. Sometimes that's easy. Sometimes that's hard."

Late that night, listening to Mom cyclically snoring inches away from me in the Brady Bunch-decorated apartment, I thought about that, over and over. Jessica's lack of bonding with a mom came back to me. Margot's tender heart toward the motherless.

By the time the sun rose, I knew what I would do for Céline, even though there would be a significant cost.

Thirteen

A person often meets his destiny on the road he took to avoid it.

Jean de la Fontaine

The next Wednesday I hung up the phone after chatting with Philippe about our dry goods order. I'd gone over the budget that morning. We might make it until August due to a couple of orders that had come in, but things were still too slow to turn the place around in a couple of months. If Monsieur Delacroix would give us another year…but he'd made it clear he wouldn't. And maybe it was just plain luck I got to work here at all, anyway. Without Dan, the lease on Bijoux would never have been signed. As Margot chronically reminded me.

"I go to La Couronne," she called out in English, for Jessica's sake, as I put the books back into the armoire. "Big order there today. I have the pastries in the walk-in for tomorrow's catering order. Good work."

I drank in the unexpected and unusual praise. It was a new corporate catering account, breakfast pastries every week for their meetings and deliveries every month to their real estate clients. *"Merci!"* I called to Margot as she exited via the back door.

Jessica had been there since that morning doing cleanup, but there was little else for her to do, so reluctantly, I sent her home. Then I took an early lunch. I had a special person to surprise and take out to eat.

I drove across town to the French-American school. I knew today was an early release day—in France, every Wednesday is a half day, and the French-American school continued that tradition. I'd decided to take Céline somewhere nice on her afternoon off. Usually, I knew, she stayed at the school for after-school care.

I parked the van and walked up to the brick administration building. The walkways were lined with the first fresh roses of spring, tough enough to bloom on the lowest ration of sunshine. I sniffed one, delighting in the tickle of perfume, and wiped away the drop of dew that brushed against my cheek.

I checked in at the main office. "*Bonjour,* I'm here to check out Céline Delacroix for lunch." I knew my name was on the approved list.

The woman stared at me in spite of what I knew was nearly flawless French after my stint in Paris. *"Encore?"* she asked me. "Again, what did you say?"

"Céline Delacroix," I said. "My name is Lexi Stuart."

"Ah, mademoiselle, *je regrette* that Mademoiselle Delacroix has already left for the day. A woman picked her up not ten minutes ago. Has there been some mistake?"

Curious. *"Non, non,"* I said. *"C'est une surprise."*

"Ah, a surprise. So sorry. Maybe next week, eh?"

I nodded and walked back to the van and the picnic lunch I'd packed. I should have thought to plan ahead. I knew Philippe hadn't picked her up—I'd just talked to him and he told me he had meetings with suppliers all afternoon. Plus, the receptionist said it was a woman. Margot was going to La Couronne.

Back at Bijoux I worked on some paperwork and made a few catering calls while waiting for Tanya and Steve to arrive. On my list was Mr. Jacques, the man I'd met last week. Should I call to follow up? If I waited too long, he might forget me altogether. If I called too soon, I'd seem pushy, overeager, and new.

I decided to call and be proactive. I was going to call before taking a cake out of the walk-in in anticipation of Steve and Tanya's arrival, but I noticed an e-mail coming in.

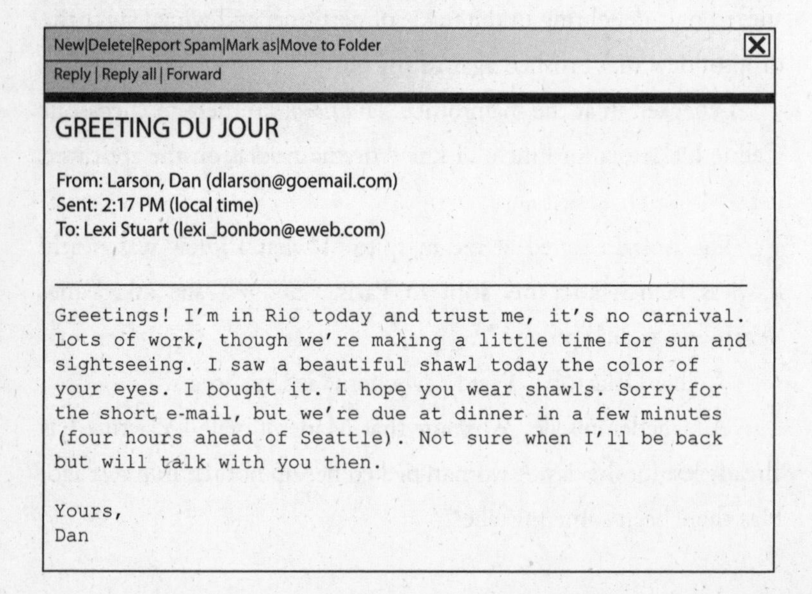
New|Delete|Report Spam|Mark as|Move to Folder

Reply | Reply all | Forward

GREETING DU JOUR

From: Larson, Dan (dlarson@goemail.com)
Sent: 2:17 PM (local time)
To: Lexi Stuart (lexi_bonbon@eweb.com)

Greetings! I'm in Rio today and trust me, it's no carnival. Lots of work, though we're making a little time for sun and sightseeing. I saw a beautiful shawl today the color of your eyes. I bought it. I hope you wear shawls. Sorry for the short e-mail, but we're due at dinner in a few minutes (four hours ahead of Seattle). Not sure when I'll be back but will talk with you then.

Yours,
Dan

A shawl the color of my eyes.

Before I could respond to his e-mail, I heard a knock on the front door. I looked up and saw Tanya and Steve waving. They looked so happy, so excited. In spite of the turmoil in my own life, I had to grin along with them. I closed the laptop and went to open the door.

"Welcome to your own after-hours private cake tasting," I said. "Come on in!"

Steve gave me a brotherly hug and I hugged him back. I showed him around Bijoux and then settled them on the leather sofa while I went to get the cakes. I peeked at them through the cutout and was surprised by a rush of unexpected feelings. I remembered seeing Tanya sitting on a couch by her first crush, remembered her sleeping over at my house, stretched out on the couch in our family room after an all-night moviefest. I remembered her on the couch at the counselor's office, and helping my mother sort through things to keep and give away by putting them on the couch of their old house.

Steve leaned into her, and she glanced up at him and beamed before leaning back against him. I was happy to see her marry, and determined not to mar this evening with any difficult topics.

"Okay, so here are the choices!" I brought out a minicake of each of the five flavors they'd picked out in advance. I didn't do so much for every couple getting married, but not every fiancée was my best friend.

"Mmm, let's get married every year," Steve said, tucking into the second cake. "Or maybe Lexi could just deliver cakes every week."

"Sure," I teased. "For a big charge!" Their wedding cake was my gift to them. Margot frowned on that decision, but I didn't care. It was something I really wanted to do.

I made some coffee for us, and we sat and talked about the wedding plans and their honeymoon in Jamaica and the new school where Tanya was applying to teach in one of the more difficult districts. I saw a mix of fear for her safety and pride in her outreach in Steve's eyes and observed how their plans so neatly intersected. I sat in a chair, slightly removed, listening to them on the couch. I was glad I had removed myself a little from my previously close position in order to let them become one.

"I think I like the almond cake best," Steve announced. "Is that okay?"

Tanya looked surprised. "Really? I thought you'd go for chocolate or the latte cake."

"I'm glad I can still surprise you. I like them all, but the cherry almond is my favorite. If you want chocolate or latte we can go for that."

Tanya shook her head. "No, almond is totally fine. I've had several of the others already."

We filled out their order sheet, and they paged through the album and chose how they wanted the decorated cake to look. I suggested something that looked kind of Japanese to tie in with their slightly Asian wedding theme, as Steve was a quarter Japanese. "It will also allow me to decorate it with Japanese cherry blossoms and twigs." I quickly sketched out an idea. After they offered exclamations of praise, we finished it off and Steve left.

"Ready for the dress fitting?" I asked.

"And Passion Fruit," Tanya reminded me, a faint pink staining her winter-white cheeks.

"Don't worry, I haven't forgotten."

She'd driven over in her seafoam blue Beetle and we got into it. I felt like Fred Flintstone, ready to use foot power riding in a car so low to the ground after my usual cruising at van altitude.

First we stopped at Passion Fruit. "I want some lingerie, of course, and also maybe a swimming suit for the honeymoon," Tanya told me as we got out. "I'm going to start tanning every week to build up a little color so I don't fry."

"Good idea," I said. "You've got, what, six or seven weeks?"

She nodded. We poked around the bathing suits first. I held up one with a coconut shell bra and mocked a Jamaican accent. "Hey, mon, you goin' to look fly in the islands."

"I don't have enough to fill the shells," she teased. "And that's just *so* me."

Eventually she found a sunset-colored tankini and then moved on to the lingerie. I hung back and picked out nothing, just gave my opinion. She found a long white piece that was both romantic and feminine for the first night and a couple of shorter pieces for the nights thereafter.

"You doing okay with all this?" I asked her.

She nodded. "I am. For now." She smiled, but it seemed a bit weaker than her earlier confidence.

Next we stopped at the wedding dress shop. She showed me the dress her mom had picked out for her mother of the bride dress.

"My mom wore her MOB dress last week to the bridal show," I said. "She still looked great in it."

"Do you think she's planning to wear that to your wedding?" Tanya asked.

"What wedding?" I said a bit more sharply than I meant to.

"Oh, I just mean, whenever," she said. "How are things going with the guys?"

"Fine. But this day is about you, not me. How about we have lunch soon and talk about me, but enjoy *your* wedding tonight?"

"Okay," she happily agreed, as I knew she would. Another discussion avoided for now.

She showed me the tea green bridesmaid dresses, which partnered prettily with mine as maid of honor, which was also green, but designed slightly differently. "It has a boat neck which I know looks best on you," Tanya said. "Is it okay?"

I held it up in the three-way mirror. "It's perfect," I said. "You have impeccable taste, as always."

The store matron came over with Tanya's dress. She went into the draped dressing room and put it on, then came out for me to help her zip up. It was styled simply and straightforwardly, just like Tanya herself. It was pure white, which would set off nicely against her newly tanned skin and blond hair. A perfect bow in the back cinched in the train.

"You're ready," I whispered.

"I'm ready," she said, then grabbed my hand and squeezed it.

By the beginning of the next week, I was planning when I'd call Mr. Jacques. What did I have to lose at this point? It was the beginning of May, and there was little else I could do to drum up business. Jessica was doing nicely in the kitchen—mostly cleaning up, doing errands and delivery, but I also had her doing a little prep work, and so did Margot. I wondered if Margot would be able to find a lower-level position for Jessica should Bijoux fold. I thought back over the staffing needs, as I knew them, at La Couronne and L'Esperance. No openings that I was aware of. And now that the country was in a recession of sorts, we were all tightening our belts.

Maybe Margot was just trying to give her as many skills as possible so she'd have a chance for placement.

I took the trash out to the Dumpster, and when I walked back into the bakery, I overheard Margot talking on the phone in English.

"I'm sorry, I won't be able to come," she said. "I have to watch my niece that night. Yes, yes, I know I said that last time. But what can I do?" She muttered a few more words and then hung up.

I couldn't help smiling. Margot had a social life. My smile faded. One that was, apparently, hampered by her care of Céline. Poor Céline, shuffled from aunt to aunt.

I should have backed away from the cutout that let me overhear, but I didn't. She'd apparently called someone else, because now she spoke in French.

"And then that one, he can never fall in love with a French girl, which would make it easier all around. No. First, it's an Englishwoman, which was bad enough. Now, apparently, it's an American woman."

Oh no. That was going to make it even more difficult to back away from Philippe.

Margot turned halfway on her heels, and I ducked from the cutout and went back to the kitchen. Jessica eyed me for a second, knowing I was eavesdropping, but then walked into the cooler. I followed her.

"I'm going to L'Esperance for the afternoon," I said. "Sophie and I have some planning to do. Margot will lock up when she leaves, so you'll have to clock out, okay?"

"Okay," Jessica said, looking at her watch. I knew what she was thinking. Another early day. But what could I do? There just wasn't anything else for her to do today.

I hopped into the white van and drove toward L'Esperance. A few minutes later, I parked next to the catering van and snuck in the back door.

"*Ooh la la,* look out, here comes the big boss," said Auguste, my friend and jovial harasser from my days as a lowly bakery assistant. One of the things I missed about not working here was the camaraderie and friendship of the other bakers.

"I'm not a big boss," I protested. "I've hardly gained a pound." He handed me an almond croissant, my favorite, and I bit into it while I chatted with the other *Trois Amis,* the three friendly bakers who rolled out the thousands of croissants L'Esperance sent out every day.

I went back into the kitchen where Andrew, Margot's assistant, was dipping coffee beans and slicing lemons for decorating the tarts. I decided I should start Jessica doing some of that. It was exactly what I was doing a year ago.

"Hi there," I said, running my hand over the stainless steel countertops. I felt a lot of love for this kitchen, and maybe even a bit of longing for what seemed like simpler days. "Do you have any crème patisserie you need me to mix up? Or maybe a torte to assemble?"

"Coming back to take over your kitchen?" he joked, but I heard a slight note of tension in there.

"Nah, never was my kitchen," I reassured him. It belonged to Patricia, and then Margot. I was only a helper. "I've heard you mix up a mean pastry cream."

"Now you've got your own place anyway," he said.

I grinned. "Such that it is."

He grinned back but didn't harass me. Everyone knew the precarious position Bijoux was in.

I walked up front where Sophie was helping a customer from behind the counter. Even though she was the assistant manager, she never lost her customer service focus. I observed her from a distance before she could see me.

She looked gentler. Her hair was lightly highlighted, and she wore the faintest edge of lipstick. Not like she'd turned into anyone she wasn't, but maybe that she'd allowed the sharp edges she'd always kept as a defense to be softened if not yet completely erased.

The customer left, and I went and joined her behind the counter. "Hey, neighbor stranger," I said. "How are you?"

"Oh, Lex, I'm so glad to see you," she said. "I agree, we should see each other much more than we do. Maybe we should set up a wine and soy cheese night once a week and catch up either at your place or mine."

"Soy cheese—yum!" I agreed that would be a fine idea, and she got herself a veggie and sprout sandwich and me a ham and cheese, and we sat at one of the tables and talked.

"By the looks of things, you're doing well," I said. Most of the day's bread was already sold, and the sandwich counter looked like it had been breached in a recent skirmish. Andrew had just popped out from the kitchen to help clean it up.

"Business is great," she said. "I worried quite a bit when Luc left, not knowing what would happen to L'Esperance or me, really. But Philippe has been wonderful." She glowed like a woman in love.

I startled myself with the thought. She did. She glowed like a woman in love!

And, like a woman in love, she kept talking about her beloved without paying too much attention to whether I was listening or not.

"It took awhile for all of us to get used to his style, of course, because he was new. But really, he smoothed things over." She took a bite of her sandwich and a sip of her iced tea. "He even came to church with me last week. I'd been kind of tapering off going a little. I mean, I liked it when I went with you and then when I had a friend or two there. But alone was kind of tough. When Philippe told me he was a Christian and had been thinking about finding a good church for him and Céline, I thought, why not? I guess the church he went to in France was kind of, I don't know, British or formal, so he felt like he fit right in with this one."

"That's great," I managed to stammer, trying to absorb everything without letting her know I was really taken aback. "I'm so glad they found a place and that you're not alone there anymore."

"Oh, well, I'm not saying we'll go all the time," she said. "But hopefully a lot more!"

Philippe opened his office door. He waved and called out a

pleasant hello to me, then asked Sophie in to talk about something specific to L'Esperance.

I sat at the table, mechanically chewing my ham and swiss and trying to process everything I'd just learned. When I looked back over things, I could see that this last bit of information made everything else slide into place like a giant Connect Four game.

Philippe's motorcycle riding away from my apartment building when he hadn't visited me.

Céline playing Sophie's piano.

The professional warmth Philippe showed me lately without the personal friendliness that had been growing in Paris.

His dwindling need for me to offer American advice.

The woman picking Céline up from school—Sophie.

And finally, Margot's conversation today about Philippe falling in love with an American woman.

I blushed furiously, hating that I had no control over it and glad that, for the moment, I was alone. How embarrassing! I had assumed Margot had been talking about *me* and, knowing I was growing more distant with Philippe, worried how it would affect us all.

Even more embarrassing was that I had assumed it would all be up to me to make the choice between Dan and Philippe. Obviously I hadn't considered deeply enough that one or both of them were sifting through choices, thoughts, and feelings of their own. I was so busy worrying about what I was going to do and how it might affect others.

Life is not a novel, Lexi. It wasn't always two men dueling over the woman who would eventually choose one of them. Then I softened a bit. *Grace, Lexi, err on the side of grace. Even with yourself.*

I glanced at the pastry counter—crème brûlée, mousse au chocolat, mille-feuille. Mille-feuille was Dan's favorite. We didn't make it at Bijoux, and I hadn't thought to take him any since I'd been home. I'd been so busy trying to solve everyone's problems and keep Bijoux afloat.

My misunderstanding about Philippe and Sophie made me worry that I'd misunderstood Dan's intentions for the future too.

Maybe.

Céline came in through the front door. "Lexi!" she said, running and jumping in my lap. "You are here. I've missed you. You came to see me today?"

"I am always glad to see you," I said, heart hurting with the truth of it. "I've missed you terribly."

"And I, you," she said. "I got a ride home from Madeleine's mother. Do you want to see my princess collection?" She dug into her backpack and began to extract some dolls.

Philippe called out to her. *"Bonjour, ma puce,"* he said. "How was your day?"

"Fine, Papa," she said.

"Would you like an after-school treat?" Sophie offered eagerly. "I can get you whatever you'd like."

Céline smiled at her but made no effort to move from my lap. "*Non, merci.* Not right now. I have to show *ma Lexi* the new princess."

I glanced at Sophie and Philippe, standing close to each other. Now that I knew what was between them, I could see the growing familiarity. In fact, if I hadn't known them but had just observed them, I would say they were a couple.

Then I looked down at Céline, so joyful and happy sitting on my lap and chattering to me in French about her day.

The gulf between us and them was wide. I knew that what I'd determined to do the other night must be done even more quickly and more sharply.

I stroked Céline's hair as she talked, and tried to impress its silkiness and scent in my memory.

Fourteen

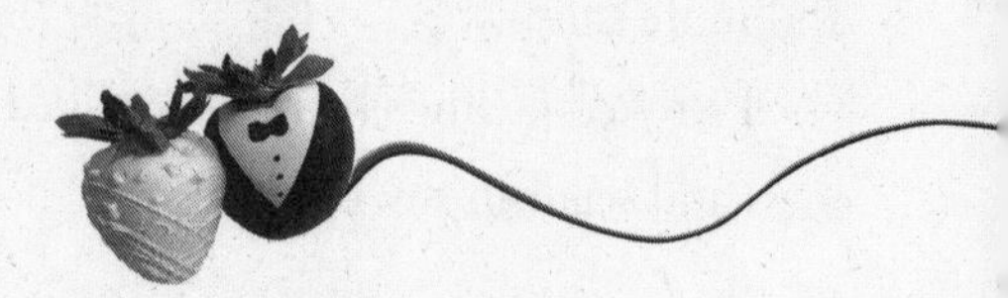

You learn to speak by speaking, to study by studying, to run by running, to work by working; and just so, you learn to love by loving. All those who think to learn in any other way deceive themselves.

Saint Francis de Sales

A few days later Margot, Jessica, and I were working together like cake and ice cream when Philippe called to say he'd be coming over to talk business with me—did I have the late morning and afternoon available? I did. Usually he wasn't that formal. Normally we didn't need such a long time to meet.

"Oui, pas de problème," I responded. I saw Margot glance at me out of the corner of her eye. She knew he was going to call. What was up?

I pulled the clipboards off the catering board and went over the week's orders. Two wedding cakes—not bad for early May, but not enough for the wedding season. A few birthday cakes that would be fun to make and decorate and that would show Jessica a few tricks.

A dozen corporate pastry trays. I also had five or six calls to make following up with caterers. This morning I was baking cakes for the next cake tasting, already advertised in the *Seattle Times.*

Should I call Mr. Jacques? He'd said he'd call me, after all, and I didn't want to be pushy. I'd been trying to manage a lot of things lately, and they hadn't all turned out so well. I'd take my hands off the wheel and pray.

Jessica sat down after finishing the dishes. I needed to increase her skills as quickly as possible, preparing her for other employment, just in case.

"Let me show you how to make crème patisserie." I brought her over to the huge commercial KitchenAid. Margot looked up at me. I wasn't sure if she was trying to signal that she thought it was a good thing or a bad thing that I was moving Jessica so quickly. At this point, I didn't care. I had to prepare the girl for her future, wherever it may be.

We pulled out the plastic-coated recipe card. "Crème patisserie is pastry cream. We use it in the other bakeries for layering between the sheets of puff pastry in mille-feuilles, or Napoleons," I said. "But we use it for a lot of other things too, like in fruit tarts—it's the soft filling between the pie shells and the fruit. And it's the cream layer in cakes like Boston cream."

"Thank you for showing me all of this," Jessica said. I glanced down at her red knuckles, raw from scrubbing dishes in extremely hot water. She'd earned it. "Where did you learn to cook and bake?" she asked.

"I learned some at home," I said, aware she'd had no such home. "And a lot of it I just experimented with, like anyone could." That she could do on her own if she was motivated. "Also, last year Monsieur

Delacroix brought me to France to study baking with the company and at pastry school."

"I've always wanted to go to cooking school," she offered shyly. "They have a good program at South Seattle Community College. I've just never had the money to go."

"Not everyone has to go to school to learn to bake. Attention!" I imitated my dad's military voice. "You can learn right here and now!"

We mixed the cream together, and I helped her fill the shells waiting for the fruit topping that would make today's pastry order. After pulling the sliced fruit out of the walk-in, we warmed up some apricot jelly and brushed it over the tops of the filled shells. She placed them on a silver tray and presented them to Margot.

"Voilà!" she said in nervous French.

"*Ooh la la,* now she speaks the French," Margot teased. "They look very beautiful," she reassured Jessica, who beamed and then wrapped them to go. Afterward, she washed the dishes we'd used.

"You are a good maman," Margot said, using a more familiar form of 'you.' We hadn't been fighting too much lately—Jessica had somehow mediated an uneasy, unspoken truce between us. I think that in spite of herself and her additional commuting, Margot was rooting for Bijoux to make it.

"I'm not the maman," I said. "More like the big sister."

Margot nodded. I *was* beginning to feel like the big sister to Jessica, perhaps as Patricia had felt toward me.

An hour or so later Philippe swaggered in looking more relaxed, joyful, and handsome than I'd seen him look for a while. He had a roguish five o'clock shadow even though it wasn't yet lunchtime. *"Bonjour, jolie mademoiselle."*

Pretty miss, eh. The Frenchman was back.

His attitude calmed me, though. Perhaps things weren't as bad as I'd feared. We went over the books line by line together, and he was encouraging. "They are looking better. However, I have to share with you, Lexi, that I am worried Luc overexpanded us a bit. Like the Starbucks, no? They bought too many places at once, and then some stores robbed the others of business."

It was true they could have continued to do the pastry catering out of L'Esperance and La Couronne. "But you don't do wedding cakes at the other bakeries," I said.

"Not the wedding cakes," he agreed. "But they have to pull their own weight. They are beautiful jewels in the Delacroix crown, but we need more diamonds, *n'est-ce pas*?"

"Oui," I agreed. I looked at my watch. It was nearly noon, and we'd only taken an hour to go over all of the relevant business. "You said you wanted to get together for a couple of hours?"

"Ah, *oui*," he agreed. "Perhaps we can eat lunch together? I will even buy the cheeseburger if you like."

"Oh, now I know I'm in trouble," I said, "if you're going to eat the cheeseburger. No, if you're paying, *Monsieur le Patron,* let's go somewhere nice."

"Bon!" He clapped his hands together. "Le Pichet."

Margot had already checked out for the day, and Jessica was just leaving after arriving at five that morning. I locked up and got on the back of Philippe's motorcycle.

"Better for the gas," he said as he adjusted my helmet. This time, while I appreciated his fine cologne and the bad boy thrill of being on the motorcycle, the adrenaline wasn't there for me. And I was relieved.

We arrived at Le Pichet—much easier to park a motorcycle by Pike Place Market than a car—and got a table on the street. The weather was lovely, the trees tentatively opening their fisted buds, leaves unfurling one by one like fingers unclenching. After ordering an iced tea, some crusty onion soup, and a fresh seafood platter, Philippe leaned across the table toward me.

"It's been quite a spring, hasn't it, Lexi?"

"It has," I said. "Busy at work, busy at home…"

"It's been a wonderful time for me and Céline," Philippe admitted. "America—it is really free. A person can make his own way, can try and fail, can try and succeed. I think we needed a new start after Andrea's death."

"I think so too," I said.

The waiter came by and chatted politely with Philippe for a few minutes—they had a professional friend in common in France—and then left the fresh oysters on a mother of pearl platter.

"Eat." Philippe indicated the oysters to me. "Please."

I dabbed some Tabasco sauce over my shooter and let it slip down my throat. We ate for a minute in the silence. Then Philippe pointed to the oysters.

"For me, after my wife died, I became like one of these oysters." He took two halves and put them together to show the oyster when fully shut. "And nothing could pry me open, see? I was tightly in myself. I took care of Céline, I worked, I went to church, and I went to sleep. I wanted nothing to come in and nothing to come out."

"Understandable," I said. Where was he going with this? Our waiter delivered hot bread and I tore off a piece of the spongy softness and soaked up some clam liquor mixed with butter and salt.

"But then you came to Rambouillet." He smiled, genuinely, expansively, and I recalled the days at the museum or restaurant in Paris. "Bringing that air of American freedom to me. And I felt—yes, perhaps it was time to try to live again. So I tried the motorcycle, and I liked it. And we went to dinner together. *C'est si bon!* It was a wonderful time. Surprisingly, I liked zesty American women."

I laughed. *"Vive le zeste!"*

"So when Luc and Marianne had to come home, I looked at you and thought, 'Perhaps the Americans aren't so bad.' Patricia had enjoyed some of you."

I grinned. He spoke of us Americans as if we were cannibalistic pagans from another planet.

"And that gave me the idea that it would be okay to come over here and try. Now, all sorts of *fantastique* things are happening. Luc wants to stay in France, I enjoy it here, and, well, *la Sophie* and I are becoming very close."

He busied himself with an oyster. So this was the point.

"I noticed," I said softly. I buttered another piece of bread and lifted it to my mouth.

"And this does not hurt you?" he said. "I wasn't sure of your feelings…"

I shook my head. "Oh, I don't think any woman likes to be set down, even gently. In all honesty, I wasn't sure of my feelings either," I admitted. "But I've become more sure of them lately, and it's okay. Sophie is a wonderful woman. Plenty zesty," I teased.

"*Oui!* And almost like a Frenchwoman, except that she doesn't speak French."

"Or eat meat," I pointed out teasingly.

"*Bien sûr,* but that means she won't be making me eat *les cheeseburgers, n'est-ce pas*?"

I laughed aloud. "*Oui,* maybe *les garden burgers* instead."

He screwed up his face. "What heresy is that?"

I grinned. "I'll let her explain that for herself. But I think she's a wonderful woman and you've made a good decision."

"We'll see how it goes," he said, but his sunshine gave him away. "Thank you for opening the oyster, Lexi." He reached across and held my hand in a brotherly way.

"Thank you for teaching me how to handle brioche," I answered. We both laughed, though I knew he didn't understand the double entendre I'd shared with my mom, about Dan being brioche.

"Speaking of that, Papa has asked that you come back for a continuing education course at the pastry school at the end of June. There is an advanced ingredients and techniques class being held, and we've got our training funds to use up for the year. He thought you might like to view the new bakery in Versailles, if you're interested, personally, with him. All expenses paid."

"Really?" I nearly dropped my fork. "For how long?"

"Oh…a week." He was kind of coy. "Patricia will meet you at the airport and you can stay with her in Rambouillet. Even though she and Xavier live in Provence most of the time, she's kept the apartment. And you can see your friend, Anne. She is doing a *fantastique* job at the bakery."

"I'd love that," I said. A little continuing education would be good.

"Bon," he said. "I'm taking Céline to visit her grandparents in London at the end of June."

"Ah, Céline," I said. "Does she know about you and Sophie?"

Philippe waited until the waiter cleared our plates. "A little. But she's very attached to you, Lexi."

"I know," I said. "I know. I...I should take her to lunch. And maybe talk to her about Sophie. But, Philippe, do you want her to get attached to Sophie before you...before you're sure about anything? It will be hard enough to wrench her away from me."

He shrugged. "When a man is of an *âge certain,* he's pretty sure when he's sure."

We sat there for a while, quiet. Every layer of this situation brought fresh pain and resolve, commingling and becoming one, like rain in the sea. Perhaps Céline was the only child I'd ever be able to mother easily, naturally. But I was not going to be her mother. By my choice, and by Philippe's choice.

Maybe Céline cracked open my mothering oyster and showed me that I really could do it. But how to transfer the pearl without doing damage?

"This won't be easy, will it?" Philippe said. "I know you love Céline. And I thank you for loving her."

"It won't be easy," I agreed. "I don't know how to do it so that it helps but doesn't hurt."

"I don't either," he admitted. "Thank you, Lexi. I hope Bijoux does what you need it to do. And if not? There will be another opportunity for you someplace wonderful. Of this, I am certain." He spoke with such confidence. "You make wedding cakes like no one that I know. Papa was impressed. You're an excellent pastry chef."

It was the first time he'd called me by the title. "*Merci,* Philippe."

He drove me back to Bijoux and walked me to the door. As he did, he gave me a long hug and I hugged him back. It was for all that had gone before us, and between us, and whatever might lie ahead.

We had no orders on Saturday, which was okay, as my parents had invited Dan and me to visit them on Whidbey Island. I hadn't been back to their house since I'd first come home from Paris, and I was looking forward to it. The early May day was warm, but as we were taking the ferry across, it would get cool. I purposely wore a short-sleeved shirt so I could pull a shawl around my shoulders later in the day. Just in case.

I felt the proverbial butterflies as soon as the security buzzer rang. Then I heard Dan's footsteps coming up the stairs, and I waited, poised, behind the door, for the knock.

I opened the door. "Hi," I said, suddenly shy even though it had only been a few weeks. Dan didn't know how tightly I'd closed the door with Philippe while he'd been away.

"Hi," he said. We just stood there for a few seconds, staring at each other.

"Come on in," I said. He walked in and hugged me.

"I missed you."

"I missed you too," I said. "I'm glad you're back."

I felt myself, and Dan too, holding back a reservoir of emotion and action. To ease the tension, we made small talk for a few minutes before I picked up my purse, my keys, and my phone. As we were leaving, Margot called to check on an order she'd asked me to prep for a catering pickup tomorrow.

"Oui, c'est fini," I reassured her. We carried on our conversation in French for a minute, and then I hung up and turned around. Dan didn't move toward the door.

"I thought you might want to open this here." He held out a slightly crinkly gold gift bag with crunched royal blue tissue paper that looked a little worse for the wear. I kept the smile off my face. Did any guy know how to wrap a gift? I was happy his assistant hadn't done it though; so much more personal to do it himself.

"Thank you," I said, sitting on the sofa. I lifted the tissue paper off the top and pulled out a neatly folded shawl of impressionist blue silk that slipped through my fingers like happiness. "Oh, it's so delicate and beautiful!" I exclaimed.

I reached over and hugged him, and as I pulled away, he pulled me back to him, gently took my face in his hands, and lightly kissed my lips. As I closed my eyes and kissed him back, I felt us fuse and the reservoir break. For a moment I breathed his breath and he mine.

Then we shakily stood up. It was time to flee.

We headed down the stairs, making small talk to steady the moment, and then got into his truck. As we started down the road, my phone rang again. After talking with Margot, I automatically answered in French.

"Bonjour!"

"Ah, mademoiselle, I did not know you spoke French." Pleasure came through the voice on the other end, a voice speaking French with a Texas twang. "It's like opening the mail and finding a check instead of a bill!"

"Mais oui," I answered, trying to place the voice and the number which had shown up as an unknown on my phone display.

He kept speaking in French. "It's Ted Jacques here, from Continental Catering. Remember me from the bridal show?"

"*Bien sûr,* of course I remember you, Monsieur Jacques," I reassured him. I glanced at Dan and gave him a thumbs-up and a smile, but since he couldn't speak French, he had no idea what was going on. He smiled uncertainly.

"I'm sorry to call on a Saturday," Mr. Jacques said. "If it's no problem, I'd like you to come by the shop early next week. I'm extremely busy, and the season is heating up like crawfish in a paella pan. One of my usual cake caterers is off having a baby weeks before she thought she would, and her staff is running behind. We had a fiasco yesterday, and I can't afford to repeat that. I thought I'd give you a call and see if you could take on a few events for me. Truth is, I'd forgotten about you until now. I'm sorry it's such short notice. I just pulled the account—you'd have to do the cakes next weekend."

"Certainly, I'd love to!" I said, not caring that my voice was more excited than professional. Authenticity demanded I was going to have to be who I was, I'd been learning. Monsieur Delacroix had given me good practice. And Mr. Jacques was certainly being honest himself.

"All right, young lady, why don't you come by Monday morning and we'll see where we go from there." He gave me his address, which I already knew. Everyone knew where they were located. I thanked him again and hung up.

"Great news!" I said to Dan as he pulled in the ferry dock. "That was Mr. Jacques with Continental Catering. Remember, I told you about him? How he was one of the chefs at Community Table and he knew Jessica and he tasted my cake and liked it?"

"I had no idea you could fit that many words in one breath and sentence," Dan said, smiling. "Yes, I do remember. I, ah, couldn't understand anything you were saying, though. What did he want?"

"He wants me to come in on Monday, and he's going to give me a few weddings. For next weekend. He pulled some events from an underperforming account and he's going to give me a chance."

"Do you have next weekend open?" Dan asked.

I shook my head. "I already have one event, but I don't care. I'll pull on extra people or go sleepless or whatever it takes to make it work."

Dan laughed. "You're singing a new tune from last year, aren't you?"

"What do you mean?"

"Last year you were Miss Anti-Corporate, looking down on the poor slobs in cubicles who had no balance of life. Now *you're* ready to do whatever it takes to make a career work."

I nodded, slowly. It was true. "I guess when I found something I really cared about, it made all the difference."

"I understand," he said. And I knew he did.

We drove onto the ferry and parked the car, and then headed up to the observation deck. We got a cup of coffee, leaned over the rail, and watched as the relentless rows of waves swam toward us like a synchronized team, winked, and melted away.

"I'm going to be doing some traveling of my own," I told him after he'd talked about his trip to South America.

"Really?"

I nodded and beamed. "Paris!"

"Oh...really? When? For how long."

"At the end of June for about a week or so. After Tanya's wedding. Philippe asked me this week when we had lunch."

"Oh."

"We went to lunch to talk about him dating Sophie. So I could talk with Céline to make things a bit easier for her."

Dan turned toward me, and even though I suspected he didn't want to look relieved, I could tell he was, a little. I was too.

"So what are you going to do?" he asked.

"Oh, I'm going to do a little continuing ed at the pastry school. Staying with Patricia—whom I love! Visiting my friend Anne. Shopping. Eating!" I grinned. "Just relishing the beauty of France. And," I continued, "Monsieur Delacroix said he wants me to visit the flagship bakery in Versailles with him."

"Sounds good," he said, and then remained silent for a minute before continuing. "But I meant what are you going to do about Céline?"

I watched the ferry bow cut through the water like a plow in soil. "Well, maybe it's like Tanya and Steve a little. I mean, Tanya and I have always been this close." I crossed my fingers and held them up. "So in order to let her do what she needed to do, what she wanted to do, I had to be the one to pull back a little. She'd never do it, worried about hurting my feelings. So even though it hurt me, I did it for her." I brushed a flyaway piece of hair away from my face. "That way she can grow into what she needs to be without me complicating things."

Dan nodded thoughtfully. "And you're going to do that for Céline too?"

I nodded. "I'll say a little, and be around a little. But basically I need to disentangle myself from her. She won't see why right away, but later she will. And I hope she'll understand that I did it out of love."

Dan nodded again. "She will. She knows your heart." We both turned to look at the approaching island. "Better get back to the car," he said. "We're nearly there."

A few minutes later we drove off the ferry and down the road to my mom and dad's house. As we pulled up I saw the driveway lined with flags—well in advance of Memorial Day—and a large flag fluttering from the pole in the front yard.

"My dad is a retired marine," I explained a little self-consciously.

Nonna came out to greet us as we got out of the truck. "Welcome to the recruiting station," she teased. "Uncle Sam is in the back starting the barbecue or starting the house on fire, I'm not sure which." She shooed Dan to the backyard to meet up with Dad, whom he had last seen about a year ago at Nate's wedding. Then she cornered me.

"So now that you don't need the old lady's house anymore, I never see you, eh?" She gave me a big, doughy hug.

"Oh, Nonna, I miss you, but business is finally kicking in—some," I said. We walked arm and arm into the kitchen, and I told her about Mr. Jacques' calling and the events I was going to have to rush home and prepare for.

My mom flurried out to greet me and give me a hug, and then welcomed me into her kitchen. The big family room and kitchen windows looked out over the backyard and the Sound. I could see my dad giving barbecuing tips to Dan, who listened intently, politely, whether he wanted to or not. I smiled and my mother smiled with me.

"He's cute!" Nonna said. "What happened to the Frenchman?"

I pointed thumbs-down. "He's dating Sophie."

"Oh, I'm sorry, lovey," Nonna said.

I glanced back at Dan and grinned. "I'm not."

"Me neither," Nonna said. "Hubba hubba."

"Mother!" Mom tapped Nonna on the behind with her frying pan. "Do something useful!" She turned to me. "You too. You only encourage her!"

Lexi's Soft Oatmeal Raisin Cookies

Ingredients

1 cup butter, softened
¾ cup packed brown sugar
¼ cup white sugar
1 tablespoon vanilla
1 3.5 ounce package instant vanilla pudding mix
2 eggs
1¼ cups all-purpose flour
1 teaspoon baking soda
1 teaspoon baking powder
3½ cups quick rolled oats
1 cup raisins (optional)
½ cup chopped, toasted walnuts (optional)
¼ cup cinnamon coffee-flavoring syrup

Directions

Preheat oven to 350 degrees. Line cookie sheets with parchment paper. In a large mixing bowl, cream together butter, brown sugar, and white sugar until smooth. Blend in instant pudding, then beat in eggs and vanilla until the batter is light and fluffy. Combine flour, baking soda, and baking powder in a small bowl; stir into the batter. Next, add oats, and raisins and nuts if desired.

Drop dough by spoonfuls onto cookie sheets. Bake for about 8 minutes, until just set but not yet firm. Take out of oven and let sit on pan for 1 minute before gently removing to cool on wire racks. When partially cool, brush tops lightly with cinnamon coffee syrup. Serve.

We three women made a caesar salad and corn on the cob, and I made some oatmeal raisin cookies while the guys were outside chatting and barbecuing. I knew Dan was in trouble when my dad took him to the shed where he kept his yard tools. Originally, Dad hadn't wanted to do any landscaping. Now he was a collector—Garden Weasel, tiller, mower, edger, trimmer, shearer, you name it.

We sat on the patio, which was breezy but sunny. I wore my shawl, which I pointed out came from Brazil, and Dan looked away, pleased but a bit shy.

After lunch Mom and Nonna went inside to take a short nap, and my dad went to watch golf on TV. Dan and I went for a walk down the shoreline, shoes in one hand and holding hands with the other, talking. He was quiet, but he probably had been talked out by my dad, who looked pleased the entire afternoon. When Dan wasn't looking, Dad had winked behind his back. Later he told me he'd rather have a grandson named Jack than Napoleon, his way of supporting me, no matter what. I'd hushed him and told him to not rush Dan—or me!

"I was wondering," I said to Dan, "would you be willing to come with me? I keep asking you to escort me to these weddings!" I said it playfully, but he didn't bite. I felt embarrassed, like maybe I'd been rushing things. "And I've got tickets to a Mariner's game the week after," I said a bit more casually.

"What's the date?" Dan asked.

"The second-to-last weekend in June," I said. "Six weeks? Five weeks?"

He nodded. "Sure."

We talked about church for a while and then sat on the patio swing again. I got us each a cup of coffee and an oatmeal raisin cookie.

Dan pointed out a few holes in the yard. "Your dad is really annoyed about the mole holes."

"My dad is a perfectionist." I looked out over the holes pocking his smooth yard like landscape acne. "Look at some of the places where those bulbs are coming up," I said. "In the middle of the yard, over by the corner. Definitely places Dad didn't plant them."

"He said he thinks the moles push them to new spots when they tunnel," Dan said.

"I think they look nice." I pushed into the concrete with my toe to give us a swing. "I have kind of a random thought. Maybe it's spiritual. Like, Dad the perfectionist planted them where he wanted them to go, where he thought they should go, and then the mole came and moved them. It messed up Dad's design, but in the end God made the bulbs bloom anyway. And they might even be prettier 'out of place,' at least to a more random girl like me."

He put his hand over mine. "I like your randomness. Maybe that's what happened with Continental Catering. You thought the first bridal show was a disaster, but God grew it somewhere you could not have known to plant."

I smiled, glad to have someone who liked me just for who I was. We tossed the softball for a while, and then I went into the house to say good-bye. If we were going to make the ferry back, we'd have to get moving.

Dad and Mom were in the family room, watching TV. I went to wake Nonna, who was spending the whole weekend.

"We're leaving, Nonna," I said gently as I sat on the edge of her pink chenille bedspread. I touched her shoulder and she rolled over.

"What? Who? Oh, Lexi. Dear, this is not good." She sat up, trying to rearrange her hair, which was plastered to the side of her head where she'd been lying.

"What's not good, Nonna?"

"This Dan, it doesn't look good."

"I thought you liked him!" I protested, confused.

"I do like him. But something is off. Something is not good with him and you. I detected it over lunch."

"Nonna, don't be the harbinger of doom. Everything is fine! He bought me this shawl. We kissed in my apartment. He likes my random thoughts. What could be wrong?" She must have been confused. It took older people longer to wake up and come fully to their senses. I'd make her a cup of coffee before we left.

"I've lived a long time, dear, and seen a lot of men and women. I've developed a sixth sense for these things, and I'm telling you, something is not right."

She wobbled to her feet, and I steadied her before leading her out to the family room. "Let's get some coffee," I said more confidently than I felt.

I poured a cup for her, and we said our good-byes to everyone. My mom caught my arm before we left and gave me a tight hug.

"A year ago you and I were both dying for you to move out and live on your own."

"Thanks, Mom," I said. "'Dying' to have me move out, huh?"

She laughed softly. "But now that you're gone, I find myself wishing you back."

I put my arms around her neck and hugged her before leaving. "I miss you too."

Dan and I headed out to the truck and then toward the ferry dock.

"Thanks for coming. I hope my dad didn't talk your ear off," I said.

"No, he was great. It was all good," Dan reassured me.

"And we're still going to your parents' house for Memorial Day in a couple of weeks, right?" I asked. "I'll make sure I have the day off, though I can hardly believe anyone would be married on that day. Nothing is scheduled now, and hopefully Mr. Jacques won't have anything then."

"Yeah, we're still going," Dan said. "It'll be a good time. I wondered, could you bring a cake? My mom wanted to know."

"Of course," I said, and then settled in for the ride.

We pulled right onto the ferry and headed home. The way out had been so bright. I looked at the sky as we departed. Clouds were beginning to gather and stick, blotting out what little was left of the sun.

Fifteen

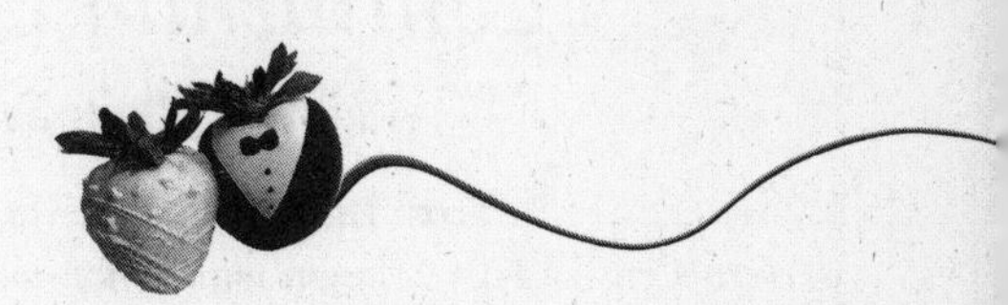

A mother who is really a mother is never free.

Honoré de Balzac

Monday morning at ten, I sat at a smooth, laminate table at Continental Catering, waiting for Mr. Jacques to arrive. Their reception room was huge, containing maybe a dozen tables for people to go over menus. Continental had sales people with culinary training whose only job was to sell and close the catering accounts. Very often they delivered a complete meal or two to prospective clients before they made a final decision. Why not? At five thousand to fifty thousand dollars per dinner order, they could afford the largesse.

I paged through their menu. They offered catering for open houses, cocktail parties, sit-down service buffets, theme parties, corporate events, and of course, weddings.

Mmm. Maybe I'd have Continental do *my* wedding.

Continental Catering

Wedding Menu Selections

Fresh Pacific Salmon with a miso glaze
Herb-Crusted Filet Mignon with pinot noir and sun-dried cherry sauce
Filet of Wellington with a rich brown sauce
Chicken en Croute with a caper tarragon sauce
Blackened Jumbo Prawns

"Hello, Lexi." Mr. Jacques breezed into the room in his chef's whites. I was glad I had worn my own. He spoke English, as most everyone around us did too.

"Hello, Mr. Jacques," I said.

"Please call me Ted." He sat next to me and opened one of the four manila folders he'd brought with him. "I have two weddings this weekend I need covered and two more the first weekend of June. Can you cover them?"

"Yes," I answered without even checking my day planner. "What days?" He showed me the folders, and all four were Saturdays.

"Good," he said. "Here's what I've got." He pulled out the first order, one hundred and twenty-five pieces of chocolate cake with a hazelnut butter cream filling, frosted with chocolate ganache. "The bride and groom are big chess players, and they want the top decorated with chess pieces. Can you do that?" He showed me the drawing the fired caterer had made. I knew where I could get chess molds and would make some white and dark chocolate chess players.

"Yes, I can do that," I said, excited by the challenge.

"The second cake is pretty straightforward—pink champagne with pink champagne icing and filling. Their florist is going to arrange flowers on the cake itself when it arrives. It will require someone staying there until the florist has completed her work, and then we'll take it from there."

He went over the other two orders, and when I added it all up in my head, we'd sell five hundred pieces each weekend. At six dollars per slice, that would be three thousand dollars each weekend in addition to the orders we already had coming in.

He stood and handed me the folders and told me the names of the managers at each event. "We'll see how these work out," he said. "I have another bakery or two I work with, but I'm growing and looking for people to grow with me. We'll talk in a couple of weeks."

I shook his hand, thanked him, and headed out to the van. During the course of our conversation, he'd implied he might be able to send me four or five cakes each weekend if he liked my work—in addition to those we'd scare up on our own. We'd be rolling in dough. Literally!

I drove back to Bijoux where Jessica and Margot waited. I ran into the kitchen and shouted, "Score!"

The three of us danced around, albeit in a somewhat ungainly manner in Margot's case.

"I'll need help for these two weekends. We need two people at each site. The wedding I've already got booked is in the morning, but then we'll have two evening ones each weekend. Can you work?" I asked Margot. "Please?"

She nodded. "*Bien.* This weekend Philippe and Sophie are taking Céline to a movie and dinner." She watched my face for a reaction. I kept it impassive, but her words reminded me that I needed to set up my lunch date with Céline.

"I can work," Jessica said. "Of course."

"We need one more person," I said, leaning over the countertop and already planning the cakes out in my mind. "How about your friend Trina?" I asked, wanting to give another Community Table grad a chance.

"I guess," Jessica said. "Should I call her?"

I should have picked up on her reticence, but I was so busy trying to mentally order the supplies I'd need for the cakes that I didn't. "Sure. You can work with Margot, and I'll take her with me. After I'm done setting up, we'll come back and pick you guys up again."

Jessica nodded. Margot prepared the day's catering orders, and I got on the phone with our suppliers to get materials delivered stat for the new cakes. I preheated my oven, texted Dan and Tanya, and got to work.

A few minutes later we heard a van rumble up. Margot patted her hair, and Jessica and I exchanged small smiles. Fred the UPS delivery man came to the door, delivered the boxes, and then indicated for Margot to step outside. We pretended to work, but I saw her write something on a piece of paper and hand it to him.

Margot came back in and said nothing at first. We all worked—I didn't dare ask her what had happened.

"Fred used to be the driver for our stores," she volunteered.

"Oh, that's nice," I said.

Jessica waded deeper. "What happened?" she asked.

"He got injured and had to take some time off. Of course, I didn't know that. I thought he'd just asked for a new route."

Ah. As in, avoiding her.

"But now he's well and back."

"I saw you hand him an order," Jessica said a little teasingly. "Or maybe a personal phone number so he doesn't have to call the bakery all the time?"

"Impertinent! Back to work!" Margot said, but her voice reflected pleasure and she left the radio on Jessica's rock station.

Saturday morning came, and several wedding cakes sat in the walk-in. It was still only half full, and I envisioned it full, the business booming. I'd worked late every day that week and still had energy to spare.

"Normally it won't be this much of a rush," I reassured Jessica as we toted pieces out to the van, "because we'll have them in advance. But everything has to go perfectly these two weekends."

Jessica and I did the morning wedding setup ourselves, and it went off without a hitch. She went home to get a couple hours of sleep, and I tailored the Saturday evening cakes to perfection. Because the weddings were at nearly the same time, I'd have to drop off Jessica and Margot to set up the first one while Trina and I set up the second, waiting for the florist.

Trina arrived silently later that afternoon, like a cat. When I turned around after packing a box, she stood right behind me. I looked at her, but she didn't blink or introduce herself.

"Trina?" I asked.

"Yes," she said, sweeping her long blond hair out of her face.

"I'm Lexi."

Jessica kept her distance, merely nodding. I had too much work to do to worry about niceties any longer. I showed Trina what to load, and we headed to the wedding site.

"Can you help me carry these in?" I asked her once we arrived, giving her the smallest pieces and the setup ware.

"Sure." She walked in the back door kind of unsteadily. I watched her go. I didn't want to be judgmental, but there was something kind of sneaky about her. I'd definitely caught an uncomfortable vibe between her and Jessica and wished that I'd paid better attention when I'd asked Jessica to call her. Too late now. It'd be over soon.

I took the rest of the champagne pieces inside, and we found the cake table between the open bar and the DJ station in the back. Continental Catering was already setting up linen, dinnerware, and silver. I met the catering manager.

"Thanks for everything," I told her. "Here's my cell number if you need anything, and we'll make sure everything is perfect with the florist before I check out with you."

"Good," she said, looking over my shoulder. I turned to look, too, and saw Trina by the bar, openly flirting with the bartender.

I walked back to the cake table and pulled her aside. "We're here to work, okay? It's really important that we stay on task."

"I *am* on task," she said in a snide voice. "What else do we need to do?"

"Just stay here and guard the cake while I help the florist for a minute," I said. I met the florist on the other side of the room, and together we chose some blooms I could use to decorate the cake. I took them back to the cake, but Trina was gone. I saw her by the bar again and waved her toward me. When she got back to the cake, I distinctly smelled alcohol on her breath.

She was definitely not old enough to drink.

I decided that, for the moment, the best thing to do was get the flowers done as quickly as possible and then leave. Should I send her to the van? What if she drove away?

"Why don't you just sit over there while I finish the cake," I said quietly. "And then we'll go."

"Sure thing," she said. She sat at one of the tables and began to toy with the silverware. One of the catering waiters came over and asked her to stop. When he bent down to replace the fork, I saw him quickly turn his head and look at me. He'd smelled her breath too.

I made the cake look as beautiful as possible and then talked with the catering manager. "We're all set," I said, keeping a positive look on my face. Had her waiter told her about Trina? She glanced at Trina. I guessed that he had. "Here's the special box I provide each bride and groom for their top layer. It's got a special lining inside to protect against freezer burn."

"What a lovely idea," she said, genuinely pleased. "I'll call if I need anything else. Otherwise, we'll deliver the service pieces next week."

"Let's go." I motioned to Trina. I really wanted to drag her out by her hair. If she'd ruined my chances with Continental Catering, I'd kill her.

I hated managing people.

Once in the van I asked her, "Did you visit the bar?"

"Yes," she said defensively. "I was talking to the bartender. Are you racist or something that you care about me talking to him?"

Don't you dare try to turn this and put me on the defensive. "I didn't notice what race the bartender was. I did notice that your breath smells like alcohol."

She turned away from me. "You're imagining things."

We picked up Jessica and Margot, and I instructed Trina to stay in the van. After thanking the manager for her business, I hustled out of there. As I'd expected, when I got back to the van, Trina was gone.

"Where's Trina?" Jessica asked.

"I think she ditched out on us," I said. "Did you know she drinks?"

"Yeah," she said.

"Zut alors!" said Margot.

"Why didn't you tell me?" I asked.

"I don't know." Jessica hung her head. Margot patted her hand but said nothing.

I wanted to feel bad for her; I did feel bad for her. I knew she'd had little guidance and training, but right now I was mad. My new account could be ruined.

Inside, though, I knew the anger should be directed toward me. I hadn't even checked Trina's references. I'd picked up on vibes from Jessica and ignored them. And, after all, I was the boss here.

I hated managing people. I hated hustling business. All I ever wanted to do was bake.

I floored it and got us back to Bijoux as fast as possible.

The next afternoon I was hosting a second cake tasting at Bijoux, and Leah came to help me out. It had been hard for us to get together, and I was excited for her to see the bakery in action now that we were humming.

"Can I help with anything else?" Jessica asked as she brought out the last of the coffee cups and set them by the café express machine.

"No," I said.

She walked back into the kitchen, reached up to the radio, and flipped her hard rock station off. She turned her sad-dog face away from me while taking off her apron.

"Don't beat yourself up over Trina anymore," I said. "I've put it behind me and so should you."

"I know," Jessica said. "She's called me again a couple of times, asking for a job."

"Unless you're running a business in your off-hours, you don't have one to offer her," I said, and she laughed at that. "You have to gather the courage to confront her."

"I know," she said, but not with a lot of power. Easier said than done, I knew, for a kid who has had to be nice to everyone her whole life in order to ensure survival.

I hugged her, and she clocked out a few minutes before Leah arrived.

"Hey, I wore black and white," she said.

"You look catering cute!" I said. "If you ever need a job, just let me know."

"I might just take you up on that," she said, tying a Bijoux apron around her waist. "It's been a really hard week."

"What's up?" I asked.

"Oh, just work. I made some mistakes on a case, and my boss had to come behind me and redo it. Which means he assigned the good parts of the next case to someone else."

"I'm sorry," I said.

"It'll pass. It always does."

I looked at her, a year younger than me but more experienced in the corporate world and thought, *Maybe she's right.* I could see how her levelheadedness was a great balance for my brother.

And maybe how I, always a bit more spontaneous and flighty, would be better balanced and partnered with someone more level-headed.

"What do we do first?" she asked.

"Bring the cakes out. They're already cut into small pieces. We'll line them up on the bar along with the scorecards and pencils. If it gets really busy, God willing, you just help people write up their names and numbers on the card. If they're ready to put down a deposit, signal me and I'll come over and help."

"Sounds easy," she said.

I put some soft jazz on the radio and got everything ready just a few minutes before the first couple arrived. Within half an hour the place was packed. It only took ten people to pack us out, but still! It gave a successful vibe to everyone coming in.

"I think this couple is ready to sign up," Leah whispered, pointing to an older couple in the corner.

I went over to help them, and as I did I saw another couple come in. I recognized them. He was a Seattle Mariner, though I couldn't remember what position he played. I caught Leah's eye, and she put on her professional poker face and went to help them.

A couple of hours later we'd shown the last couple to the door, and I looked over the scorecards to assess the day's gains.

"Seven people want me to call for weddings in August or September," I said. "That's not bad. And Mr. Pitcher's fiancée left her number too, though I noticed there is no date."

"Four deposits!" Leah said triumphantly. "One for a wedding of three hundred. All right!" She sank into one of the chairs and took a large plate of cake with her. "I don't know how you stay 'on' the whole time they're here."

"It's getting easier," I admitted. "I want their wedding cakes to be memorable. People hardly ever remember what the meal looked or tasted like, even though it's more expensive. They always remember the cake."

"It's da trufe," Leah said through a mouthful. She got up and refilled her plate.

"Are you eating for two?" I teased.

"Yeah, me and Nate," she said. "As always. Though your mom would love for me to be eating for three. Hurry up and get married so the pressure can be off me to have a kid."

"She promised she wouldn't bug you!"

"Oh, she doesn't say anything," Leah admitted. "It's just the longing glances when we're together and pass a baby stroller or kids at the park or..." She began laughing and I did too.

"Actually, I have a kid outing myself today," I said. "I'm taking Céline to dinner."

"Oh, right, I remember you told me that. Are you ready?"

I sat in the chair next to her, kicked off my shoes, and threw my legs over the armrest to get comfortable. "No. But it has to be done. She's a kid, so I can only say so much. I want her to know I'll be there for her in some capacity, but help her to love me a little less so she can love Sophie a little more."

"Do you want that? I thought you didn't like kids," Leah asked, sitting up to look me in the eye.

"I don't know. I still don't like them all. I told you about the anthill I fell into when I was teaching Sunday school, right?"

Leah laughed. "Yes, you told me."

I took a bite of almond cake before continuing. "Maybe I didn't love kids until I had one I started to think of as maybe becoming my own. Kind of like I didn't care about having a real career until I had one I loved and might lose. You know?"

She nodded.

"I want them all to be happy, I want what's best for Céline...and for me," I said quietly. "But I'm going to miss her a lot."

"You'll still see her, though?"

I nodded. "But it'll be different. I have to make it so. And just when I thought I was going to make such a good mother!" I joked to lighten the mood.

Leah set down her plate. "That's exactly why you'll be a good mother, Lex. It's a very motherly thing to look out for Céline's best interests when you know she needs to bond with Sophie instead."

"Yeah, yeah, I know." I stood. "I guess I'd better get going."

"You want me to pray for you before I go?"

I opened my mouth to say no, that that was making a big deal about it, but then I remembered my verse from this morning. *Do not be anxious about anything, but in everything, by prayer and petition, with thanksgiving, present your requests to God. Philippians 4:6.*

"Yes, please," I said instead. Leah and I held hands among the remains of the day—the nearly empty plates, the dregs of cafés crèmes, the wailing of a saxophone, the forward-looking dreams of the couples who'd passed through—and prayed for a six-year-old girl and a twenty-five-year-old woman who needed His arms around them.

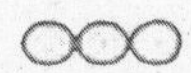

An hour later, I arrived at Margot's condo, where Philippe and Céline lived for the moment until Philippe bought something. Céline had the door open before I even rang the bell.

"Ready to go?" I asked.

"Oui!" She grabbed her fur and feather purse. Philippe walked her to the door. "You can't come, Papa, this is an outing just for girls," she admonished.

"*Bien sûr,* I will stay here and clean the bathrooms, *n'est-ce pas*?"

At that she broke out in laughter. I couldn't envision Philippe doing a whole lot of housework. He grabbed Céline and kissed her on the face, and then he took me by the shoulders and kissed each of my cheeks too.

"Merci," he whispered to me as we left.

"De rien," I answered casually, knowing it really wasn't "nothing at all."

I strapped her into the back of the van, and we took off.

"Do you hate driving this big thing?" she called. It *did* seem like a big thing, and she sat way back there in this vehicle.

"Oh, it's not my favorite car in the whole world, but it's only for a while. Then I'm going to get something really cool."

"Like what?" she asked.

"A convertible."

"Ooh, like in California."

"Yeah, it makes more sense in California, where it doesn't rain so much, doesn't it?" I said. "Anyway, I can dream."

A few minutes later she asked me, "Did you give your car to Sophie?"

I took a right turn and headed toward the waterfront. "Yes."

"Why?"

"I was going to France and didn't need my car anymore, and Sophie is my friend and did need a car. And I got this van when I came back, so it all worked out okay, didn't it?"

"Oui," she said, and then she clutched her purse in a prim lady-like way and waited while I parallel parked the van—no small feat in itself.

I got her out of the backseat, and we held hands as we crossed the road to the wharf. I loved coming down to the docks. It was touristy, but it was also quintessential Seattle. There were docks promising water tours and water dinners, creaky ferry landings, salt water taffy that could pull out the best dental fillings, and the smack of saltwater, fish, and sweat commingling in a Washington brew. The savory stew of people from all races and many languages hailing horse-drawn carriages or hawking T-shirts or creating street art reminded me that I did not live in a cultural wasteland.

"This is different," Céline said.

"Do you like it?"

She nodded but held my hand tighter, until a balloon twister offered her a pink poodle balloon. She laughed with delight, and we took it with us into the restaurant.

When we got to the door, she looked up at the entry sign. "That's a British flag," she said, automatically and unconsciously, I suspected, switching to English.

"It is!"

I held up two fingers and asked for a table by the window, and we were promptly seated.

"My mum was British," Céline said.

"I know. I thought you might like to come to a British restaurant today since you're part British. You're going to visit your grandparents at the end of next month, right?"

She nodded. "Right."

We ordered a basket of fish and chips to share, two Cokes, and some tartar sauce, and then giggled at the seagulls squabbling over a scrap of bread on the dock in front of us. A young boy lost his hat in the wind, and the seagulls took off after that too. Céline and I laughed even harder.

"I thought it would be fun for us to have dinner together," I said.

"And talk about Sophie?" she asked.

I smiled in spite of myself. "You're such a smart kid."

"I know," she said without a trace of arrogance, and then flashed her gap-toothed smile.

"What made you think we were going to talk about Sophie?" I asked.

"I heard Papa and Tante Margot talking about it, a little," she admitted. "Papa and Sophie are lovey-dovey." She made a romantic face and rolled her eyes.

"How do you feel about that?" I asked her.

She shrugged. Little Philippe.

"Do you want to know how I feel about it?" I asked.

She nodded enthusiastically.

"I think it's very nice. Your papa is a very good friend of mine and Sophie is a very good friend of mine, and I'm happy they're happy together."

She picked at a feather on her purse before speaking. "Did you want to be lovey-dovey with Papa?"

I smiled. "No. For a while, maybe, I wasn't sure, but then I knew that wasn't the right thing."

"I wish it could be the right thing." The honesty of children. Maybe that was one reason the Lord said we all must become like children. They had no shell of pretense.

"I know you did," I said. "But you don't always know how wonderful things are going to turn out. Remember how you didn't like Anne-Marie at school? And now?"

"She's my best friend!" Céline said.

"Exactly. Let me tell you a few things about Sophie." I waited while the waitress brought our food, and when Céline took a bite, I continued.

"She's very artistic. She plays the piano beautifully."

"I know that!" Céline said, bouncing in her seat. "She even taught me something new, and then I surprised Madame at school with it. Do you play the piano?"

"Nope, not a bit," I said. "I like to spend my time baking."

Céline screwed up her face, as I knew she would.

"Sophie, on the other hand, doesn't like to bake at all," I said. "So if your papa is busy baking, why, Sophie would have lots of time to do something with you!"

"C'est vrai," Céline said thoughtfully, slipping back into French.

"Of course it's true." Now to drop the biggest bomb of all. "Did you know Sophie was a cheerleader?"

"Non!" Céline exclaimed excitedly. I knew that would be a big draw because Céline was into all things girly Americana. I also knew that if there was one person who could jolly Sophie into talking about her cheerleading, it would be Céline.

"Oui!" I said. "So, you see, there may be many adventures ahead for you and Sophie."

She nodded, agreeing, but wasn't ready to totally write me off yet. "But what about you, Lexi? Are you going to move away?"

Why would she ask that? *"Non,"* I said. "I'll still be around. I can be like an aunt. Like Tante Margot or Tante Patricia."

She laughed. "Oh no, your voice isn't so rough."

"Should I start smoking so I can be your aunt?" I lowered and roughened my voice to imitate Margot. "*Bonjour,* niece."

She further dissolved into giggles, and I knew that we had passed the critical point. *"Non, merci,"* she said. "*Pas de* smoking."

After leaving the restaurant, I turned my phone back on and quickly checked to see if I had any messages. I thought maybe Dan would call to see how the cake tasting had gone.

I waited for it to sync up—sometimes it took awhile before the messages came through. When two minutes had passed, it was clear there was no message from Dan waiting, though there was a missed call from Jessica. Strange. I sighed and put the phone back into my purse.

We stopped in front of a candy shop to watch the taffy pullers as they mechanically drew farther and farther away from each other, stretching the bond between them thinner and thinner as they did. Poignantly, it reminded me of the situation I'd just brought to a close. I bought Céline some taffy, and we walked back to the van.

"You've had a wonderful mum, you're going to get a wonderful mom someday, and you've got many tantes who love you. What a lucky girl you are!"

She smiled and began chattering away again. The contentment in her heart was worth the pain in my own.

Sixteen

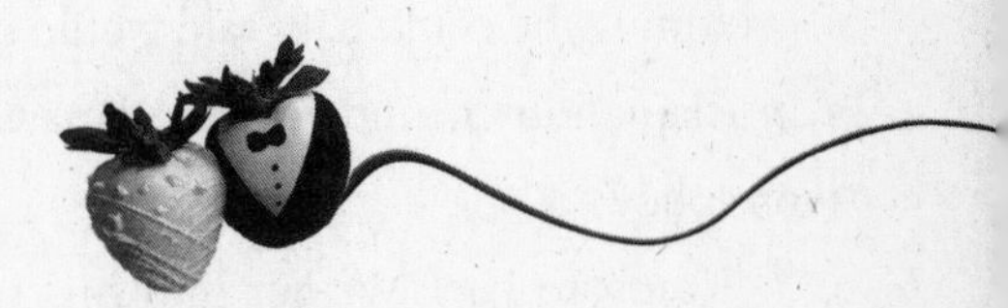

Courage is like love; it must have hope to nourish it.

Napoleon Bonaparte

When Dan and I talked about his family's annual Memorial Day barbecue, he asked if I'd make a cake for the occasion. I wanted to make something that wasn't too showy but was also different. I wanted it to taste good—of course—and make a good impression. I hoped his family liked me as much as my family liked him.

I hoped he felt about me the way I felt about him.

On Memorial Day I took the cake out of the walk-in for the final touches. I'd made a large, two-layer chocolate sheet cake. I frosted it with milk chocolate icing and smoothed it so it was nearly flat. Then I used a piping bag and drew lines across the top so it looked like a barbecue grill. On top of the "grill" I laid bamboo sticks upon which I'd skewered gummy candies that looked like veggies. I also frosted chocolate cookies with a bumpy technique so they looked like burgers.

When Dan came to pick me up, I showed him the cake before boxing it. "Like it?" I asked. "I wanted to do something different than just a typical flag cake."

He grinned. "It's cute and whimsical, Lexi, like you."

Nothing he could have said would have made me happier. Well, a proclamation of undying love, maybe, but perhaps that would soon follow.

"Ready to go?" We got into his truck and headed out to Cle Elum, in the country foothills east of Seattle.

"So who's going to be there?" I asked.

"A lot of people. It's my mom and stepdad's house, so of course they'll be there. My sixteen-year-old half-sister will be there. My other sister is in Belgium, you remember, so she's not coming. Aunts and uncles, some cousins. They have a big place, a pool, lots of acreage. There'll be lots to do."

"Sounds fun," I said.

"Maybe," he agreed.

"Will your dad come?" I asked. "Do your mom and dad get along?"

"He won't be there. He's a good guy, and my mom is a nice lady. I love them both, but they've never been close since their breakup. Understandable." He kept his eyes on the road, and I understood from this and other conversations that nearly seventeen years later, his heart was still riven with the effects of his parents' divorce.

The day was thankfully sunny and warm—not always a given for late May in Seattle—and we talked comfortably all the way to Cle Elum. As soon as we turned down the country driveway, I felt my stomach clench. It felt like an audition. It *was* an audition.

Dan must have noticed my face go pasty; he reached over and caressed my cheek. "Don't worry," he said. "I'm sure they'll love you. How could they not?"

He came around and opened my door—Dad would approve—and took the cake from my hands. I'd boxed it well and we'd had the air conditioning on the whole way, so it was in perfect shape.

We walked up the driveway to the home's entrance. It was a huge stone rambler that flung its arms wide in each direction. The front door was big enough to let Barnum and Bailey pass through, though you couldn't imagine any kind of animal, save a well-behaved, truly obedient family pet, anywhere nearby.

"Wow, big house," I said admiringly.

"Bigger than my dad's house," he said. "My stepdad is a contractor. My dad is a teacher. My mother always wanted more than he could give her, so she found what she wanted instead."

"Oh." I said nothing more and neither did he, but I could feel the unresolved pain lying beneath the surface.

We walked in and Dan called out, "Hello!" A teenage girl with strawberry blond hair to match Dan's ran in and hugged him. I held back a little, standing in the foyer, feeling like Gertrude Good Housekeeping holding my cake.

"How are you? I've missed you. I'm driving!" she said to him all at once.

"Heaven help us and clear the roads," he said. "Amber, I want you to meet Lexi. Lexi, this is my sister, Amber."

"I'd shake your hand, but I've got the cake." I felt a little tentative. Sometimes sisters didn't appreciate other women coming into their brothers' lives. I needn't have worried.

"I'll take the cake, no problem," she said. "I'm so glad you could come. I have a lot of questions for you. Dan said you lived in Paris last year." She kept chattering and led me into the kitchen. Dan rolled his eyes, but I could tell they were close and he was glad she had taken to me. I was glad too. Extra large piece of cake for Amber.

"Mom, this is Lexi," Amber said. I grinned. She was apparently astute enough not to call me a girlfriend without Dan referring to me that way. Another attorney in the making. Great.

Was I a girlfriend? That kiss in my apartment had certainly said so.

A woman in her midfifties wiped her hands off on her apron and came to greet me. Her hair was expensively colored and I could tell that her clothes were expensive, but there was nothing snobby in her attitude. "Welcome, Lexi." She hugged me. "We've heard some about you but certainly not enough. I've been looking forward to meeting you for myself."

"Thank you for inviting me," I said. I had the feeling the dozen or so people milling around were sizing me up. Since we were in horse country, I felt tempted to open my mouth and ask if they'd like to check my teeth, but I didn't think that would play too well right off.

The crowd regrouped into smaller clumps, thankfully, and Dan took me around with him as he greeted everyone, introducing me on the way.

"This is Aunt Linda and Uncle Roy," he whispered to me. "Remember?"

He'd prepped me on the way about who would be there and what to expect. "The one who is always selling something?" I whispered back. He winked and nodded.

"Hi, Aunt Linda," Dan said, leaning over and kissing her cheek. "You smell wonderful!"

"It's Feathers by the Sea," she said. "It's one of the premier fragrances in the line I've just started selling." She reached into her handbag and extracted a brochure. "Here. Every woman can do with new cosmetics. Can I spray the sample on you?" She dug into her handbag again.

"Oh, no thank you," I said. "I'm afraid that with the scent I already have on, it wouldn't do it justice. But I'll look at the brochure."

"I hear you cook," she said. "I also represent a home kitchen products company. Call me."

Uncle Roy drained his beer and caught my eye with a smile. I shook his hand and made small talk with him for a few minutes before Dan put his hand at the small of my back and steered me toward the crowd that had drifted outside.

"That was very gracious," he said. "Please don't start wearing Feathers by the Sea. I appreciate your efforts to have my family like you...but I like that alluring scent you already wear."

I didn't dare look him in the eye. He found me—or at least my perfume—alluring. It felt like a secret revelation in the midst of the crowd.

"Hey, it's Dan," an older man called out. "How come we only see you when there's food or a new girl you want to introduce?"

I noticed Dan grimace. "Lexi, meet my mom's cousin Scott. Scott, Lexi."

Scott pumped my hand. "Pleased to meet you, missy. I hear you've been to Pair-ee!"

"Yes, I spent six months there last year," I said.

"Well, you won't find frogs' legs or goose livers on the grill today, just good old American beef. I hope that's okay."

"I'm the daughter of a marine," I said politely and pointedly. "Good old American beef is just fine."

"I'm Enid, dear." A large older woman came alongside me. "Come sit down with me."

Dan smiled and indicated he'd be right back. Enid pulled me into the chair next to hers at a nearby table and proceeded to tell me about everyone there, only nice things, and I liked her immediately.

Finally she said, "I don't want to give you the wrong impression, dear. We all want you to like us. But do stay away from the macaroni salad. My sister Marcia makes it, bless her heart. She stores opened mayonnaise in the pantry and not the fridge."

"I'll be careful," I promised, and she leaned over and kissed my head in a grandmotherly way.

Dan was talking with the guys by the grill, and I didn't want to appear needy or unable to stand on my own, so I went back into the kitchen where the women were mostly gathered. Amber took me under her wing, which was very sweet, and introduced me to the other women in the room.

Dan's mom pointed to the cake box, now set on the countertop. "Can I look at it?"

"Of course."

She opened the box lid and peeked in. "Oh, how dear," she said. "This is adorable, Lexi. Is that your full name?"

"It's Alexandra," I explained. "But almost everyone calls me Lexi."

"Lovely," she said. "Thank you for bringing the cake."

"You're welcome. Is there something else I can do to help?" I guessed not, seeing that the other women were milling around chatting. The table was set, the silverware was out, and when Dan's mom opened her fridge, I saw everything neatly organized in matching Tupperware containers. I mentally compared it to my fridge at home—dozens of bottles of partially used condiments, half-eaten cooking experiments, a veritable United Nations of cheeses. But no Tupperware. Maybe Aunt Linda repped Tupperware too.

"Not now, thanks," his mom answered. "Just stay and chat with us for a minute."

Amber sat on a bar stool at the island. I did likewise. Dan's aunts were all very kind to me, asking what I did for a living and where I'd gone to school. One of his older cousins was a Western Washington University grad, like me, so we felt an instant bond. I tried not to overeat chips and salsa as a coping mechanism, but I did anyway.

"Oh, darn, I could use some more cilantro," Dan's mom said.

"I'll go get it!" Amber offered. I smiled, remembering how eager I'd been to do errands as soon as I'd gotten my driver's license. "Lexi, do you want to come with?"

Dan's mother frowned a little. "Maybe Lexi would rather stay here."

"I don't mind," I said. "I remember what it was like to first have my license."

His mother smiled and handed some money to her daughter. "Okay, don't be gone long."

Amber walked out to the driveway where a small Corolla was parked under a nearby tree. "This isn't really my car, but it's our oldest one so my dad said I could drive it. I'm still mastering the stick shift. I hope you don't mind."

Ah. Maybe this was the reason for her mother's reluctance.

Amber started the car, backed out, tried to put it in first gear, and killed it with a lurch. "Sorry," she said, fumbling with the keys again. She shoved the car in first gear again, and we drove about fifteen feet at five miles an hour before the engine begged at high pitch to be switched into the next gear. She lagged for a minute and switched it into second. I didn't want to brace myself against the dashboard, but putting my hand there was an automatic response.

"Are you okay?" she asked breezily.

"Fine, fine," I said. Had I been Catholic like Nonna, I'd have been imploring the patron saint of driving to watch over us. We got on the road to town, Amber shifted into fourth, and things smoothed out. I took my hand off the dash and began to relax until she started fumbling for her sunglasses.

"Can I find them for you?" I offered.

"No, no, I got 'em," she said.

I promised myself that if she whipped out her phone and started texting, I'd say something.

We walked into Safeway, got her mom's cilantro, and went back to the car. I thought back to the wild ride I'd had with Patricia in France. "You drive like a Frenchwoman," I said.

"Really?" She lit up. Clearly, it was a compliment to her. I didn't disabuse her of the notion, just sent up a prayer for a safe ride home. Someone was listening. We made it.

"You returned in one piece," her mom said to me in a low voice as she relieved Amber of the cilantro. "Was it a wild ride?"

I caught the sparkle in her eye and risked a humorous response. "A bit like breaking a bronco. But we made it back."

Dan's mom broke out in laughter, and I laughed along with her. They must have heard us outside, because Dan looked in and saw us laughing, and I could see him relax a little. Whether he felt better because I was more at ease or because his mom was or just in general, I didn't know, but it felt like we'd turned a corner.

A softball game was underway in the backyard. I'd loved to have played but didn't want to interrupt, so Amber and I decided to play Scrabble until the next game started.

She shuffled the tiles and handed them out. "Dan said you lived in Paris last year. Did you like it?"

"I loved it," I said. "It was always my dream to go there as a girl, and I was thrilled to do it last year."

"Was it beautiful?" Amber asked.

"Beyond imagining."

"My sister lives by France," she said. "She lives in Belgium. She went there as an exchange student, fell in love, and now she lives there forever. I wish I could do that."

I laughed. "Maybe you will. It's a little different than Cle Elum."

"I know." She made a face. "That's why I want to go."

"You'll love it. It's dreamy, it's wonderful, there's no place in the world like it. It's the City of Lights and the City of Love. Just like I said." I pointed to the Scrabble board.

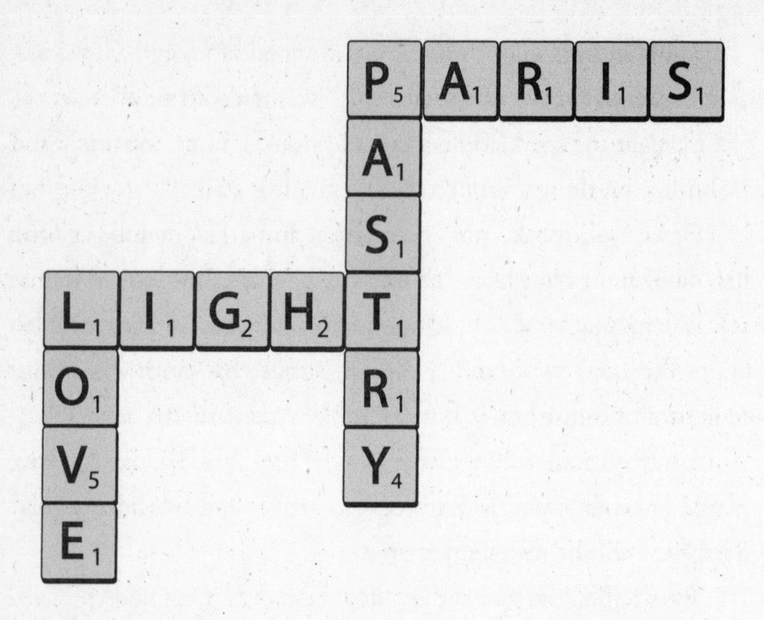

I remembered what it was like to be a young girl dreaming, and I saw that reflected in Amber's face.

I heard a cough behind me and looked up to see Dan looking over the board. "Dan! How long have you been here? Your sister is killing me at Scrabble," I said.

"A little while," he said, flushed and handsome but sounding a little reserved. "I came to see if you want to play softball."

"Only if I can be on your team," I said. At that, he smiled.

After two games I sat on the patio drinking iced tea and watched Dan roughhouse with his younger cousins on the grass, turning them upside down and pretending to be overwhelmed when they tackled him. He called out, "Lexi!" and passed the football to me out of the boys' reach, and they groaned. They clearly adored him.

So did I.

Lunch was served on their extensive patio. Dan and I sat together, chatting comfortably at a table with his aunt and uncle and a cousin who was serving in the military. I was glad my own dad was in the military, as it gave us a common topic to talk about. The food was excellent, and our conversation flow was natural and comfortable. We felt like a couple. Dan's stepdad was a master barbecuer, and his mother's ambrosia salad recipe was excellent. I may not have had cooking competition from Nancy, but I would definitely have something to live up to with his mom.

After lunch, some people scattered to play croquet, but I'd spied something else on the side of the house I'd rather do.

"Whose ATVs are those?" I asked Dan.

"Everyone's," he said. "Why? You interested in riding?"

"Sure," I said. "If you are."

He grinned. "I'd love to. Let's see if we can escape for a while."

He hitched the ATV trailer up to his truck, and we drove a few short miles to the area around Cle Elum Lake. We put helmets on and after he fastened mine under my chin, Dan showed me how to start the machine. I took off before he could get ahead of me.

We drove around for a bit, in and out of the trails, and I had to duck a few times to keep from getting clocked by low-hanging branches. It felt so good to be outside, to be in the sun, to be away from the pressures of the bakery. The baking itself was wonderful. But the business part, the management, the staff issues, the money issues, all of them had taken a toll that I felt falling away with the mud and dust behind us.

After about an hour we were returning to the truck, and I made a daring move and passed Dan again. I reached the truck just ahead of him. We took off our helmets, laughing.

"Trying to make me chase you?" he teased.

"Maybe," I said. This time we were both definitely aware of the double meaning, but I didn't care. I felt free and flirty and was enjoying the day. "Is it working?"

He laughed again. "Yes. But you don't need to try any more."

He loaded both ATVs onto the trailer and then opened the truck door for me. After I settled in the seat, he used his hands to wipe away the dust on my face, more a caress than a cleaning. It brought back the moment in the rain in Paris.

"My mom would never ride an ATV," he said. "But you did."

"Is that a good thing?" I asked.

He traced my lips with his fingertip. "Yes."

My body melted like a candy bar on the dashboard.

Seventeen

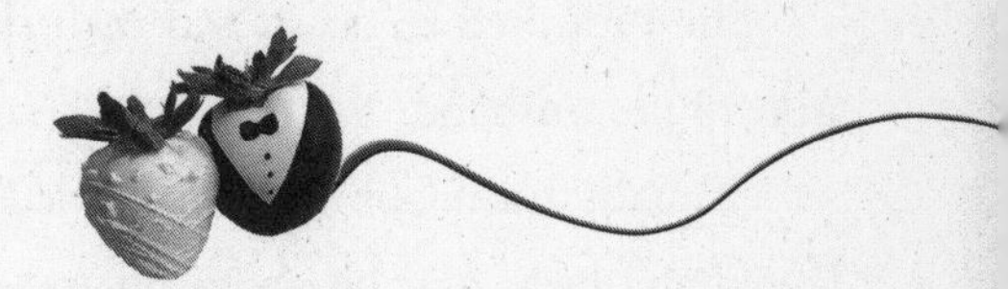

How many cares one loses when one decides not to be something but to be someone.
Coco Chanel

I slipped into church Sunday night. The room was dim and soft, and somber praise wafted from the back. I'd missed church that morning due to an order that had been confused and reworked at the last minute. "These things happen," Leah had told me about her recent job faux pas, and I was learning to take mine more in stride too.

I saw someone across the sanctuary wave at me. Tabitha! The woman I'd taught Sunday school with. She stood and headed my way. What if she asked me to help out again?

"Hi, Lexi," she said. "I've been looking for you for a couple of weeks. We must attend different services."

"Good to see you!" I said, and I meant it.

"Would you like to get together sometime?" she asked. "We can meet for coffee instead of juice in Dixie cups." She smiled knowingly, and I liked her immediately for knowing my limits and wanting to reach out anyway.

"I'd love that." I jotted my phone number on a slip of paper in my Bible and handed it to her. "Call anytime."

She promised to do so and then slipped back to her own seat next to her husband.

Tonight was a Communion service. I slipped into an open seat, closed my eyes, and began to lift my prayer requests to God. So many things to ask Him for. Dan. Business. Jessica. Money. But my heart stilled.

Was God a giant Dear Abby I wrote questions to and He had to stay within the confines of answering them? Or was He a partner in the relationship, able to initiate conversations as well as take questions?

I'm sorry I talk so much, Lord. Tell me what's on Your heart.

I sat with my head in my hands for a few minutes, glad I'd arrived early enough to meditate and have time to myself. Every time my mind wandered into another lane, I steered it back between the lines.

A few minutes later the music slowly faded, and the pastor called our attention to the Communion table at the front. "We come to this table, invited to eat a meal that we did not pay for, but one that was provided for us at a sacrificial, personal cost."

I made my way up to the candlelit table with the others in my row, and as I knelt to take the bread and the cup, I clearly heard the Lord speak to me. "*Feed My sheep, Lexi.*"

After making my way back to my chair, I bowed my head again.

I felt Him like a warm rush in a cool room, like syrup, almost, enveloping me with His presence. I wanted nothing so much as for that moment to never go away. But it receded, an appetizer for eternity, and I was left with the residue of aftertaste, an almost tangible memory of our momentary intimacy.

As I left, I looked down the hall toward the Sunday school rooms and knew those weren't the sheep I was to feed. I remembered God whispering that very same phrase in France, and I'd thought He'd meant Céline. And maybe He did, but I'd handed that baton off. With an unexplainable clarity, I suddenly knew who my sheep were.

I'd make the call tomorrow.

"Chef, it's good to see you again!" Max showed me into his tiny office beside the Community Table kitchen. A shelf full of cookbooks, county regulation manuals, and a picture of his family lined one wall, and a beat-up computer percolated on his desk. I could hear the cleaning crew working in the kitchen next door—lots of work to do after a weekend feeding a thousand or so people. I wondered who the guest chef had been, and whose restaurant had sacrificed financially and personally to feed that weekend's homeless. I'd seen the menus. They didn't offer blue green meat or day-off chicken. It was always their best.

"Thanks for having me in," I said. "The end of the weeks are busy for me and you too, so I thought early in the week would be a good time to stop by." The rattle and clatter of pans banging in the next room brought a working-kitchen vibe to the whole place. Rap music boomed out from the radio. I heard someone turn it to hard rock, some playful shouting ensued, and then a third station was settled on.

"No problem," he said. "How is Jessica working out?"

"Great!" I answered with unbridled enthusiasm. "She's doing a fantastic job and is very reliable. She's one of the reasons I called you."

"I'm glad to hear it," Max said. "She was a hard worker here, and our guest chefs enjoyed working with her. How else can I help?"

"Actually, I'm wondering how I can help you. I know you've got guest chef programs, but frankly, we're not in the financial position right now to donate the food required for the weekend meal programs. However, what I can donate is my time. I held a cooking class at my bakery a couple of months ago. That was for nonchefs, but I'd be willing to open up my bakery one evening a month for a training day. It would allow some of your staff to see if baking or cooking is a career they'd like to pursue. It's something they can do without advanced education, which I know is beyond the means of many of your guests."

Max grinned. "What a great idea! I'd thought of that at other times, of course, because we can only provide so much training here, and in order to get more people through the door and stabilized, we can only keep them for six months. Some, but not all, of our clients are interested in cooking and baking. This would be a good way for them to figure it out. But what's in it for you?"

Feeding sheep, I thought, but I kept that to myself. "It's a way for me to give back to the community," I said. "As I grow, I'll be looking for new employees too. This will give me a way to see who might work out...and who might not."

Max was savvy enough to hear the tone behind that. "Did something happen with one of our clients?"

I nodded. "Did you know Trina has a drinking problem?"

Max shook his head. "No. She'd have been immediately released from the program if she had shown up inebriated. I'm sorry—did she show up drunk on the job? I thought you weren't going to hire her."

I sighed. "I wasn't, but did for one gig. Unfortunately, she took alcohol from the wedding's open bar and then disappeared. Just thought you'd want to know. I hope she gets some help."

Max looked grim. "Me too. We get a lot of people with abuse backgrounds here—substance abuse, physical abuse, sexual abuse. It breaks your heart, but you can't fix them all. You can only put a Band-Aid on and pass them to the next doctor for another set of stitches."

I glanced at the clock above his head. "I'd better get going. I've got a huge dry goods order that will be delivered in a bit. Four big gigs this weekend—cakes serving fifteen hundred total. Time to bake."

"I don't know how you guys consistently cook for so many week after week," Max exclaimed. "I marvel at it every week. So—we'll talk soon?"

I grinned. "Sounds good. I've got a busy June, but I'll call you in July to see when we can have our first training session. I'll try to hook up with South Seattle Community College's cooking and baking programs ahead of time and see if I can get some brochures too."

Max walked me to the door, and after saying good-bye, I headed down the street to check on my order.

"Can you help me count pieces?" I asked Margot. I had two huge cakes going out this afternoon and Jessica hadn't arrived yet. She wasn't officially late but she was usually early.

"Oui," Margot said resignedly, stubbing out her cigarette and washing her hands. She was supposed to be on her way home, having already baked the pastries for Sunday.

I went into the walk-in and began pulling out the many pieces of the first cake, a complicated structure with Grecian statues in addition to the cake itself. My cell phone buzzed in my pocket. It was a text message from Jessica.

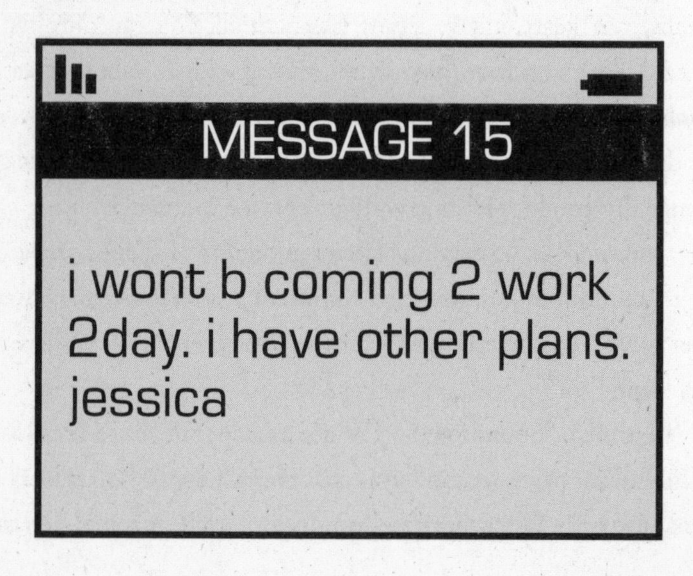

What? Was she kidding? I had two enormous weddings to set up. This was so unlike her. I deleted the text message and tried to call her, but it went to her voice mail immediately. I left a message asking what the text message was all about, then headed back out to the kitchen.

"Have you talked with Jessica today?" I asked Margot.

"*Non,* why?"

"She just texted me that she's not coming to work today—at all."

Margot's eyebrows shot up in alarm. "Did she say why not?"

"She has 'other plans.'"

"*Ooh la la, mal, mal.* And I cannot help you," she offered before I asked. "I have other plans I've been putting off for many Saturdays. I have to keep them today. A date."

"A date!" The mood lightened momentarily and she turned back to the oven, but not before I saw her smile.

I could call Max at Community Table and see if he could recommend anyone, but after Trina, and now this, I wasn't sure I was ready to take on anyone from Community Table. Or maybe it wasn't them. Maybe I was just a poor manager.

"How about Andrew?" Margot suggested. "He's not really creative with design, but he's a good worker and dependable. A good backbone baker."

I nodded. "Yes, please call him."

Margot turned to use the phone, and I went back in the walk-in to finish pulling out pieces for my huge Grecian cake. Of course, this was the day I had two back-to-back orders for Continental Catering.

I glanced at the back of the walk-in door. A couple days ago I'd posted my last meditation verse there. People always say to place them on your fridge. Well, this was the fridge I went to the most.

> Finally, brothers, whatever is true, whatever is noble, whatever is right, whatever is pure, whatever is lovely, whatever is admirable—if anything is excellent or praiseworthy—think about such things. Whatever you have learned or received or heard from me, or seen in me—put it into practice. And the God of peace will be with you.

What was noble was the idea of hiring and helping Jessica—no matter her minor problems—and mostly it had been good. What was right was that I made the best decision I could at the time. What was pure was the plan God had for me to reach out to others with the skills and passions He'd given me. What was admirable was that Margot, whom I was beginning to like, was on the phone right now helping me.

Excellent and praiseworthy? God bringing a potentially business-sustaining account out of the ashes of the Bridal Show Disaster. I took a minute to calm myself in the cool, refrigerated air before walking back into the kitchen.

"Any word?" I asked.

Margot nodded. "He'll be here in ten minutes. He's at L'Esperance right now."

I hugged her, which made her very uncomfortable, so I switched to kissing each cheek. *"Merci."*

"It'll be good for Andrew," she grumbled as she got ready to leave. “I hope she’s okay,” she said as she fumbled for her car keys. I knew she was just as worried about Jessica as I was.

Good as his word, ten minutes later Andrew arrived on his little scooter, which he parked and locked up outside the bakery’s back door. “I’m here,” he said.

I showed him into the walk-in and asked him to get a large latte cake on the counter so I could make sure I had all its pieces and props. Then I went to the front room to get the topper out of the display case.

Before I could close the case again, I heard a knock on the front door. It was Jessica.

I set the topper on a table and unlocked the door. “Hi…,” I said tentatively.

“Hi.” She set a small plastic container on the counter. “I can explain.”

I looked at my watch. “It’ll have to be very fast, because I have two weddings to get to.”

She nodded. “Trina came to my house this afternoon. I finally got up enough courage to tell her that our friendship was over. Really, it never was a friendship. I tried to help her out once when we met at Community Table. She was a big mooch.”

“More like a leech,” I said.

Jessica shrugged. “Yeah. You’re right. Anyway, she was really hacked off when I told her that and showed her the door. I told her she needed to visit AA and find a life on her own.”

I smiled encouragingly as she refilled her lungs before continuing.

“I started getting ready to come to work, but I couldn’t find my phone. I was running a little behind because I made something for you." She glanced at the plastic tub. "When I finally found my phone and turned it on, I heard your message. So I looked at my texts. Trina must have sent one when I was out of the room helping my cousin for a minute." I could see her working hard to keep herself together. "I'm really sorry, Lexi."

I put my arm around her. "It's okay. I'm really proud of you for standing up to her. Are you going to keep worrying about if she gets a job, or finds a place, or whatever?"

Jessica shook her head confidently. "That's not my problem anymore."

"It never was your problem," I told her.

"Do I still have a job?" she asked.

"I'd dock your pay for being late, but you're already making minimum wage," I teased her. "I do think there needs to be some consequence, though."

"I totally agree," she said.

"I've got it. You have to listen to smooth jazz in the kitchen for the next week."

"Please, dock my pay instead," she said, relief relaxing her face. We laughed together and headed toward the kitchen.

"What's that?" I pointed to the plastic tub.

"Oh, I made it for you. Remember how you told me you practiced at home when you were learning how to cook?"

I nodded as we stepped into the back. She stopped talking as she caught an eyeful of Andrew. Andrew apparently caught an eyeful of her too, because he almost tripped over the rubber mat in front of the doorway.

"Andrew, Jessica. Jessica, Andrew."

"Nice to meet you," Andrew said.

Jessica returned the greeting and then turned back to me, slightly less focused than before we'd walked into the back. "So I wanted to make some tapioca pudding from scratch—you know, not a mix," she said.

I glanced at the clock out of the corner of my eye. I wasn't exactly sure where we were going, and wanted to leave soon.

Whatever you have learned or received or heard from me, or seen in me—put it into practice.

"Well, what are you waiting for?" I asked. "Get some spoons!" She grinned and opened our big drawer. Most of the spoons were industrial sized, but she found a couple of coffee stir spoons and brought them over. I tasted the pudding.

"Very nice. Creamy. Tapioca cooked just right," I said. "Good work!"

Jessica beamed as Andrew came into the room. Bolstered, I guessed, by my praise, she offered him some too. "Do you want to try the pudding?"

"Sure," he said, and she spooned some into a nearby ramekin and offered it to him.

I stepped back to watch him react. He'd had some culinary training, and I knew there was no way he wouldn't taste the slight scorch.

Without blinking he said, "Really good."

Jessica turned happily away, and I winked at Andrew behind her back. He grinned and pinked up. I wasn't the only one afflicted with blushing!

"Let's go," I said. The three of us climbed into Odometer.

First stop, My Big Fat Greek Wedding Cake. The couple wasn't actually Greek but had PhDs in ancient studies from Columbia. They'd ordered their cake well before Ted Jacques' baker had her baby early, and he was particularly concerned that I might not be able to pull it off. I'd preassembled it yesterday and sent a picture to the managing caterer for the event, and she'd sent me back an e-mail full of exclamation marks. So I knew I was right on.

We set the cake up and I arranged the linens just so. Next to the cake were urns that, I assumed, would be used to pour wine.

"No Greek gods?" Andrew asked after he'd set up the other statues.

"Thankfully, no," I said.

"I have the body of a god," he said. Jessica and I both looked at him, ready to give him a hard time. "Unfortunately, the god is Buddha."

I shook my head and rolled my eyes, and Jessica laughed appreciatively. He felt confident joking about it because it wasn't true. The pastries hadn't gotten to him yet.

He regaled Jessica all the way to the next job and back, and she laughed every time, on cue.

A whole new kind of staff problem, I thought wryly. I looked at Jessica in my rearview mirror. Her face had high color and her eyes sparkled. She already seemed more lively and self-assured since shedding Trina. It was a pleasure to watch her grow.

As for Andrew, I'd have to tell Sophie to keep her apprentice in check. We were having lunch on Friday. It would be the first time we'd been out together since Philippe had shared about their relationship.

I expected it to be awkward.

We met on Friday afternoon at Café Flora, one of Sophie's favorite restaurants—vegan, of course. A server, Jeanne, greeted her by name. I think they saw each other frequently. "Atrium?" she asked.

"Sure," Sophie said. She looked breezy in a light green sun dress. She hadn't gone too mainstream, though. She wore hemp sandals, and I could see the thin tattoo coiling around her ankle.

"Want to order for both of us?" I asked. "You're the pro."

"Of course," Sophie said. "I'll even order vegetarian for you."

Pâté Platter:
Lentil-pecan pâté, gherkins, apple, marinated olives, and red onion confit with croccatini crackers.

French Dip:
Caramelized onion, swiss cheese and Portobello mushroom on an herbed baguette with roasted garlic-mushroom jus and wild green or yam fries with cayenne aioli.

Oaxaca Taco:
Roasted corn tortillas filled with mashed potatoes, cheddar, and smoky mozzarella cheese with lime créme fraiche, cotija cheese, black bean stew, pico de gallo, and wilted greens.

"How's business going?" I asked.

"Good. Picking up. I heard you did a few big orders for Continental Catering," she said.

"Who told you?"

"Word gets around." She grinned. "Margot. She came back the day after the first delivery and told me all about it. About the girl who drinks…"

"Ooh la la," I said. "Did Philippe hear about that too?"

Sophie nodded. "Of course. We're a family. There are no secrets. I think he was impressed with how it all ended last week, though. I was too, Lex. For someone who didn't want to handle staff…"

"I still don't," I grumbled good-naturedly. "But I was proud of Jessica and how she came through."

Jeanne brought our pâté platter. After she left, Sophie continued.

"But she's not able to take the cakes for you when you go to France in, what, ten days?"

"Something like that," I said, putting a melon ball in my mouth. "Jessica can't handle it yet. Someday, maybe. Speaking of that, thanks for letting Margot stay full-time at Bijoux while I'm in Paris."

"You're welcome, but I don't *let* Margot do anything. She does what she wants. *Ooh la la*…Paris in June. Maybe you won't come back." She took a long drink of her iced tea.

"Margot would kill me," I said. "Thankfully, I've got cakes lined up for a couple more weeks, and I hope Continental Catering will give me some full-time accounts. I'm going to call Mr. Jacques before I go, just to follow up on the events I've done. Do you…are you upset that I'm going to Paris? That Monsieur Delacroix is paying for my continuing ed and I'm going again?"

It had been bugging me. Margot could go whenever she wanted, and the Trois Amis never had any desire to leave their little Seattle enclave. But Sophie…

Her eyes twinkled. "Maybe I'll get to Paris another way this year."

Ah, yes. The elephant in the room.

"You mean with Philippe?" I asked.

"Yes," she said. "He told me you two had lunch."

Jeanne slid a plate of tacos in front of me. They looked and smelled fantastic. "Wow, just because you're doing without meat doesn't mean you're doing without, eh?"

Sophie grinned. "To tell the truth, I was pretty much a soup-and-salad girl until I started dating Philippe. The vegan thing was almost a deal killer, but I scouted out a few places that satisfy his gourmet taste buds and my no-animal convictions. It hasn't been bad. Did you notice almost everything I've ordered has a French twist?"

"What did he say about you being a vegan?" I asked, biting into the incredibly rich taco. Since he'd thought Garden Burgers were heresy, I was dying to know.

"He was…hesitant. I've made some adjustments, but I am who I am at the core of it. If he was ever going to like me, he was going to have to like the real me."

"That makes sense," I said.

She dunked her French dip before continuing. "I had to decide if I was going to, you know, get my honey where I get my money, but so far it seems to have worked out okay. Were you…sad when he talked to you about…us?"

She looked shy and girlish at that moment. I reached across the table and rested my hand on her arm. I looked at her again, this time with fresh eyes. I'd been noticing for months that she looked softer, but she was still the same alternative Sophie. What had made her softer was love.

"No, Soph. I think you're a good match."

"You do?" she asked.

"I do."

"He's really kind," she continued. "One morning when I was sick he came over early, got my paperwork, opened the bakery, and did my job for the day without a second word."

Ah. The day I'd seen him drive away from my building so early in the morning.

"And...he rides a motorcycle." She laughed out loud. "I know, I know. I have a thing for bikers. What can I say? At least this time it's an employed, clean, Christian biker."

She'd not mentioned anything about her faith at all since I'd been home except to talk about going to church with Philippe.

"So the Christian thing is going okay?" I tried to sound casual.

She smiled. "It's growing on me. Philippe told me that you kind of 'opened the oyster' for him as far as dating women again after Andrea died. So—thank you. I think you kind of 'opened the oyster' for me too, with Christianity. I'm drawn. I feel myself being drawn more and more. I'm seeing where it goes. You oyster opener, you."

There was only one thing I could say. "Ah, shucks."

She offered me a bite of her sandwich bread. "Wanna try?"

"This is good too! I'll have to bring my meat-eating date here sometime."

She grinned. "The attorney?"

I nodded.

"Ah ha! I thought it might not be such a tragedy if Philippe and I were together. That man has always had a thing for you. And you for him too, right?"

"Yes," I said. "And it's only grown since I got back. At least on my part."

"Oh, from what I hear, it's on his part too," she said, and I smiled and blushed and didn't even care.

"And who did you hear this from?" I asked.

"Margot!" we both said at the same time.

"That woman has too much time on her hands," I said. "I'll keep her busy with the shop work next week while I make the cake for Tanya's wedding."

I explained the cake to Sophie, and she oohed and aahed. I wondered if I'd be making a cake for her sometime in the next year.

"Didn't Dan escort you to your brother's wedding last year?" Sophie asked.

"Yes."

"Is he taking you to Tanya's wedding too?" she asked.

"He's meeting me there—again. Since I'm doing the cake—again. But he's been a good sport about it. We just talked earlier today." I still heard his voice in my heart.

"Cool," Sophie said. She drained her tea. "He has a sister who lives in France, right? Does he have a lot of French connections?"

"No," I said. "You've got France on the brain, girl. His sister lives in Belgium. He's pretty much a through-and-through Seattle kind of guy."

Jeanne brought our check and Sophie paid for it. "My treat this time."

We hugged outside and she got into my old Jetta. I felt a pang of affection as I saw her start it up. Then I got into my van. I noticed my Bible on the passenger seat along with a take-out bag, a coffee cup, and a catering contact. For once, my Bible didn't have a sticky note marking my spot.

I was done with Philippians.

Sophie drove away.

Eighteen

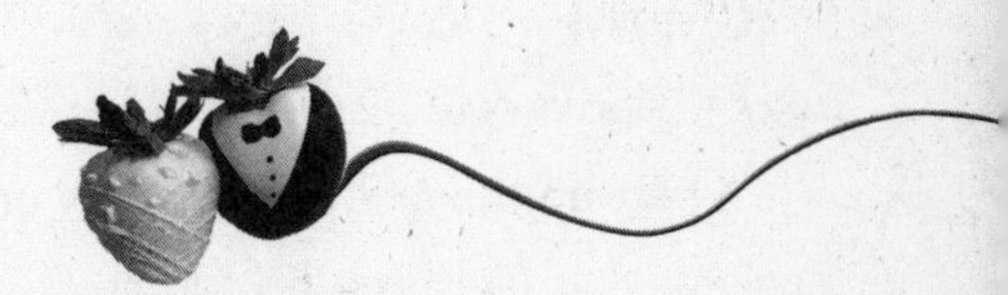

A thought which does not result in an action is nothing much, and an action which does not proceed from a thought is nothing at all.

Georges Bernanos

Thanks for coming to help," I said to Jessica. "I know you've got other plans."

We'd arrived at the reception area early to set up the cake. It was a beautiful clubhouse on Lake Washington. Not a cloud to be seen, thankfully, and the wind was low. Tables for dining were set out on the dock and patio side and would be cleared later for dancing. The catering company bustled about, snapping linen and polishing silver. The smell of dinner's genesis drifted across the room. My stomach grumbled. I hadn't eaten all day. Only coffee.

"It's okay," she said. "I made no plans for next weekend and the whole week afterward when you're in France. Margot said she'd show me a couple of things when you were gone, if it's okay. Some baking stuff and pastry things."

I raised my eyebrows. Maybe Margot was turning into the *maman.* "Of course it's okay," I said.

"She said just not on Saturday night." Jessica grinned and shook her hand as if fanning off some heat. *"Ooh la la."*

I tapped her chef's hat—which we all wore when setting up cakes—sideways to tease her for her French.

We set up the table. I'd specially ordered some Japanese cherry blossoms that had been held in cold storage so they would bloom late, the week of the wedding. I set them up near the cake table and laid out everything else just so. The caterer would do the cutting, so I didn't have to worry about it. I had other, more important, duties today.

Jessica dropped me off at the church, and I sent her back to Bijoux in Odometer and told her to bring the keys in on Monday morning, early. I knew Dan would drive me home tonight. I couldn't wait. The day promised nothing but pleasure.

"Knock, knock!" I opened the door to the "bride's room," where Tanya and the other bridesmaids were getting ready. Our dresses hung in long plastic sheaths in the back. Tanya's mother had hired hairdressers and manicurists and makeup artists and just about everyone except plastic surgeons to make sure we all looked good for the day.

"No one is waxing me," I made her promise.

"No one will wax you," Tanya had laughed. "I swear it."

"Lex!" Tanya screamed and came over to me in her slip, hair bouncing with thick, old fashioned caterpillar curlers.

I hugged her and held her at arm's length. "You look beautiful already!"

"It's the day," she said.

"It's the day," I agreed. I said hello to her other friends and then sat in a chair. A beautician came up to me and held back one of my eyebrows with one thumb and forefinger.

"Yes, yes, too thick," she said in a Russian accent. "This will not do. I wax, okay?"

I jumped up. "Ah. Let's think about that." I caught an eyeful of Tanya and the others giggling just a few feet away. "Okay, the joke's over," I said. "Very funny." Then I laughed along with them.

One of the bridesmaids brought a playlist full of bright, summery, chick music and played it rather loudly. It added to the general hubbub of the room.

After makeup and hair it was time to slip on the dresses. Tanya had four other bridesmaids and a junior bridesmaid, who was sweetest of all. She was Steve's younger sister, the one who introduced the two of them when Tanya had been her teacher.

"I guess we should call her cupid," Tanya said, leaning over to kiss the cheek of her new, about-to-be sister-in-law.

"Calling me 'sister' is good enough," she answered shyly, and the room hummed with a collective, "Awwww."

While the other bridesmaids chattered and slipped into their dresses and out of their hot rollers, I pulled Tanya aside.

"This might be the last chance we get to talk privately," I said. "Wedding, reception...honeymoon. Are you ready?"

"For which one?" she teased.

"All three!"

"I've got my dress, my dancing shoes, and my coconut shell bra." She smiled, her newly tanned skin making her teeth even whiter. "Yes, Lex, I'm ready."

I hugged her. "I knew you would be. Steve will be your number one, but I'll always be your best girlfriend."

"And I'll always be yours." She pulled away. "I'm going to talk with my mom and Steve's mom for a minute before I put my dress on. You look ready…are you?"

I nodded. "I'll be back in a few minutes to help you into your dress. Do you mind if I slip out?"

"Dan?"

"Yes. Just want to make sure he got here okay."

"Of course."

She turned to get her mother's attention, and I slipped out and walked to a side door of the auditorium. I scanned the crowd and then locked in on him. I willed him to look back at me, and by some metaphysical miracle he caught the vibe and turned around. I waved to him to come back for a minute.

He slipped out of his seat. "Hi," he said softly. "You're not supposed to be prettier than the bride, you know."

I grinned. "And you're not supposed to be finer than the groom. I just wanted to make sure you were here. Otherwise I'd have to find another ride to the reception," I joked.

"I'm here." He looked gorgeous. He'd worn gray green suspenders over an ivory shirt so he'd match my outfit, which was very thoughtful.

"See you afterward?" I asked.

He nodded. "I'll wait in the back."

I turned away and headed toward the bride's room again.

He'd seemed a little troubled. I wondered if he'd had a problem at work or if something was up with his family. For some annoying reason, Nonna's warning from the day at my parents' house loomed in my mind.

In the bride's room, I helped Tanya into her dress. She turned to look at us, and without planning we spontaneously broke out clapping.

"Don't make me cry," she begged. "My mother just paid a fortune for me to have my makeup done!"

The clapping turned to laughter, and we spilled out of the room and into the foyer in front of the sanctuary.

One by one we paired off with groomsmen and stepped down the runner toward the pulpit. If I'd been a woman with more self-control I might not have turned to look toward Dan as I filed past his row, but I did, and I caught his eye and winked. He smiled back. I couldn't help letting my own mind wander and wonder as I walked down the aisle.

As Tanya stepped forward to the rail, I took her bouquet from her, set it down briefly, and arranged her train before stepping back. The service was blessedly brief—there's a time to preach and a time to refrain. Wasn't that in Ecclesiastes? Tanya and Steve exchanged the beautiful vows they'd written and the rings they'd picked out and were pronounced husband and wife.

They kissed and the moment was broken, and then they triumphantly led us down the aisle. After picture-taking, which took longer than the ceremony itself, we were off to the reception.

Dan drove to the lake club, and I took off my shoes and wiggled my toes the whole way.

"I picked these shoes out two months ago, when it was cool outside," I said.

"Maybe your feet are just getting fat," he said, keeping a straight face.

"Ha!"

"Do we have to sit by your grandmother again?" he asked when we arrived at the club. I recalled my brother's wedding last year when we'd spent some time with Nonna and her friend, Stanley.

I turned to him as I slipped my shoes back on. "Don't you like my grandmother?"

"I do, I do. She just scares me," he said. "She's always coming out with something and I'm never sure how to answer."

"I think that's why Stanley mostly keeps his hearing aid off," I said, laughing. "But no, we're going to sit at the head table—you too."

His visible relief tickled me, and we walked arm and arm into the reception.

It was great fun to mingle with Tanya's family—we'd been best friends for a dozen years and they seemed as much my family as hers. I knew she felt the same way about my family, which was why my mom and dad, Nate and Leah, and Nonna and Stanley were there.

We sat down to a delicious dinner, and afterward the caterers cleared the tables. I snuck over and checked the cake. Perfect! Tanya was talking to someone across the room but saw me as I looked it over, and smirked from afar, giving me a thumbs-up.

I watched the cake get cut from a distance and then stood and celebrated my friend as she was feted and toasted. Afterward, the tables were moved aside, and the DJ and band warmed up.

Tanya and Steve danced the first dance, of course, and afterward her dad joined her on the dance floor. Dan and I stepped out with many others.

"Going to do the chicken dance?" I teased him as we waltzed around the floor.

He shook his head. "No, but I'll do the dollar dance since she's your best friend."

He was a remarkably smooth dancer. Sometimes he seemed so down home and comfortable that I forgot there was a lot of polish beside the spit. He could ride an ATV, but he could also close a deal. He could tip little boys upside down in a garbage can, but he could also lead smoothly in almost any dance.

"May I?" My dad stepped in and tapped Dan on the shoulder.

"Of course," he said, graciously bowing out. I saw Nonna making her way across the floor, ready to pin him into a dance, I was sure. Swiftly, but surely, he turned to my mother and asked, "May I?"

"Of course!" my mother echoed him. I knew my mother well enough to know she enjoyed foiling Nonna. I knew Nonna well enough to know she'd pay them back somehow in her own subtly evil way. She nabbed an unsuspecting groomsman instead.

Tanya snuck up to me during a rare free moment. "See Jill?"

I looked across the dance floor. Jill was in a corner, chatting rather intently with a man I didn't recognize.

"Steve's cousin," Tanya said. "Really laid back."

"Good!" I said, glad for her. Who knew if anything would ever come from it, but it probably took the edge off her heartache.

A few dances later, Dan and I were back for something a bit more lively. Within the hour, Tanya and Steve were ready to say good-bye.

"We'd like to thank everyone here for coming to our wedding," Steve said. "But as I am sure you can understand, I'm ready to sweep my bride away to someplace a little more private." Catcalls rose from the crowd. "I think my...wife"—he relished the word—"would like to throw her bouquet before we go."

Tanya nodded and took the small tossing bouquet from her mother's hands. My mother pushed my back to get me closer.

"Go forward!" she said to me.

"Mom!" I whispered to her, hoping that Dan, on my other side, couldn't hear her.

Nonna was nearby. Most of the bridesmaids were in the inner circle. Tanya turned her body almost forty-five degrees to aim that bouquet right at me. She lifted her arm and tossed it.

It seemed to fall in slow motion, twirling through the air, ribbons and petals lifting and swirling. Instead of a rush of women heading toward the bouquet, as would be typical, it seemed like they all dropped back and let it come, unencumbered, right to me.

If I didn't reach my hand out and grab it, it would have seemed odd. Besides, I was a catcher. It was instinct.

I caught it neatly by the stems. A rush of applause lifted from the crowd, the loudest of which was Tanya's. For once, I was at a loss for words. I also didn't have the courage to look up at Dan.

Tanya and Steve left, and my parents took Nonna and Stanley back to Soundview.

Dan had been extremely quiet until now. "Would you like to take a walk along the lakeside before we go home?"

"I'd love to," I said. I looped my little purse around my wrist, kept the bouquet in that hand, and took my shoes off and carried them too. I was glad for Tanya's mother's insistence on pedicures. My toes were pearled and polished in the summer moonlight.

We walked down a paved trail that followed the shoreline. Jasmine perfumed the air with its exotic spice. For some reason, jasmine, like moonflowers, grew more beautiful and memorable at night.

"It was a nice wedding, don't you think?" I asked.

"It was," he said. "Everything was perfect. Especially the cake."

"It did taste rather remarkable," I teased. Then I became a little more subdued. "I remember all the times we dreamed, when we were girls, about what kind of weddings we'd want. Tanya always wanted something traditional, and she got it. I always wanted big yellow sunflowers and blue plates and something unexpected."

The talk of my wedding hung between us. We came to a bench.

"Lexi, let's sit down," Dan said. I looked at him, and his face seemed so strikingly serious.

We sat on the wooden bench and watched the moon's reflection ripple across the water. I set the bouquet on the bench between us. Dan gently took the purse and shoes out of my hand. Then he took my left hand in his right.

"Is everything okay?" I asked.

"Yes. But I have something I want to say to you. I've been thinking about it for a while."

"Sure." My heart throbbed.

"Lexi, I'm in love with you." He turned to look at me. "It's something I've known and felt for a long time."

I opened my mouth to speak in the pause, but he put his finger to my lips to hush me.

"You are magical in every way. You're smart, you're funny, and you're spontaneous. You can cook. You're spiritual in a fresh and conversational way, and I love that. You're beautiful. But…"

"But?" I had just bathed in the most beautiful moment of my life, and that one word splashed cold water over me in a split second.

"I've had a few concerns lately."

"Is it the Sunday school incident?" I asked. "Because really, I think I'll probably be really good with kids once we get used to each other."

Dan laughed. "No, it's not the Sunday school incident. I am sure you're fantastic with kids. Look at how you handled Céline. And my sister!"

"So…is it Philippe?"

"Not really…but kind of. I know you don't have anything going with or for him. He just brought to the surface something I had been thinking about, maybe even worrying about, lately. If I'm honest, it's not just lately. Maybe it's been a concern since the last wedding I escorted you to. When you were leaving to go to France. Just like you're going next week."

"But I'm going for less than ten days this time."

"I know," he said. "That's not it. I'll miss you each of those ten days, though I'm going to try to distract myself with an important case. It's that, well, Lexi, I think you really love France. And French culture and French cooking and speaking French. And French people."

I didn't disagree with him; it was true. "But that's not all I love."

"I saw you speaking French with that guy at my company dinner and with the new caterer. I heard you talking about Paris with my sister, and, well, I don't want to rob you of that dream."

He continued. "Do you remember how I told you my mom married my dad, but she was never satisfied with what he could provide? She wanted another lifestyle, and while she's a good person and she's happy with Dennis, it might have been better if she and my dad had figured out before they got married that there were other issues at play. Issues that would make long-term happiness unattainable."

I kept my hand steady and under the cover of his own, though I felt it tremble from the inside. "I'm not your mom."

"I know that." He was silent for a moment. "My plan was to just say nothing, let us drift apart. I thought that would be best for both of us. Kind of like you with Céline."

"What?! She's a child."

He hung his head. "It was the coward's way out," he admitted. "Born out of fear. But I didn't take it."

"Are you saying you don't want to see me anymore?" I asked. I needed to know right now where this was headed.

"I want more than anything to be together," he said. "I just want you to take a long, objective look at the whole situation and make sure you're going to be happy with a man who doesn't speak French, one whose idea of gourmet is to mix ketchup with mayonnaise before dipping his fries. Who likes a cold beer as much as a pinot noir."

We sat quietly for a minute. "I think your trip to France might even be divinely inspired. It'll give you time to think it over, to pray about it, and to make the comparisons firsthand. When you come back, you can let me know what you think."

I nodded, still taking it all in. "Are we still going on our date on Friday? I have the Mariner's tickets...and I leave Saturday."

"Yes," he said. "I took the afternoon off. I'm looking forward to it."

"Me too," I said. He stood and then held my elbow so I could steady myself as I stood.

"I meant what I said." He kissed me softly, lingeringly, as if this might be the last time he did so. "I love you enough to want the best for you even if that doesn't include me."

Nineteen

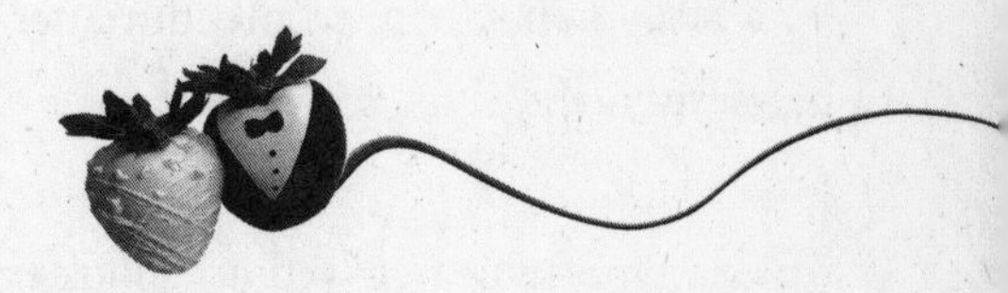

Out of difficulties grow miracles.

Jean de la Bruyère

I took Monday off. There wasn't a lot going on at work, and I needed to get a few things in order for my trip to Paris on Saturday. I ran some errands.

At the library, I noticed a couple with their heads together, shoulder to shoulder, looking at a book. Their hair touched, blurring the lines between them.

At the post office I stood behind a couple filling out a postal hold for their mail during their honeymoon.

I ran to the mall for a minute to buy a new pair of shoes. A kind salesman helped me. I sat in the chair, and he knelt down and slipped the shoe on my foot. I couldn't get the image of Cinderella out of my head. Maybe it was all that California Disney talk with Céline.

I stopped at the grocery store to buy a carton of juice and a sandwich and saw an older husband and wife selecting a variety of fruit and some salmon. The wife urged her husband to try pomegranates for his heart health, reminding him that he'd like to be around to see their grandchildrens' kids.

I drove home and wrote out my packing list for Paris. It should be a really happy trip for me, but after the talk Dan and I had on Saturday night, it felt so heavy.

Tuesday morning I arrived at Bijoux early. I wanted to make sure everything was properly prepped for the week, and I had three cakes to bake for weekend weddings. I'd get them all made, Jessica and Margot would set them up, and Margot had the catering under control. The weekend I was in France held only one wedding, and Margot said she'd take care of it. After that, well…things looked thin. A couple of weddings each weekend, a slowly growing catering business.

I turned the iHome to my Paris combo mix and got to work.

God, what should I do? Dan definitely has a point in asking me about France. I do love France. I love the language, the art, the food, and heaven help me, even their techno music. But when I came home, I was ready to come home.

I dumped flour and cocoa powder into the huge KitchenAid mixer.

Keep your mind straight, I reminded myself. *Don't mess up the recipe.*

I focused on mixing the batter and pouring it into the huge prepared pans lining the counter. Margot came in, and I barely nodded to her before returning to my task. She didn't bother me. We were used to working quietly side by side. In spite of our growing warmth, we each knew when to respect secure boundaries.

Jessica arrived. I greeted her quickly but, I knew, distractedly. She set about getting out the materials for the cake filling and icing. I'd laid the recipe cards out in advance for her.

I popped the cakes into the first three layers of the huge wall oven. "How was your date on Saturday?" I asked Margot.

"Bon," she answered, a little taken off balance, maybe, by the personal question.

"Was it with Fred?"

"Oui," she answered. "Am I filling out a new visa here?"

I laughed. "No, no. I'm asking for my own reasons, actually. Sorry."

"De rien," she said good-naturedly. Then she started whistling. Whistling! "What is this?" She pointed to the bouquet I'd placed in a large vase full of water.

"I caught the bouquet on Saturday."

"You did?" Jessica lit up. "You know what that means!"

"Supposedly..."

"Ah yes, I know what this means," Margot said. "Catching the bouquet."

"Well," Jessica said, filling in any blanks she thought Margot might have, "after the wedding, when the bride is getting ready to go on her honeymoon or whatever, she throws her bouquet into the crowd. Actually, I think only the single women are supposed to come up close, right?" She looked to me for confirmation and I nodded. "So then, whoever catches it is the next to be married. Which means *you,* Lexi. Who's the lucky guy? The guy on your cell phone screen?"

"Jessica! You've been peeking at my cell phone screen?" One time Dan and I had been kidding around and had taken a picture of ourselves with my phone. I used it as my background.

"Hey! I can't help but see it every time you talk on the phone," she explained.

"Get to work," I told her.

I busied myself in the kitchen and heard Margot whistling "Here Comes the Bride."

"How do you know that song? Do they sing it in France?" I demanded, throwing a towel in her direction.

She shrugged and kept whistling, pretending to take measured steps down the aisle with my bouquet in her hands as she headed back to roll out her pastry dough.

"Bah!" I said, imitating a frustrated Frenchwoman. Margot enjoyed pestering me about it. I enjoyed it too.

But was he the man?

I finished assembling the rest of the ingredients for cake number two and then excused myself. I stepped into the walk-in, my favorite refuge, and pulled my phone from my apron pocket. I flipped it open to the wide screen and looked at Dan and me grinning for the camera.

I loved the way his hair was professionally styled and yet a little lock slipped out, boyishly, in our picture. I loved the crinkles around his eyes when he smiled. I loved that he'd had to crowd next to me to take the picture and our heads touched, blurring the lines of separation yet remaining distinct.

Yes, he was the man. I thought about vegan Sophie and meat-eater Philippe. Sophie'd told me that she'd made some accommodations for Philippe, but if he truly liked her he was going to have to truly like *her.* I thought about matter-of-fact Leah saying that things that would annoy her in someone else only endeared her to my hypochondriac brother Nate.

Then I took a long look around my walk-in filled with food, which was my calling. Each of the ingredients was too sweet, too bland, too sour, too creamy, too dry in and of itself. But put them together and *voilà*! A masterpiece.

Suddenly, I had the answer.

Dan had asked me not to talk to him about this until I returned from Paris. Okay, I wouldn't "talk" to him about it. But I'd give him my answer nonetheless, and I'd answer him in food. I'd make my thoughts and feelings very clear on our date on Friday afternoon and evening. If he knew me as well as he thought he did, he'd get it. If he wanted to be together as much as he said he did, he'd make a decision. The next move after that would be his, if he'd risk taking it.

Please, God, let him be the man I believe him to be.

My phone, still in my hand, rang. It startled me. Dan and I disappeared from the screen, replaced by the contact name. Continental Catering!

"Lexi Stuart here."

"Hello, Lexi. Ted Jacques here."

"Hello, Mr. Jacques," I said. "How have you been?"

He was cutting out a bit; I willed my connection to stay clear. I didn't want to take a live call into the clattering bakery.

"Fine, fine. I've been meaning to call you, but I've been so busy you'd think I was twins. Anyway, I heard you pulled off some fine wedding events. Every one of my catering managers was more pleased than a catfish at high tide."

"Thank you," I said, thankful the manager who'd been on duty when I came with Trina had said nothing about her.

"Well, now, the woman who had a baby is going to be out for a few months. I told her we were going to reassign her contract to someone else because her staff just wasn't up to par. I'm thinking that contract might go to you. How'd you like that?"

"I'd be happier than a firefly who's been let out of the jar." I took a stab at a Texasism and he roared his approval.

"I like your spunk. Now—a few things. I'll be sending three or four wedding cakes your way every week. Do you have the time to handle that many?"

Three or four cakes a week! Put that together with the cakes coming our way from word of mouth and the monthly cake tastings, the catering business that was already in place and growing, and we'd be at full operational capacity within a few months!

"Absolutely, we can handle that," I said. "*Pas de problème.*"

"Good," he said. "The other thing is I hire bakers, not companies. My contract will be with you, not Bijoux. I don't trust staff chefs and so I expect that you'll be overseeing every cake I do. I'm not gonna run into the same kind of problem I had with the other woman's staff."

"I'll be here, certainly," I reassured him. "I'll oversee every cake we ever do for you."

"Fine, fine," he said. "I know people take holidays and such, but with some preplanning it can be done. Good! Let's plan to start say, mid-July, shall we?"

"Great timing. I'm going to France next week but will be home in plenty of time."

"I'll call you for a contract sit-down sometime after you get home and we'll get all our t's dotted and our eyes crossed," he said.

"Thank you, sir," I said. His down-home manner belied the business savvy he was known for. "We appreciate your business."

"I know you do. *Au revoir!*" he said as he signed off.

I ran screaming out of the walk-in. "We did it! We did it!"

"*Zut alors,* what is the *crise*?" Margot asked. Jessica said nothing but looked a little uncomfortable at the sight of me running from the walk-in.

"That was Continental Catering. They're assigning us three to four wedding cakes a *week* starting in a few weeks. We're set, we're in the black, we're afloat!"

"Chouette! Extra!" Margot pulled out a couple of Céline's happy vocabulary words and I agreed with her.

"Extra! Chouette!"

"Cool! Great news!" Jessica chimed in with English. The incongruity of it made Margot and me laugh. I was especially happy because this meant Jessica would remain employed with no need to cut her hours. In fact, maybe I could soon give her a raise.

She knew it too. I could tell by the smile.

"Okay, ladies, close down the ovens. We're going to an early lunch to celebrate."

"Good! Where to?" Jessica asked.

"I'm not sure. Get ready and I'll think about it." They began to get things to the point that they could leave them for lunch—Margot for the day—and I made a few calls.

First, I called my mom and dad. Mom wasn't home, but Dad was. "I am so pleased and proud, Lexi," he said. "Just like Frank Sinatra said, you did it your way."

"Thanks, Dad," I said.

I called Dan, but his assistant said he was out for the morning, and did I want to leave a message? I decided to text him instead. Then I texted Tanya—who had already texted me once that the honeymoon was A-OK. I texted my brother and Leah. I called Nonna. She was out, but I left a message.

Then I called Philippe. "Guess what?" I said, switching naturally to French.

"Quoi?"

"Monsieur Jacques called me today and offered me three to four wedding cakes a week—every week! That means in the off-season too."

"Très bon!" Philippe said, his excitement coming across the lines. "Can you handle it? The work load, I mean?"

"Yes. If I don't have to spend so much time trying to find new accounts, it'll give me more time to bake. And I can always hire someone to help if we need it."

"Good, good," he said. But he sounded just a little distracted.

"I've decided to take everyone out to lunch, to celebrate. On the company."

"Bien sûr," Philippe said. "Where will you take them?

I thought hard and then grinned. "Dick's Drive-In. For cheeseburgers."

Philippe laughed with me and promised he'd share the good news with Sophie. "Enjoy your time in France, if I'm not over to Bijoux before you leave," he said. "There may yet be a few surprises for you. This month, Lexi, the world is *your* oyster."

By Thursday I had the weekend cakes all prepped, set in the walk-in on shelves according to event, with a hand-drawn map showing how to assemble them. I'd taken a picture of each cake at my preassembly and printed it out, then put it by that specific cake. Margot and Jessica would have no trouble putting them together. I'd also put the address, contact information, and anything else they'd need in a folder by the cake. I knew Jessica would keep them organized.

The catering orders were ready. The kitchen was ready. My bags were packed. I had only one thing left to do. But it was the most important thing in the world to me.

Thursday afternoon I shopped for ingredients, and Friday morning I arrived at Bijoux and began to assemble the meal. I was planning a picnic before the evening baseball game.

"What time should I come get you?" Dan said when he called in the morning. "And what should I bring?"

"How about two o'clock?" I said. "Just bring yourself and casual clothes. I'll have the meal and the tickets."

"Looking forward to it," he said, his voice softer than when he'd first called.

"Me too."

I set about boiling potatoes and tuned in to the rock station on the radio. I'd given this day a lot of thought and prayer in the six days since we'd talked at Tanya's wedding.

I can only be honest and be myself. I tried to be what my parents wanted me to be and didn't find my career until I let go. I tried to make Philippe and Céline happy and they were well able to make themselves happy. I tried to teach Sunday school knowing I'd be less successful than a blind chauffeur, as Mr. Jacques would say, but now I've found what God meant for me in feeding His sheep.

That morning I'd called Max at Community Table and told him to schedule our first training session for the last Monday night in July, traditionally a dead night in food service. He was delighted, and so was I.

The first recipe in my armory—my new *Lexi*con—was ready. I put it into a pretty, portable bowl—Tupperware, as a nod to Dan's mom—and stuck it in the cooler.

I folded a picnic blanket into the bottom of a large tote and then set the potato hamburger buns, some paper plates, some napkins, and portable condiment containers inside. I had a small bag of charcoal ready. I went back to the walk-in, took out the ingredients for the burgers, and mixed them up.

I put the chopped vegetables into the divided plastic container and then nestled the little dip container next to it. I loaded all of these into a cooler. Last, but not least, I added the pink, wax-lined box that held our dessert.

Franco-American Burgers

Ingredients

1½ pounds ground chuck or hamburger
1 packet Lipton's onion soup mix
6 strips bacon, fried crisp and then chopped fine
4 tablespoons finely chopped cornichons (small French pickles)
1 egg
salt and pepper
American cheese slices

Directions

In a large bowl, mix together the ground meat, soup mix, bacon bits, cornichon bits, egg, and salt and pepper. When completely blended, form the meat into patties the size of the bun and about ½-inch thick. Grill until desired doneness, then top with American cheese and leave on the grill a minute or two until the cheese melts. Serve with your choice of condiments and soft hamburger roll.

I was ready. I stood back and spied my dartboard. I pulled the old tags out of the utensil drawer and affixed them next to some of the new ones. I stepped back several paces and took a shot. I aimed true and threw the first dart.

Job.

The cakes were lined up, the money was going to come in. I threw the second dart.

Home.

Okay, so the apartment wasn't perfect. But once the business was humming, I'd find something else. I threw the third dart.

Man.

Man, I hoped so. The last three throws explained it best.

Zut alors. Zut alors. Zut alors.

Dan knocked on the back door a few minutes later. I hadn't seen him all week, and by the look on his face, he was as glad to see me as I was him. I opened the door and hugged him. I'd have liked to have held on to him longer, but with things kind of up in the air, I walked the middle line.

"Hard at work?" he teased, nodding toward the dartboard as I scrambled to take the papers down before he could read them.

"I'm ready to go." I handed him a map to the park I'd picked out next to the Sound. He lugged the cooler out to the truck, and I took the bag.

"How was your week?" I asked.

"Good…but not as good as yours!" he said, navigating the light afternoon traffic. "I'm really excited about your good news with Mr. Jacques. Now maybe Margot will stop sending poisoned vibes in my direction."

"It's not that bad, is it?"

"No," he admitted. "But she's not easy to win over."

We got to the park and found a shaded spot near a tiny grill. We spread the blanket and started the grill, then chatted some more while I laid out the food.

"Looks delicious," he said. "What did you bring?"

"I've got the short answer and the long answer." I held my breath to see which he'd choose.

"The long answer, of course!"

He'd passed test number one.

"First," I said, "I have some Coke. Four very cold cans. Coke is known the world over as a symbol of America. It's a very American drink, and one I indulged in anytime I was homesick last year in Paris."

He cocked his head a little, catching on partly but not completely yet. "Good, good..." he said hesitantly. "I like Coke."

I popped open a can and handed it to him, then popped one open for myself. Then I fished the cut vegetables out of the cooler. "Homegrown in Washington," I said. I took the lid off the dip. "But served with French dressing."

"Ah..." A little smile lifted the corner of his mouth. "Next?"

I took out the potato salad. "Can you imagine a more American dish than potato salad? Okay, okay, forget the Germans for a moment. But this potato salad is as American as the Fourth of July. Want to taste it?"

He nodded, and I dipped a plastic spoon into the container and handed it to him. "Fantastic!" he said with unrestrained enthusiasm.

"Secret recipe," I told him. "But made with mayonnaise. Did you know that the French invented and refined mayonnaise?"

"No." He grinned. "I didn't. Is there any meat to this meal?"

"Ah yes, the meat," I said. "Hamburgers. What could be more red, white, and blue than hamburgers?"

"But there's certain to be a French ingredient in there, right?"

"*Bien sûr!* There are tiny little cornichons, French pickles, chopped up inside for a little extra zest!"

"And I suppose the paper plates are 'Chinette'?" He changed the pronunciation to sound French.

I laughed. "I hadn't thought of that."

I turned my back to him as I served the potato salad. *He got it.* I knew he would. Now let's see what he did with it.

We ate dinner together and when we were done, I said, "I have one more thing, if we've got time."

He checked his watch. "We do."

I cleared the food and the plates and then brought out two small plates and the pink box. "Here. Open it." I handed it to him.

After prying the piece of tape off the box, he opened it up. "Napoleons. I mean, mille-feuille." He lifted them out. "My favorite!"

I grinned. "I know, and I'm sorry I haven't made them for you for a long time. I got so busy with work…"

"That's okay," he said. "Now these are purely French. Right? Nothing American in them?"

"Only the baker," I said.

He smiled and held out a fork to me, and we shared the pieces before packing up and heading off to watch the Mariner's game.

"That was delicious," he said after starting the truck. "I mean,

I won't forget this meal for a long time. Delicious. Can I take the potato salad leftovers home since you're leaving in the morning?"

"Of course!" I was pleased. But he'd said nothing aloud about my *Lexi*con.

We pulled into the stadium, and he took his glove from the spot behind his seat.

"Oh," I said. "I forgot my mitt. And we have such good seats." I was bummed. I always brought my glove in case there was a pop fly in my direction.

"You can use mine if you want," Dan offered.

"Thanks," I said. We walked hand in hand into the stadium, where we enjoyed the game under the starlight and the open roof. I even convinced him to do the Wave.

On the way home, he said, "You had a pretty good theme going here tonight."

I beamed. "You think?"

"I think," he said as he pulled up to my apartment. "Leave anything out?"

"I was going to bring my CD with Lenny Kravitz singing 'American Woman,' but I thought that might be a bit over the top."

Dan laughed. "Maybe. Maybe not."

"He lives in Paris, you know," I said. "Lenny does."

"I know. I do music copyright law, remember?"

"Yeah." I sat for a minute. "I'd better get going. I've got an early flight tomorrow morning."

"I'll walk you up," he said. We got to my door. "I'll see you when you get home?"

"Yeah," I said. "I'll see you then. Remember, there are three ways to say good-bye in French."

"Remind me..."

"There's *adieu,* which is good-bye in a more permanent way. There's *au revoir,* 'until we meet again.' There's *à bientôt,* 'see you soon.'"

Then I leaned forward and kissed him, initiating for the very first time.

I'd leave him to figure out which good-bye that meant.

Twenty

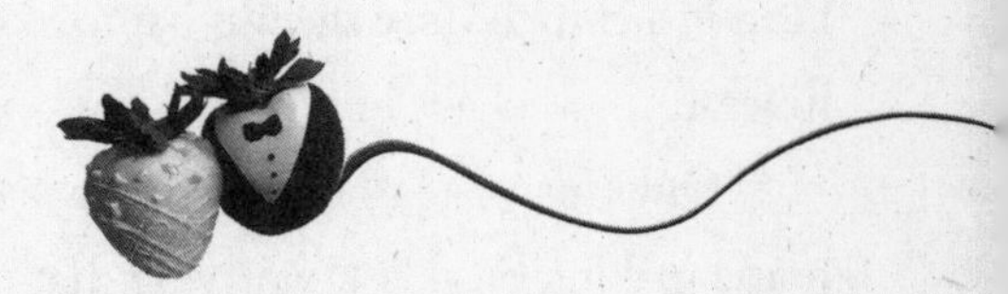

Everything happens in France.

François de la Rochefoucauld

B*on matin, Paris,* I thought as I touched down. Good morning, indeed. Every morning landing in Paris would be a good morning. My flight was delayed, and I hoped Patricia had checked the arrival times.

I hopped on the minibus that took me from deplaning to customs. After a short wait in line, I stood in front of a customs agent who looked like Inspector Clouseau. He glanced at my passport, looking over last year's French stamp.

"Welcome back, mademoiselle," he said. "Enjoy your stay in France."

"Bien sûr," I answered. He looked happy, as all Frenchmen are, to hear their lovely language spoken.

I walked through customs and saw Patricia waiting just down the hallway. She opened her arms as she saw me, and I ran right into them. She kissed me on each cheek. *"Ça va?"* she asked. "Everything all right?"

"*Ça va.* It's fine. I'm sorry my flight was late. I hope I didn't make you miss church," I teased. I knew very well that she hadn't been in a church since she was baptized as a baby, except for the odd funeral.

"Only for you," she teased right back. "Come on. Xavier is at home making breakfast, worrying that you won't like him."

We got into her Renault and she lit up right away, then dashed into the torrent of traffic whirling around the airport.

"So, tell me all about everything. Bijoux. My brother and Sophie. Céline. My sister. That lawyer."

I laughed, glad to be back in her forthright company. In many ways she was like her sister, Margot, but more like a filled chocolate: a shell on the outside but liquid on the inside.

"First, Bijoux is in good shape. We are going to be making serious money soon."

"Vraiment?" She looked surprised. "Really? I thought things were a bit...touchy."

"They were," I said. "Until last week. Right before I left to come here, we got a major order of several wedding cakes every week. Putting that together with the work we've already done, I think we'll make it!"

"Extra," she said, still taking in the fresh information. Philippe must not have relayed it to her.

She navigated *le Boulevard Périphérique* and headed us toward Rambouillet. After a few choice words and hand gestures, she jockeyed her way onto the road and then calmed as we were on our way.

"And your brother, well, *ooh la la,*" I said, shaking my hand. "I think he and Sophie are heating up."

"I would never, in a million years, have guessed that," Patricia said. She'd worked at L'Esperance with me when her cousin Luc had been in charge, so she knew Sophie well.

"Sophie has changed," I said. "She's softer, more confident. She's grown up."

"Just like you, *ma petite.*" She called me by a term of endearment, like an aunt or a big sister would. "And does she like *ma* Céline?"

This, I knew, was the big question. And I could smooth the way into the family for Sophie. "*Oui,* she does. She's teaching her how to play piano. She's picked her up from school and taken her to lunch. She's even agreed to pull her old cheerleader uniform out of the mothballs for her."

"Cheerleader? Sophie?" Patricia looked as shocked as I did when I first learned that.

"Yes. Does that show you the depth of her devotion?"

Patricia nodded. *"Ooh la la."*

"And she makes sure she has her *goûter,* her after-school snack, each day."

"Bon," Patricia said, satisfied for the moment.

I thought I'd drop the next bomb before she asked. "And Margot has a boyfriend." But Patricia surprised me.

"I know," she said. "She even sent me his picture."

We laughed together.

"How do you and Xavier like Provence?"

"Ah, *ma chère,* it's perfect. The sun, the lazy days, the Provençals who truly enjoy good baking and aren't in a hurry. Xavier and I enjoy our days together."

"The evenings together?" I teased.

"Mais oui, certainement," she agreed. Like all French people, she found honest discussion of intimacy normal and nothing to hide. "I liked living in Seattle, I liked living in Rambouillet. But I am Provençal, so I belong *en Provence, n'est-ce pas*? How is your lawyer?"

"I don't know," I answered honestly. Because we had grown close over the past year, and because I had no big sister of my own, I found myself pouring my heart out to her on the way to the apartment in Rambouillet. I ended by telling her about my food message.

"Clever, clever," she said. "So what will he do? Does it depend on what you say when you go back?"

"Maybe, but...I kind of hope not," I said. "I hope it depends on his own heart."

"Je comprends," she said. "I understand."

We pulled into the parking lot of her apartment in Rambouillet. Even though she no longer lived there, the family kept it for anyone working nearby in the bakeries in Rambouillet and Versailles.

"Come on," she said. As I walked down the garden path, I could smell breakfast.

"*Bonjour,* welcome," Xavier greeted me as I walked into the house. He kissed my cheeks and then headed out to the car to get my suitcase.

"Très beau," I whispered to Patricia.

"I think he's handsome too," she said. He brought my suitcase back in, putting it in a small bedroom off the living area.

"And now—breakfast. I assume you haven't had a proper omelette since you left France. And so—*voilà,*" Xavier said, setting a plate before me.

Patricia put some brioche on the table. "And I assume you haven't been making brioche, either, with all of those cakes?"

"No." I shook my head, and for a moment, a whiff of longing crossed my path as I recalled telling my mom that Dan was kind of like brioche.

"Let's eat. Today you can rest and relax, but tomorrow, you're back to work. Four days of continuing education at the pastry school—advanced cake decorating techniques, more ganache work, and marzipan. Papa is going to take you to the Versailles bakery tomorrow during your lunch break. The weekend," she continued, "is for you to revisit the city in any way you want."

"Thank you, Patricia," I said. "For having me back for continuing ed, and all that."

"Pas de problème," she said. "Remember, France asks all of its employers to spend one percent of their budget on training. You speak French, so you get to come here. It's fine. Enjoy!"

After unpacking that afternoon, I walked over to the bakery in Rambouillet to surprise my dearest friend from pastry school, Anne. When I left Paris, she took the job I'd been offered at the Rambouillet bakery.

"Oh!" She ran forward and kissed me on both cheeks. "I wondered why Patricia asked me to stay late and do prep work I could have done tomorrow. *Quelle surprise!*"

"Can you have dinner tonight?" I asked. "Monsieur Delacroix has me all planned out for the next few days, but at least we can catch up."

"Oui," she said, and then switched to English. "And we can even speak in English!"

"Oh, you sound good! Still going to the English classes at the church?"

"Yes," she said. "It's been very enjoyable. Maybe someday I will come and visit you at Bijoux, *non*?"

"Non!" Patricia answered behind her. "I'm not losing my baker here too."

We laughed; Anne took off her apron and went into the office to do a little paperwork before we left together. I stood in the nearly quiet bakery, recalling my time there. I wandered into the cool room and remembered Patricia's lesson on only handling chocolate when I was in a good mood. I lightly touched the cool oven that had once burned me. I looked up at the shelves of dry goods and saw one of the shrunken apple heads I'd made with Céline, still hanging out in the back, a mascot of days gone by. I smiled at the memory of it.

I walked down the hallway and saw the aprons and jackets hanging on the pegs, all neatly embroidered with names and "Boulangerie Delacroix." How I'd coveted having one of those of my own—and I'd earned one. Mine hung on a peg at Bijoux, in Seattle.

I waited outside the office. I saw Anne taking care of a few details, so competent, so in her element. It had been good for Patricia to hire her to manage the place. At one time I'd stood outside and watched

Philippe handle the bakery business, attracted to him, wondering if he lay in my future. The attraction had evaporated, and in its place was a mist of affection and respect. I glanced at the phone.

Dan had called me, accidentally, on that phone. I felt a pang of longing.

"Ready?" Anne asked, turning the lights out in the office and leaving final instructions with one of her employees, someone I didn't recognize.

"Ready," I said. We walked together, heading toward one of our favorite bistros to dine and catch up.

After a few hours I was ready to call it a day. Jet lag was a serious problem at that point, and I had to be at the pastry school early tomorrow.

"Are you coming for continuing ed?" I asked.

"Not this time," she said. "Monsieur Delacroix is sending me for some more bread baking education in the fall, so that's fine. Cakes aren't my thing. They're yours."

I smiled. "But I'll see you again. Maybe after the tour of the new bakery at Versailles?"

"Sure," she said. "You're going to love it, Lexi. It's divine. The nicest bakery in Paris, I think. Though I'm sure I'm prejudiced. As beautiful as Ladurée, which *used* to be the most beautiful bakery in all of Paris."

I couldn't wait.

"So, mademoiselle, you have returned to France for further education?" Monsieur Desfreres greeted me less glacially than when I'd been an inexperienced baker with an uneasy hand not so long ago. It'd been six months since my graduation.

"I have," I agreed. "Monsieur Delacroix was kind enough to have me come back."

"And are you baking the cakes in the United States?" he asked.

"*Oui,* monsieur, I am. I am busily working to help educate the American palate, to civilize it. We'll never reach the level of French civilization..."

"Bien sûr," Monsieur Desfreres agreed readily.

"But I think I can make a positive impact with the assistance of the Delacroix," I said. "And, of course, we Americans have other strengths of our own."

"Bon," Monsieur Desfreres said. "Welcome back."

After that he greeted several other students, only one of whom I knew from my original class. We forged forward into the course, advanced pastry work. That day and the next we spent on cakes, each of which had to contain a minimum of four components, such as cake, sable, mousse, and ganache layers. We worked together to ensure that each flavor, texture, and element worked together to provide the best taste. I was already thinking how I could apply this at home.

The classmate from my former course and I teamed up with two others, one of whom he had known professionally. With such a short course, it was important to make alliances quickly and we did. I felt free this time, knowing I had a job and that I wasn't going to be graded. I could simply experiment and create. The thought occurred to me that if I always lived under the certainty of God's provision instead of the certainty of Lexi's worry, I might always feel this free.

Knowing the French preferred traditional flavors, we agreed on a champagne-flavored cake with a chardonnay jelly brushed on the layers and a lightly whipped white chocolate mousse between them. Ivory ganache coated the entire cake, and we set about making grape vines and sugared grapes for decorations.

At the end of the training day on Monday, Monsieur Delacroix stopped by the school. He spoke with Monsieur Desfreres for a while, then came over to my station as I was cleaning up the sugaring materials.

"*Bonjour,* mademoiselle," he said. "I trust your education progresses?"

"Oui," I said. "Thank you for bringing me here. I'm learning some very valuable lessons which I will immediately put to use for the Boulangeries Delacroix."

He smiled. "You're welcome, it's nothing at all." But it was, and he knew it. Just flying me over was costly. I knew Patricia was behind lobbying for it, and I appreciated that.

"Monsieur Desfreres tells me you're doing well. Tomorrow, I would like to take you to the Versailles bakery for a tour. It was not yet open when you were here, correct?"

I nodded.

"Bon," he said. "May I drive you home?"

"Non, merci," I said. I was meeting Anne for a glass of wine and a salad. "I'm meeting a friend."

The next morning we whipped up a variety of fillings and learned new layering techniques. Monsieur Delacroix arrived precisely at eleven o'clock.

The first topic of conversation, *naturellement,* was Céline.

"And how does my granddaughter do?" he asked.

"Well, according to Philippe, she's a musical genius," I said.

Monsieur Delacroix smiled and I could see a bit of Philippe in him. I wondered what had made him such a hard man that Margot left home as a teenager. I wondered why he held so tightly to the reins that Philippe felt he had to move to Seattle in order to have a life of his own. He, too, was like his daughters, one thing on the outside and another inside, except perhaps backwards. Soft on the outside but stern at the heart, where it mattered.

"She does well in school. She charms everyone she meets. Including Sophie, of course," I said.

Monsieur Delacroix didn't answer that at all. I wondered if he knew about Sophie.

"And Bijoux...she is doing well?"

"Yes. Did Philippe tell you we just secured a big contract?"

"Non." He took his eyes off the road for the first time and looked at me. "Tell me about that."

I explained about Mr. Jacques, but I didn't tell him the contract was dependent on me staying at the bakery. "I'm sure the training you've provided made all the difference."

"You are on your way to becoming a fine chef."

I grinned. In France, I would never be a real chef until I'd worked for at least ten years.

"Ah. We're here."

He pulled his smart little car into a tight spot and came around to open the door for me.

The bakery, of course, was already in full swing. It took up almost half a city block, which was saying something in Versailles. The bricks on the outside of the building were buffed clean but somehow still retained the look of newly molded sand, like all old Parisian buildings. The glass was so clear it nearly seemed invisible, the Boulangerie Delacroix emblems etched on them.

We went in through the front door. A long line of people waited for their early afternoon bread, the croissants so expertly created that the butter remained trapped within the flour and didn't leak out of the bottom even fresh from the oven.

"*Bonjour,* monsieur." An obviously star-struck young lady greeted us as we walked in the door.

"*Bonjour,* mademoiselle."

The walls were lined with wicker baskets holding long fingers of baguettes. Crown-like loaves and rustic loaves and pillowy brioche each nested on high-quality linen-lined shelves. In front of the store was a long, glass counter filled with croissants and pastries of every kind.

"Mademoiselle?" Monsieur Delacroix offered me a pastry.

"Pain au chocolat, s'il vous plaît."

The young lady put a chocolate croissant on a blue-rimmed porcelain plate and then put a raisin and nut roll on a plate for Monsieur Delacroix.

"Deux cafés crèmes?" she asked.

"Oui," he answered. Then he beckoned me back toward the bakery.

I'm not exaggerating when I say it was a minivillage. At least ten bakers worked side by side doing various tasks. Some gently rolled long wooden pins over supple croissant dough; others slapped bread dough with open hands.

"Venez-vous ici." Monsieur Delacroix called me over to the cool room. The room for making chocolates and icing final cakes was as big as Bijoux in its entirety. "Like Louis the Fourteenth, eh?" he said. "Dominates."

"Yes," I said. I wondered who the chef was who got to work in this room.

After introducing me to a few people and finishing the tour, we returned to the front room and sat at a sturdy little table edged with gold leaf, like the rest of the bakery. The young lady behind the counter had placed our coffee and pastries on the table. The coffee was still piping hot.

"So, mademoiselle, what do you think?"

"I think you've done a wonderful job, monsieur. It's an absolute dream."

"Oui," he answered after taking a sip of his coffee. "It has always been my dream to have a large, opulent bakery in Versailles. And now I do. Tell me, Alexandra, do you miss France?"

"Sometimes," I answered honestly.

"I have been thinking," he said. "For some time, I've wanted to expand the kinds of cake work we do here. In particular, wedding cakes. We make many *croques en bouche,* the traditional French wedding cake of filled chouqettes."

Ah yes, the air heads. I suppressed a smile, knowing that nickname had once been given to me. The name really meant "crunches in the mouth," and it was made of tasty cream puffs carefully balanced to make a beautiful, chocolate-drizzled tree.

"Would you be interested, mademoiselle, in coming to live in France again and working as a sous chef to the pastry chef at Versailles?" Monsieur Delacroix calmly set his coffee cup down and tore off a small piece of croissant.

"Moi?" I asked in amazement. "Work here?"

"Oui," he said. "You could stay at the apartment in Rambouillet for a time, if you wish, until you got properly situated."

"What about Bijoux?" I asked.

"Margot can continue to run it," he said. "And while you are a promising chef, we could find someone else to make the cakes in Seattle."

"Oh," I said. "Of course, of course, this is completely unexpected. I—I thank you for the honor. I don't know what to say."

"We would make sure the pay is adequate, of course," he said. "I could find someone here, but I like your style. And I like to promote from within the Delacroix bakeries whenever possible."

"I will certainly think it over. Thank you! If…if I decide to stay at Bijoux, is there still a job for me there?"

"Bien sûr," he answered smoothly. "As long as it's making money, it will be there. It's just that this is an unprecedented opportunity to work in Versailles and study under some of the best chefs in France."

I nodded. "How long…when would you like an answer?"

"By the end of the week," he said. Boy, he wasn't wasting any time. "You can call me." He handed me a card with his personal cell number on it.

I agreed. "Thank you, sir, for everything. The job in Seattle, the job offer here, the training." We stood to go, and I took my purse. A thought crossed my mind. "Monsieur Delacroix? Would it be possible, at all, under the French law, to use some of that one percent of the money you must set aside for training of the U.S. employees?"

He cocked his head as if considering that for the first time. "I don't see why not. Of course, they will have to study in Seattle, which is bound to be somewhat inferior—unless they speak French." He opened the door and I followed him out. "It's certainly something to contemplate."

Wednesday morning as I prepared to go to class, Patricia stayed home until I was ready to leave, rather than going to the bakery early as she usually did.

"Lexi," she said. "I have a change of plans for Friday. I know that you were going to sightsee, but I wonder if you could do some errands for me tomorrow instead. That still leaves Saturday and Sunday for sightseeing." She seemed a little awkward and uncomfortable.

"Sure," I said. I'd been planning to go to a museum and do a little shopping, but I could do that on Saturday. "What's up? What can I do for you?"

She shook her head. "I'll explain in the morning."

"Okay," I said, trusting her but curious about the mysterious vibe.

At class that day we learned advanced decorating techniques. I took copious notes in my journal to transfer to my laptop later. I'd been too busy to be on the computer very much. I'd sent Dan an e-mail when I arrived, and he'd sent me a quick one back. I knew he was busy with his big deal this week.

Thursday afternoon we assembled our cakes and walked around looking at everyone else's, taking photos and asking questions. Monsieur Desfreres told us he would donate the cakes to a retirement home that afternoon, and we heartily approved.

I walked back to Patricia's apartment, mulling over Monsieur Delacroix's offer. The apartment was empty. Patricia was at the bakery for the day, Xavier no doubt in a café with a friend.

For fun, I decided to make chocolate tube cakes with a Nutella layer tunneled throughout. My French friends had never eaten a Tunnel of Fudge cake. Of course not. This was not Betty Crocker land. But I bet they'd love it. It would be made a bit more French, of course, with the addition of the omnipresent European Nutella.

I set the cake to cool and decided to take a break while waiting for Patricia to come home. Had she known before I came to France that her father was going to offer me a job? I hadn't asked her, not wanting to pry into family business. I told her about the offer, of course, and she seemed delighted but offered no advice on if I should take it or not. In that, I appreciated the French. They weren't always telling their friends what they thought they should do.

I spent the afternoon walking around Rambouillet, drinking in the music of the French language, absorbing the rough touch of the stones on my fingertips, reflecting on the way the colors seemed brighter and stronger. Maybe it was because it was deepening from afternoon to evening, but the cypress trees seemed to shade things a bit darker than I expected them to. And I was tired.

I walked back to the apartment, took out my Bible, and thought about what to read. I'd finished *Philippe*-ians. Why not *Daniel*? The thought gave me the giggles, and then I laughed aloud in the quiet apartment, releasing the tension of the day.

What should I do, God? Is this what You have for me?

I sat quietly for a minute and heard Tanya's voice echoing from months ago.

"What will make you *happy, Lexi?"*

Twenty-One

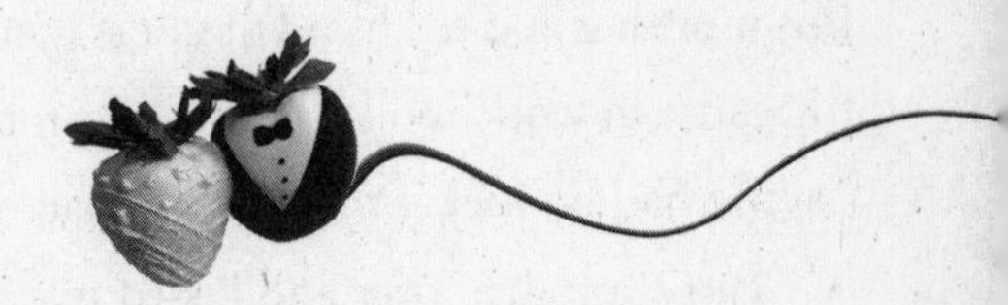

Life is a flower of which love is the honey.

Victor Hugo

"So, you need me to run some errands for you today?" I asked. "Shall I take the train, or are they local?"

"They are in Paris," Patricia said.

Paris?

"Okay, you're the boss. You paid for me to come here, so you get to call the shots," I said.

"Oh, I like that," she answered, nudging Xavier. "Did you hear that?"

"Bonne chance," he grumbled, heading back toward the kitchen. The two of us laughed.

"Take the train into Paris," she instructed me. "And then I want you to get on the Big Red Bus that stops at nine o'clock at the *Arc de Triomphe.* The driver will tell you what to do next."

"The Big Red Bus tour?" I said. "I don't need to tour."

"Yes, you do," she said. "Don't ask me any questions. I'm paying you today. Just do what I tell you. *Arc de Triomphe.*"

"All right." I nodded, more confused than ever. "But…" I grabbed her hand before she left the room. "I plan to call your papa this morning and tell him I'm not staying in Paris. I need to go back to Seattle to work. Will that cause a problem with your plans for the day?" I had no idea if this was a Delacroix bakery event or what.

Patricia leaned over and kissed my cheeks. "*Non, cherie,* I think you've made a good decision. Even though I would rather you stay *en France,* for my own sake. I do understand."

"Bon," I said. "See you later this afternoon?"

"Peut-être," she answered coyly. "Maybe."

She took off for the bakery, and I was left alone. I dialed Monsieur Delacroix before I left.

"Oui?" he answered.

"*Bonjour,* monsieur," I said. "This is Lexi Stuart."

"Ah, *bonjour,* mademoiselle. *Comment allez-vous?*"

"I'm fine, thank you. I wanted to get back to you as soon as I'd made a decision on the job offer."

"Oui."

"Well, sir, the bakery in Versailles is marvelous. It's the finest bakery I've ever been in, really. And it's tempting for me to stay and learn under master bakers. But…I have work of my own at Bijoux. I think we've started a good thing there, with your help and Margot's, of course. I have a new apprentice I think will make a fine addition to our business. I've made a commitment to bake for a man counting on us for wedding cakes this summer." I took a breath. He waited politely. "Finally, I guess, I'm just an American at heart. I belong in Seattle, though I'd like to come back to my second-favorite place often for training."

"*Oui,* I understand," he said. "I suspected as much when I didn't hear back immediately, but I do understand. *Bon.* Continue your good work at Bijoux, and I will depend on you for increasing financial stability...and a good cup of coffee whenever I come to Seattle."

I grinned. "Thank you, sir."

I breathed a big sigh as I hung up. Once the decision was made, I felt only a tint of regret but mostly relief. I looked at my watch. I'd better go if I was going to make it to the *Arc de Triomphe* station in time.

I watched Rambouillet pass by, and then Versailles. We were almost to Paris. What did Patricia have in mind?

I got off the train, took a quick Metro to the *Arc,* and got off. The buses were lined up—one taking off, one standing still. I looked at my watch. Almost nine o'clock. I walked up to the driver.

"Is this the bus that leaves at nine?" I asked.

"Oui," he said. I paid my fare and walked up the steps to the top of the bus to sit outside and enjoy the day. At the top of the stairs, I stopped and stared at the man I loved, who sat a few seats back, grinning at me.

"Dan!" I ran over and hugged him. "What are you *doing* here?"

"Same thing you are," he said, kissing me. "Sightseeing. Last time I was in Paris, I had a really cute guide who could speak both English and French. It helped out a lot. Do you think I could convince her to help me again?"

"How did you get here?"

"I drove," he teased.

"Your big account..."

"Is being handled by someone else. No more questions for now."

I settled into my seat. "You keep dropping these bombs on me and then asking me not to talk."

"Is it working?" he asked. "If so, I should write a book."

"Ha," I said. "How did you get Patricia to get me here?"

He looked a little shy. "I asked Sophie and Philippe to help me early in the week. And then I flew out. And now it's my turn to plan the day."

I leaned against him as the bus took off. The day was warm but not hot, with a slight breeze that blew through our hair. Suddenly, the city seemed light again. The laughter more joyous, the car noise not so annoying. Everyone seemed happy. We got off at the Louvre stop, and Dan bought us each a crepe from a stand.

"Taste good?" he asked.

"It tastes wonderful," I said. The strawberries seemed brighter, the crepe more tender. "Yours?"

"Good," he said. "Let's go in." This time we wandered through some of the lesser known artworks, ones we hadn't had time to look at last year when we'd done the highlights. It was my complete pleasure to show him my favorite pieces and explain the background on many of them. He was a more astute art student than I thought he'd be too. He knew many schools and styles and even shared a fact or two I hadn't known.

"Lunch?" he asked afterward.

"Sure," I said. He hailed a cab, and I asked the cabbie to head to the address Dan had written on a piece of paper.

We were seated outside. We ordered a smoked duck breast and apple salad to share and then a flaky chicken pot pie and some cheese.

"Two Cokes, please," Dan asked. "On ice." The waiter offered us dessert, but Dan declined and paid the bill. "We have somewhere else to go," he said.

We walked down the street, and soon I recognized where we were going—we were in the same district as the last time he'd visited. He must have asked Patricia—or Philippe—where to go for pastry.

We walked into the shop and I ordered for us. "Mille-feuilles?" I asked.

He nodded. "But of course," he said in a fake French accent. The couple ahead of us looked a bit disconcerted and grumbled about American tourists.

"Thank you for noticing," I said to them in flawless French. "We're truly enjoying your wonderful nation—the food, the sights, and the people."

"Ah, bon," the woman said, perhaps a little embarrassed that I'd understood her comment. But like any good Frenchwoman, she wasn't about to show her fluster.

Later we strolled along the banks of the Seine, hand in hand, and arrived at Mille Feuilles, the bookshop that sold Dan the book he'd given me last Christmas.

"This time, you find something," I told him. "To remember our day!"

After browsing, we headed back toward the Big Red Bus stop. Once seated, I told him, "I can't believe you came all the way here to share the day with me."

"I can," he said. "Will you have dinner with me tonight? Or do you have other plans?"

"No plans," I said. "Is it…upscale?"

"Yes," he said. "Is that okay? I hadn't even thought that you might not have anything dressy to wear."

"It's fine, no problem." I checked my watch. If we got off at the *Arc* in the seventeenth district, I'd be very close to the eighth district, which was where that swank little resale shop I'd visited several times last year was located. "Do you have plans for the rest of the afternoon? I have something I'd like to do."

"No," he said. "If you can get back to Patricia's on your own, I'll pick you up this evening. I've rented a car with GPS. In English."

"Okay," I said as we got off the bus. We held hands for a long time, reluctant to let go. Maybe he'd disappear as easily as he appeared. "I'll see you tonight," I said.

"Until then," he agreed. I finally let go of his hand and headed toward the Metro.

I took the connection and then quickly walked the few blocks to the resale shop. When I walked in, the same chic woman greeted me. "Polka-dot dress, wedding cancelled," she said. "Correct?"

"How do you do that!" I marveled at her amazing customer service memory. *"Oui!"*

"What can I help you with today?" she asked.

"Something *fantastique,*" I said. I had no idea what Dan had in mind, but I suspected he hadn't chased me halfway around the world for no reason.

She brought me a few different selections, but my eyes locked on one of them immediately—a shimmering gold dress, one that caught the light from every direction but whispered tasteful instead of screaming bling. It had short little cap sleeves and a scoop neck that showed off the color of my skin, close-fitting rather than form-fitting. I slipped it on and, as usual, Madame had chosen exactly the right thing.

"Shoes?" She held up a pair of new gold strappy sandals.

"Parfaite!" I said, hoping I'd have time at home to give myself a quick pedicure.

"Jewelry?" she asked.

"Non," I said. "No jewelry."

"Good," she agreed. "Understated. Maybe mademoiselle has something of her own she'd like to wear."

Mademoiselle was out of cash.

I put the purchases on my card and headed back to the Metro, which would take me to the train, which would take me back to Rambouillet. On the way, I texted Tanya even though I knew it was going to cost me a fortune: "Dan's here in Paris. Woo hoo!"

When I got to the apartment, Patricia was grinning like the proverbial Cheshire cat. "You knew all along," I teased.

"But of course. Patricia knows all," she said. "It seemed like a nice surprise for you. Off to dinner tonight?"

I showed her my dress and she clucked approvingly, as a big sister would, then pushed me off to take a nap and get ready.

I woke up, showered, and did my hair with care. Dan arrived, and Xavier greeted him at the door. That was a sight to see. Dan spoke no French and Xavier no English, but they managed to grunt a greeting to each other.

We got into Dan's rented car and headed toward the City of Lights and Love.

As soon as he pulled into the seventeenth district, I knew where we were going. The day had been retracing our visit of last year, and tonight was no different.

Dan got out of the car and helped me out. I noticed he carried a large, pink box with him. I was hoping for a rather small, jewelry-sized box. I smiled at myself, glad he couldn't read my thoughts.

We took the elevator to the top of the Eiffel Tower. "Now, how did you get reservations here on such short notice again?" I asked. "Don't tell me it was your assistant."

"Kind of," he admitted. "Actually, I asked her to contact our new partner—remember, the man you spoke with at the party? He had some contacts, and, as you'd say, *voilà*!"

"You're going to owe him," I said.

He agreed. "I will. But it will be worth it."

We were seated at a table for two, and the view was like no other view in the world. The sun was just starting to dip into the summer horizon.

The waiter brought over a wine list. "No Coke tonight," Dan teased. After we'd agreed to the *prix fixe* menu, Dan asked, "How was your training week?"

"Good," I said. The waiter slipped an *amuse-bouche* in front of us, a tiny taste to whet our appetites. "The classes were good. And Monsieur Delacroix offered me a job in Versailles."

Dan's eyes widened. "Really?"

"Really. He said they like to promote from within and I speak French and have potential."

"So what do you think about it?" he asked.

"I turned him down," I said. "It was tempting, but my place is in Seattle."

Throughout dinner we talked about Bijoux, and I told him about the work I'd be doing once a month with Community Table.

"I decided to read the book of Daniel while I was here," I said. I wanted him to know that while I may have stumbled upon Philippians, I had chosen Daniel. "I was looking for direction."

"Hopefully I wasn't weighed in the balance and found wanting," he teased, paraphrasing a part of the book.

"No," I laughed. "Not at all."

He told me about handing off the account this week. But both of us were dancing around the unspoken topic.

"So why did you come?" I asked. "I'm so glad you did. This was a perfect day. But I thought we were going to talk when I came back from France."

He pushed his plate a bit to the side. I put my utensils on mine and set it aside too. "Last year when I came to visit you, I wanted to give you some space. You'd looked forward to coming to France your whole life, so I wanted to make sure you didn't feel any pressure and just got to do the things and make the choices you wanted to make. Without a lot of interference or whatever."

"Thank you," I said. "Though I'm glad you interfered enough to give Luc the idea for Bijoux." I smiled.

"I'm not a total fool!" he said. "Anyway, when we talked at Tanya's wedding a couple of weeks ago, I told you I had planned to take the coward's way out but didn't. Later, after you left, I realized I really had taken a half-fearful way out. I put the decision totally in your hands. I didn't want to do that. You gave me three kinds of good-byes to choose from. I wanted to make sure it was *à bientôt.*"

"I'm glad you came," I said. "I'd hoped that, after our date, you'd know how I felt."

"I knew," he said. "And really, I knew in advance. But it was good for me to hear it from your own lips. I would have followed you anywhere this time to make sure you know how I feel about you."

"If you'd known about the job in Versailles, and if I had accepted it, would you have come?"

"Sooner," he promised. "But I had a few things to do before I could leave Seattle. I had to stop by your parents' house."

"You did?"

"I did. I talked with your dad."

Oh man. I knew where this was going. I'd only had one glass of champagne, but I felt my head and heart lifting.

"And then I had something to buy. The *pièce de résistance.*"

Dan handed me the medium-sized box from the side of the table. It was beautifully wrapped in pink paper with pink raffia on it. It was heavier than I expected it to be.

"Open it."

I tore the raffia off, gently peeled back the tape, and took the wrapping off a cardboard box. I lifted the lid.

"A pink catcher's mitt!" I was both delighted and surprised. Okay. Maybe a little disappointed too. "You want me to play on your team?"

"Try it on, Lexi."

I lifted it from the box and slipped my left hand inside. It fit neatly except for the fourth finger, which seemed to have something inside it. I pushed my hand in a little deeper, and a ring slipped onto my finger.

I smiled then and laughed, though softly, aware of the others around us. Then I pulled my hand out and looked at it. It was a thick gold band with a beautiful diamond set in the middle of a row of smaller ones.

"I bought it at the jewelry shop we visited last year. Did you notice we didn't visit there today? The one where you got the idea for your exhibition?"

"I noticed," I said timidly.

He leaned across the table and took my hand. "Lexi, will you marry me?"

Suddenly the shyest I'd ever felt in my life, barely able to look into his eyes for the intimacy I knew I'd find there, I looked up and answered. "Yes, Dan, I will."

"I love you, Lexi."

"I love you too, Dan."

He leaned across the table and kissed me, then indicated to the waiter that he could bring over our dessert, a *gâteau* made of white cake, blueberries, strawberries, and whipped cream.

"Red, white, and blue. Like the American flag. And the French one." Dan grinned. In the middle were two toothpick flags, one French, one American.

"I guess you can speak a food language of your own," I said.

"Indeed I can. And if that's the language you need me to speak, I'll learn it." He cut a small piece, put it on the fork, and then held it up. "May I?"

"You may." I ate it before reciprocating. *Délicieux.*

I looked out the windows to the lights of Paris. Never in my girlhood chats with Tanya, lying on the floor during our slumber parties, had I imagined this. Dan touched my hand, calling me back to the present.

"Two more days of sightseeing, then let's go home," he said.

"Yes," I agreed. "Home."

Sunday afternoon we'd checked in through customs, and were waiting for our flight. I got a text message from Tanya. "Need to borrow my ear shaver?"

I texted her right back. "Yes!!! But my man doesn't need one. Yet." I put a smiley face on the text and sent it off.

A few minutes later, I texted Patricia. "We made it through customs and now are waiting to board the plane home. I will miss you, my friend. Even though I know we'll see each other again, I will say, '*Adieu,*' because that really means '*go with God,*' doesn't it? *Adieu.*"

We boarded the plane, and just before I had to shut my phone off, I received a response message from her. I read it and took Dan's hand in my own.

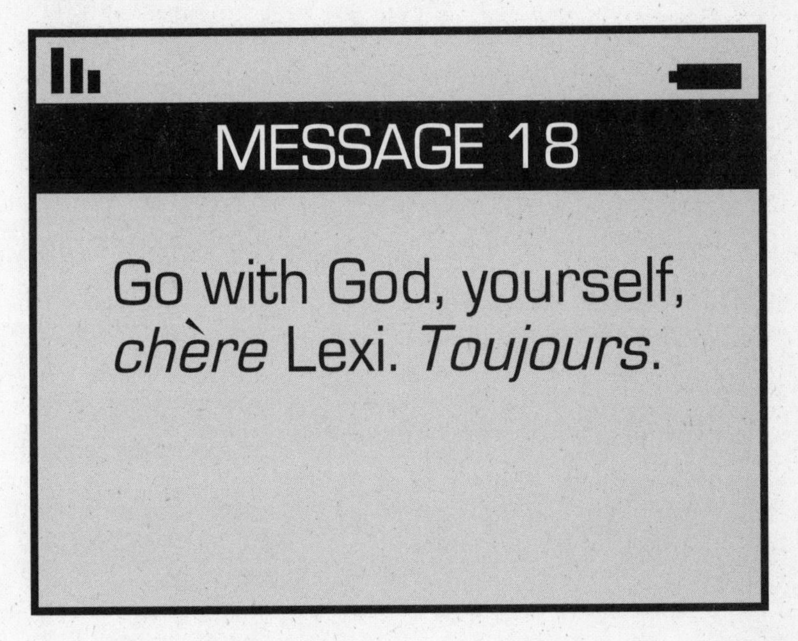

I will Patricia, I will. Always.